Wooden Spoons

A Novel

This book is a work of fiction. Any resemblance to actual events or persons, living or dead, is entirely coincidental.

"Wooden Spoons," by Dennis Ruane. ISBN 0-9787484-0-9 (hardcover); 0-9787484-1-7.

Published 2006 by Virtualbookworm.com Publishing Inc., P.O. Box 9949, College Station, TX 77842, US. ©2006, Dennis Ruane. All rights reserved. No part of this publication may be reproduced, stored in a retrieval system, or transmitted in any form or by any means, electronic, mechanical, recording or otherwise, without the prior written permission of Dennis Ruane.

Manufactured in the United States of America.

*I went to the woods because I wished to live deliberately,
to front only the essential facts of life
and see if I could not learn what it had to teach,
and not, when I came to die, discover that I had not lived.*

Henry David Thoreau

Wooden Spoons

by
Dennis Ruane

-1-

Nostalgia and melancholy overcame him that afternoon. Looking beyond books and paper on his desk, the professor stared out a window into another Wisconsin winter. Months had passed since this last happened and it seemed the problem had been worked out. When he resumed a full schedule in December, it was with the confidence that he had moved beyond an embarrassing era along an otherwise stellar career path. Whatever insight he thought he had gained then was of no use now. Confidence was disappearing like sand sifting through a hole somewhere beneath him, and he was sinking.

The pressure of a headache was building at his forehead, another of those peculiar headaches that had plagued him over the past year. Yet something was different this time. He was hearing a strange sound, a low-pitched murmur. At first it seemed to be a faint drumming inside his head, and then it became more of a vibration that seemed to emanate from somewhere outside his body.

A sudden knock sounded on the office door to which he turned but did not respond. The professor saw hesitation behind frosted glass, heard shuffling feet, and then another knock. Still, he offered no response. He was done with science today. Waiting until the figure faded, he moved to the door,

Dennis Ruane

turned the lock and switched off lights. Returning to his chair, he rolled it to the back corner of the room, to an area where there were no bookcases or filing cabinets. With his back to the wall, he turned toward another window.

He desperately wished to be at his home, in the study, but for now, this corner would serve his need. In another hour, people would leave the building and it would be dark. Until then, he could hide here. Behind the Biochemistry building were two enormous elm trees, as old as the University of Wisconsin itself. The professor stared through a web of branches into the pale afternoon sky. The weight of years gone by and the burden of love grown cold pressed down upon him.

-2-

Tom Reilly stopped sawing when he noticed his dog sit up and stare across the meadow toward Hemlock Road. "What is it, Emma?" he asked as he turned to follow her gaze. He looked across brown grass accentuated with broad swaths of snow and saw no one on the road.

Tom resumed his sawing, an endless job on a homestead where one is dependent on wood for heating and cooking. He did not doubt that someone was coming, but knew they were still beyond his human senses. After a few minutes he looked up again and this time saw a figure on the road, still at a great distance. When he strained for recognition, a smile came to his weathered face.

Tom cut a few minutes longer. The sharp teeth of his buck saw raked across a small oak log and pink dust sprayed to the ground with each forward thrust. Soon he heard the sound of footsteps scuffling on the lane. Shaking his head and grinning mischievously, he turned. "Hello, Daniel. I wouldn't have cut all this firewood by myself if I'd known you were coming."

"Hi Paw," the boy replied. He had stooped to greet Emma, who had broken from her rigid pose on the porch and sprinted to meet him. Daniel was skinny and nearly as tall as Tom. He had wavy brown hair and handsome features that were punctuated by penetrating blue eyes.

Dennis Ruane

"Must be spring if you're roaming the mountain again. How's the road?"

"Bad. There are two big trees down and it's washed out bad at The Bend," Daniel replied enthusiastically.

"Well, it was a rough winter," Tom said, smiling.

The boy thought he seemed pleased with this report.

The road, as Tom Reilly referred to it, was the section of Hemlock Road that led from the village of Lick Hollow, Pennsylvania, to the summit of Hemlock Knob. He lived at the summit on a one hundred-acre homestead named Mountain Farm. Hemlock Road actually continued to the east through the Forbes State Forest for another three miles and ended at Furnace Road. Besides Tom's house, there were only two dwellings on this dirt road; both located a mile and a half below on the west face of the mountain. In the winter, the section of road from these homes to the summit was often impassable. Beyond Tom's place where the road wound through the State Forest, it was usually worse.

"Come on in the house. You must be hungry after hiking up here. I have some stew on. You still like rabbit?" The boy nodded and eagerly followed the man up the steps of a log building. Daniel was fourteen years old. Tom Reilly, his great-grandfather, was eighty-four.

Tom was six feet tall, slightly stooped in the shoulders and had a lean, rugged build for his age. He had a wrinkled, leathery face and sported a wild shock of coarse, white hair. Tom always wore baggy jeans, a tan long-sleeved shirt, and leather work boots.

Daniel loved Tom's old log house, strange and mysterious as it was, with no electricity or telephone and water coming in by a small hand-pump on the kitchen sink. The spring out back was the reason Tom's father had built on this particular site more than eighty years before. The boy peered with obvious curiosity into the corners of the room as Tom dipped stew from a large pot on the wood stove. One thing that impressed him about his great-grandfather's residence was how quiet it was, especially in comparison to his own home. A fire had been necessary in the morning and now all the windows were open to offset the heat of the stove. The breeze, wafting through the house, blended wood smoke and food aromas with the scent of the new season.

The house was a masterwork of log construction, built of massive, hand-hewn hemlock planks, eight inches thick and some as wide as two feet. They were in The Great Room, as Tom called it, which for its large size served as both the kitchen and living room. There were two smaller rooms on the west side of the house. One was Tom's bedroom and the other, a food pantry. The rooms upstairs were empty, but Daniel knew that they had once been bedrooms for Tom and his two sisters. The boy had liked the log building since the first time he stepped inside and often wondered why his Grandmother Kelly spoke of it with disapproval.

Daniel stopped to stare at an odd-shaped piece of wood above the front doorway. It was something he had noticed before but it never aroused his curiosity until now.

Tom carried two bowls to the table, the smooth handles of some antique silver protruding from each. "That's a bata, sometimes called a fighting stick. It was one of the few possessions my father brought with him from Ireland," Tom explained as he sat down. "It's made of blackthorn, a wood cut from the Shillelagh Forest of County Wicklow in Ireland."

The object above the door was about three feet long, with a crooked handle and an enlarged, gnarled end. To the boy it looked like an ill-shaped wooden sledgehammer.

Dennis Ruane

"Did he fight with it?"

Tom shook his head. "Not that I know of. It was a ceremonial type thing used at festive occasions such as weddings or wakes." Tom grinned. Daniel missed the humor.

"Why did he hang it there?"

Tom paused, considering his words carefully. "My Pap, your great-great-grandfather, fought in a war, the American Civil War, and experienced many terrible things. He never would talk about it, not even with me. When he settled here, he made a pledge that he would never fight again. As a sign of that he hung his bata above the doorway."

Daniel accepted this explanation without comment and joined his great-grandfather at the table.

Tom smiled, wondering what the boy had garnered from his words. "So Daniel, what news do you bear from down below? How is your mother?"

"She's pretty good, I guess. She went back to work at the hospital."

"That's good," Tom said, and then he paused, once again choosing his words. "She has to keep moving. Life goes on. That was a terrible thing, your Dad dying like that, so young and with you kids. He was a good man and a hard worker, a good pap." They ate their stew in silence for a few minutes.

Daniel had first visited Hemlock Knob eight years before with his father and his older brother. Allen Whaley, Daniel's father, had been an industrious man, self-employed at a small retail coal business. Traditional in most ways and conservative in his politics, Allen never fully understood the rationale behind his wife's grandfather living alone on Hemlock Knob. However, he had liked to visit Tom very much.

Tom came to expect them in early spring, usually on the first Sunday afternoon of fair weather. Three years ago, when they didn't come, he sensed that something was wrong. A month later, he learned that Allen had died of a rare vascular disease. The following spring Daniel came alone and over the years, Tom and his great-grandson had become close friends.

"The best way to deal with death, Daniel, is to concentrate on living and your mother is doing that."

Daniel nodded but said nothing. He was concentrating on his food, obviously as hungry as Tom had suspected.

"More stew?"

Daniel nodded, immediately handing Tom his bowl.

"And how is your grandmother?" Tom asked, somewhat cautiously, from across the room.

"She's still in Florida," the boy answered.

Tom nodded.

"Oh," Daniel exclaimed, suddenly remembering the news he had for Tom. "President Kennedy was killed."

Tom looked up and turned his head to one side. "When?"

"November twenty-third."

"How?"

"He was shot by Lee Harvey Oswald and␣Lee Harvey Oswald was shot by Jack Ruby and then he died too."

Tom shook his head and looked at the floor for a few seconds before he spoke. "My word, and so who is president now? Johnson, I suppose?"

"Yes, Lyndon B. Johnson."

"Good grief," Tom said, and then stopped talking. They concentrated on their meal and did not discuss that news again.

After lunch, Tom and Daniel went to the building that Tom called the woodshed. Located forty yards behind the house, it was the most intriguing part of the homestead to the boy. Thirty-five feet in length by thirty feet wide and built of

7

hemlock planks, the woodshed was actually a small, rectangular barn. Just inside the door was a collection of firewood, stacked in neat rows that were as tall as Daniel.

"Remember, Daniel, it takes at least five cords of firewood to get through a Hemlock Knob winter," Tom said.

"How much is here Paw?"

"Oh, I guess there are about six cords."

"You have more wood here than you need for a whole winter and winter is almost over."

Tom softly laughed. "I'm always putting more in behind what I use, and that way it's always drying ahead of the need for it. Over here is wood that's been in nearly a year now," said Tom, pointing at the stack to the far left. "Over there on the right, that stack was finished up last week." He turned and looked at his great-grandson and with a somewhat ominous voice said, "You can never have enough firewood, Daniel. Winter is always coming." As he often did after a statement such as this, he cleared his throat and smiled. It was difficult for Daniel to know if he was serious or joking. In truth, as he often did, Tom was joking about something serious.

As curious as Daniel was concerning the firewood supply, the real draw to the woodshed was Tom's workshop, which was the opposite end of the building. The dominant feature was a massive workbench constructed of heavy squared oak timbers. The bench bore numerous scratches across its surface, and all the edges were rounded smooth from many decades of use.

Beyond the workbench, on the back wall, was a collection of woodworking tools neatly hung on iron pins and arranged along a wide shelf. Daniel had learned the name of each tool. He also knew that most of the tools had been made on Mountain farm by either Tom or his father.

Daniel's gaze went first to the cluster of tools in the center of the wall. The broadaxe, carpenter's adze, auger bore, drawknife, and froe were the principle tools employed in log building construction. Tom had carefully instructed his great-grandson in their use. The marks from these very tools could be traced on all the buildings at Mountain Farm.

To the right of this was a collection of saws, including crosscut saws, a turning saw, and a dado saw. An empty peg represented the buck saw that Tom was using. Surrounding these were framing chisels, rasps, axes of various shapes and sizes, mallets, mauls, gluts for splitting, spokeshaves, and a large collection of block planes.

The two-man crosscut saw, with its six-foot length of jagged teeth and perpendicular handles, was the boy's favorite. With his great-grandfather pulling at the opposite end, Daniel had cut many logs into firewood-length sections with this saw. A few generations before these tools were a necessity on any homestead. However, the advent of power tools had rendered them not only obsolete, but in most settings, nearly forgotten.

As he approached the workbench, Daniel noticed a collection of smaller tools that he had not seen before. It included gouges and chisels of various shapes, a wooden mallet, and two odd-shaped stone object. The tools were arranged neatly in pouches on a piece of canvas. He moved close to the interesting array of tools until he was hovering directly over it. In a small open area at one corner were faded words, stitched onto the canvas in a language that Daniel did not understand.

Tom observed his great-grandson's reaction with interest and waited until Daniel looked up before he spoke. "I never showed you these before because they have been tucked behind things in here. Haven't used them in a while and got them out over the winter to fool with. These are woodcarving tools that belonged to my father. His brother brought them to America

Dennis Ruane

from Ireland. Their grandfather was a woodcarver, and when he grew old and couldn't work, he wanted Pap to have them."

"They're really cool, Paw."

Tom grinned. "My pap, your great-great-grandfather, was a woodcarver, among many other things. He made spoons and bowls and did some nice carvings of animals and people."

"Where are they now?"

"Some he sold, some he gave away. They're scattered wide."

Daniel rubbed the handle of one of the gouges. "What did you make with them, Paw?"

"Mmm, well now. I made the occasional spoon, but, I uh, never seemed to have the knack for anything too complicated beyond that. These tools were Pap's prize possession and he gave them to me a few years before he died. I know that he hoped I would use them and be a woodcarver like him, but so far it hasn't happened."

"How do you use them?"

"Whew, I'm not much help there. I never knew a lot, and I've probably forgotten some of what I did know. This one is called a spoon gouge and is the tool used for shaping the bowl of a spoon." Tom held a gouge which had a crook at the end of the blade. He then picked up the mallet and struck the end of the gouge handle, chipping a small piece of wood from the leg of the workbench.

Daniel stared as if it were magic.

"The different gouges and chisels take out different shaped chips," Tom said as he shrugged his shoulders. He knew that it was pitiful instruction. "I'll tell you what my father told me. He said that when the time is right and you're ready to use these tools, you'll learn."

"I'd like to learn to carve, Paw."

Wooden Spoons

"Eh, well now, that's good Daniel, I . . ." Tom hesitated and stared at the tools. Then he looked at Daniel and smiled. "Next time you're up here, I'll show you what I know. That reminds me, do you have a jackknife?"

Daniel shook his head.

Tom pulled a knife from his right pocket and quickly put it back. "That's mine," he said. Reaching into his left pocket he withdrew another knife, which appeared to be newer, and handed it to his great-grandson. "Here it is. I put this in my pocket several days ago, figuring you'd be up this way soon. Pap made it. He made the best jackknives in the area and made this one a few years before he died to replace the old wore-out one he had. Poor old guy, got sick and never used it. I have my own so I don't need it."

Daniel opened the knife carefully. "Wow, Paw. Thanks."

"Well I been saving it for years for sentimental reasons, but I'm of the opinion now that it's silly to save things for any reason. Besides, you need a knife. I don't know how a man can make it through a day without a good jackknife in his pocket." Tom cleared his throat and smiled. "Play around with it, sharpen some sticks, cut some notches in them. Get a feel for wood and how it cuts. We'll work with the carving tools another day."

Daniel nodded.

Tom looked out the window at the sky and then down at an antique watch he had taken from his pocket. "Say Daniel, since you got out of cutting firewood, would you like to help Emma and I check the sap buckets?"

Daniel nodded eagerly. This was pleasant work, and the boy looked forward to it on his early spring visits. In Tom's ancient pick-up truck they would wobble along the rough dirt road that wove through the grove of maple trees, or *the sugar*

Dennis Ruane

bush, as Tom called it, stopping to empty metal buckets that hung from the taps.

In late February or early March the weather was usually right. With nights, during which the temperature dropped below freezing followed by days when the temperature rose above it, pressure built within the maple trees. Sap flowed out the tap hole, a deliberate leak in the system, and collected in the buckets. Each tap yielded about ten gallons of sap over the five-week sugaring season. Tom hung one hundred and ten buckets, usually one or two to a tree. There was one old matriarch that had stood at the edge of the meadow for more than a hundred years, and around its massive girth hung ten buckets. From a distance, it looked like a string of beads around her rugged neck.

Tom and Daniel poured the sap or *sugar water* through a screen into a metal trough in the back of the truck. Then it was driven to the boiler shed to be concentrated into syrup.

"Depending on the sweetness of the sap, it can take anywhere from twenty-five to seventy-five gallons of raw sap to make a gallon of finished syrup," Tom instructed. "The usual amount is about forty gallons of sap to one gallon of syrup."

The sale of maple syrup provided Tom with the cash he needed for basic necessities, and so he was meticulous about his business. But it was his great pleasure as well; he worked all year managing the sugar bush and knew the maple trees individually.

While they collected the sap, Tom talked about practical matters, which were relevant to the management of Mountain Farm. Through stories about the Reilly family, Daniel learned the history of the homestead. The boy loved to hear his great-grandfather talk of such things. He listened carefully and remembered all that he was told.

Wooden Spoons

After the sap was collected, they passed another hour walking the property. Tom and Daniel inspected the spring house with its large stoneware crocks sitting in a trough of flowing water, then the forge, a rough plank building with open spaces between the boards, the spring garden, and finally the little cemetery where their ancestors were buried. As the afternoon wore on, the boy grew uneasy and finally inquired about the time. Tom pulled out his pocket watch and looked at his great-grandson slyly.

"Does your mother know you're up here?"

"Yes, honest, she does. But I can't be late for supper again, especially today. My Uncle Nolan is coming."

Tom laughed. "It's four-thirty, so you better get out of here. I don't want your mother blaming me. Tell her I'm still alive and I send my regards. I'll be down one of these days."

As Daniel walked up Reilly Lane, he turned and waved to Tom, who was beside the saw horse again preparing to cut more firewood. As he turned toward Lick Hollow, the boy saw a deer grazing at the far edge of the meadow in the apple orchard. As he watched, it stopped and raised its head. With twitching ears and erect tail, the animal watched Daniel until he was out of sight.

-3-

Daniel was not in a hurry after he left Mountain Farm because he knew that if he took his shortcut, he could easily make it home by supper. He was often late or absent for the evening meal on the days that he journeyed to the mountain. This was never his intention, but the woods had a way of distracting him and distorting his sense of time.

A mile from the Log House, Daniel turned left onto a wide trail that abruptly ended at a rock outcrop on the west face of Hemlock Knob, a place commonly known as Point Lookout. From the rock outcrop, he had an unobstructed view of the undulating hills of the low country to the west and of Lick Hollow, Daniel's hometown. From this height and distance the town appeared to be a giant relief map, especially interesting to someone who grew up on Main Street.

Directly ahead was a fifty-foot drop. To continue down the mountain, a person had to angle in a northwesterly direction, following the rock outcropping. This was a shortcut because eventually the rock trail crossed Hemlock Road. Along with the physical challenge this route presented, it lessened the walking distance to Lick Hollow by over a mile.

Before he started down, Daniel chose a seat upon the most prominent rock. Whatever uneasiness he felt over time was overcome by a desire to sit upon this wonderful spot and examine the jackknife he had just received. He took it from his pocket and carefully pulled out the blade. At his age, he could not appreciate the time and skill that went into creating an instrument such as this, but he was thrilled with the knife all the same. Daniel turned it over and over in his hands, studying the walnut handle and carefully running a finger along the blade.

Impulsively, he pulled a small piece of oak from the brush behind him. Daniel began to taper one end, slicing thin shavings from the weathered piece of wood, revealing an almond color just below the gray surface. The knife felt good in his hands, he reveled in the ease with which it quickly shaped the wood. There was a small hump on the surface of the oak branch, where it had absorbed the end of a broken twig. The twisted wood grain in this area stopped the flow of his cutting so suddenly that Daniel lost his hold and the knife fell from his hand. It slid across the smooth stone surface and disappeared over the cliff.

Daniel froze momentarily in disbelief. Then he jumped to his feet and scrambled down the rock trail in desperate haste. When it was possible, he cut back along the base of the cliff toward the area where the knife had fallen. About fifty yards in, he was stopped by mountain laurel so thick and twisted on itself that he could not push through. Momentarily, he thought of giving up and searching on another day, remembering the promise he had made to his mother that he would be home on time. But Paw gave him that jackknife, and it had been made by his great-great-grandfather. He had to find it.

Eventually Daniel discovered that if he got right against the rock wall and crawled, he could work his way into the interior of the sprawling laurel. At a spot where he could see the cliff through the leaf canopy, he searched the ground on

Dennis Ruane

hands and knees. Twenty frantic minutes passed and then suddenly the knife was there. It was directly in front of him, lying near the base of the rock wall on a cluster of brown laurel leaves. Daniel snatched it up with a whoop of elation.

At that moment he noticed a dark aperture underneath an overhang on the rock wall. It was a cave, so close that he could smell its earthy, moist interior. The boy instinctively recoiled. The opening was about three feet in diameter, and Daniel would never have seen it if he had not been on hands and knees. He folded back the knife blade and returned the tool securely to his pocket while staring at the opening. Regaining his nerve, Daniel approached the cave and could see that there was a wall a few feet inside. The passage seemed to continue to the right.

He turned to go, realizing that if he did not start immediately it would be impossible to be home in time for supper. But then he turned back, unable to restrain his curiosity. Dozens of small caves could be found along the outcrop, created by the prehistoric rock upheaval that formed Hemlock Knob. Daniel was fascinated by these caves, and while he had explored many of them, he had never found one as obscure as this. For that reason he lingered. A nervous smile crept onto his face as he crawled into the opening. The inside temperature was cool and the stone surface moist to his touch. At the back wall, Daniel turned his head to the right and saw only darkness.

It was a simple rule, which Allen Whaley had insisted upon, that for at least one time each day, for dinner, the entire family sit down together. Daniel's mother continued the practice after her husband's death. With her busy schedule, she appreciated the opportunity to account for her children.

Stephen was easy. An aspiring basketball player, he spent most of his young life at the Lick Hollow basketball court, one block away. Abigail could go to the back porch and see the running bodies, hear their shouts and eventually spot her son amongst them. If her daughter, Megan, was not in the back yard with her best friend, Karen Neil, she was in Karen's backyard. Abigail only needed to look to the right of the basketball court to see the Neil residence.

She had to look to the east to search for Daniel this evening, although there was little chance that she would see him. There would only be Hemlock Knob in the distance and the knowledge that her son was up there, somewhere. For this reason, it was Daniel she most anticipated at the table.

Daniel had been different from other children since he was young, exhibiting a quiet loner personality that had troubled his sociable father. It seemed to Abigail that after her husband died, these traits became more pronounced. He did not play sports or participate in school activities such as clubs or dances. Although some people considered him sneaky, Abigail thought 'elusive' was a better word to describe Daniel's habit of disappearing. She smiled as she recalled one occasion when he had played hide-and-seek with other children in the neighborhood. Later, they complained to her that Daniel had only hidden once and was not found for the rest of the afternoon.

Her son's best friend was his eighty-four-year-old great-grandfather, and Daniel's favorite activity was to visit him at Mountain Farm. She was fond of her grandfather as well, and had loved Hemlock Knob since her first visit to the Reilly homestead as a child. These were some of the reasons Abigail convinced her husband to raise their children in Lick

Dennis Ruane

Hollow. But now she worried that Daniel spent too much of his time on the mountain. She wanted him to participate in activities which were more typical for his age.

Abigail moved from the stove to the kitchen window. *He certainly takes after the Reilly side of the family,* she thought as she gazed up at Hemlock Knob.

-4-

When Daniel burst through the door, scratched and disheveled, his mother was in the kitchen with Nolan Whaley. This was good for Daniel's sake, because his uncle's presence would certainly soften the impending reprimand. Daniel had missed dinner. His mother glanced at the clock when he came in, and then back at him. He could see that she was angry.

When he had told the tale of his visit with his great-grandfather, including the near loss of the knife at the cliff, Abigail shook her head. She was not surprised because she had heard many adventures such as this. Nolan, who had never spent much time in the woods, listened as if it were a tale brought back from the jungles of New Guinea. Both adults were impressed with the knife; especially so, when they learned that Adam Reilly had made it.

"How is Paw?" Abigail asked.

"He's good. He said to tell you that he is still alive, and that he will be down sometime."

"Well that's good news," she replied, finally smiling. "Fix yourself a plate and take it out on the front porch. Your uncle and I have some things to talk about. And, Daniel, for three weeks, you take no trips to Hemlock Knob."

Daniel's expression did not change but Abigail could see

Dennis Ruane

the effect of her edict in his eyes. Daniel prepared a plate and went out through the living room.

"Don't look so surprised, Nolan. This is happening far too often with him. I've got to start being firm with Daniel."

"Oh, I wasn't questioning your judgment. I'm still thinking about the story of the knife and the cliff," Nolan said, shaking his head.

Abigail laughed. "I've heard many stories like that over the years, stories of caves, tree houses, cliffs, bear encounters, not to mention the occasional rattlesnake. There's always some interesting reason for not making it home on time." Abigail went to the kitchen window as she spoke and looked at Hemlock Knob.

"It's hard for me to imagine your grandfather living up there alone."

She turned to her brother-in-law and nodded. "Paw is an unusual person."

Nolan hesitated, curious to know more of this eccentric man who lived on Hemlock Knob but at the same time, not wanting to cross that line where a polite in-law should stop. He was also aware of how fond Abigail was of her grandfather, and so Nolan worded the next question carefully. "Abigail, I've spoken with Mr. Reilly on several occasions over the years and I've always thought he was an interesting and charming man, very sociable once he gets talking."

Abigail smiled and nodded.

"So how *did* he come to live up there alone? I know some of the story, bits and pieces that Allen told me over the years. Allen was very fond of your grandfather."

"Oh, I know," Abigail responded, laughing. "Wasn't that an odd pairing, Allen with his conservative views and Catholic faith hobnobbing with the old, anti-government, atheist mountain man on Sunday afternoons? Those two loved to argue with each other."

They both laughed and then grew silent, thinking of Allen Whaley, the man of simple beliefs and strong convictions. Everybody missed him.

Abigail lifted her head suddenly. "Well Nolan, the popular story is that after my grandmother died, Paw turned his back on the world: denouncing his religion, quitting his job at the Fire Department, selling or giving away everything he owned and returning to the old family home on Hemlock Knob. All that is true to some extent, but I believe that my grandmother's death released him from a life that was contrary to his nature. It was a life that he lived for her and their family."

"Contrary to his nature?"

"It's a long story, Nolan, and it begins with his father, Adam Reilly. Adam is the one who chose Hemlock Knob as the site for the family home and instilled a love of self-sufficiency in his offspring. And even today, Adam Reilly is a legendary figure to many people in this area"

"I don't know much about him."

"I don't know everything, but what I do know would still make a long story, so maybe we should save it for another time."

"Right. I need to be back in Morgantown this evening, but I do want to learn more about both him and Tom Reilly, if you don't mind. Actually, the information would be very relevant to my research."

"Speaking of which, where were we, Nolan?"

"Oh yes, the test results. As I was saying, just before one of the subjects walked in the door, the results of the second test confirm those of the first. There was no mistake. His scores are at a very high level, a genius level."

Nolan Whaley was working towards a PhD in Psychology at West Virginia University. His current research involved the relationship between intelligence and creativity. With their mother's permission, he was using Daniel and his brother Stephen in the preliminary studies. He had administered an intelligence test to the boys five weeks before. When the results were assessed, Daniel's score was so high that Nolan and his colleagues felt there had been a mistake. A variation of the test was then given to Daniel and this time, the results were slightly higher. Nolan was trying to put this into perspective for Abigail in a calm manner, but he could scarcely contain his excitement.

"It makes sense to me; he fits the profile in many ways. The story he just told us, for instance. It's another example of that loner behavior that has been evident since he was very young."

"But what does it mean, practically?" she asked with weariness in her voice. "What does it mean in day-to-day terms?" Since her husband's death, Abigail had been kept busy enough raising her three children and now she was working full time as a nurse. She would rather not face any new or unusual challenges at this point.

"Well, the truth is, most in the field believe it's better if he is never told. You might consider getting Daniel into the best school you can. He shouldn't be steered in any particular direction, but certainly it would be desirable that he be exposed to as many options as possible."

Abigail turned her head, smiling. "I may be one step ahead of you there. I have been seriously considering moving back to Philadelphia, so a change of schools would definitely be in the plans."

Wooden Spoons

"Really, when did this come about?"

"Oh, actually I've been considering it since I started back to work. I could get a better-paying job in nursing there, and I would be closer to my sister and her family. And of course, closer to my mother."

"Sounds good to me," Nolan said enthusiastically. "There would be many good schools to choose from. Your mother will be delighted," he added with a grin.

"Oh my, yes. She has wanted me to move back for the last fifteen years, ever since I married Allen and came here. If I move back, then she won't have to worry about her father turning Daniel into a mountain man."

They both laughed. Abigail's mother, Janice Kelly, was a stern and controlling matriarch, as well as generous and protective with her children and grandchildren. Daniel had been special to her since he was born. It concerned her that he had come under the influence of her father, whom she had not spoken to in many years. Considering that she lived in Philadelphia four months of the year and in Miami the remainder, her elderly father's life alone on Hemlock Knob was insanity to her. She did not want that condition passed down to her favorite grandson. However, Janice's problem with her father went well beyond a question of his residence. In truth, it would be difficult to imagine a father and daughter more politically and philosophically opposite.

When Abigail's head finally rested upon her pillow that night, it was stirring with thoughts as a result of the conversation with her brother-in-law. The idea to move to Philadelphia had been in her mind for months, but she had kept it to herself until now. She did not want to cause her

Dennis Ruane

children any unnecessary anxiety, nor did she want her mother taking charge too soon. Stephen had always been drawn to crowds and lights and besides, Philadelphia would be a better basketball environment. He would be fine with this change. Megan was twelve years old. The separation from Karen Neil would be rough for a while, but she would adjust. It was Daniel that she was worried about, and it was mostly for him that she kept the plans to herself.

In her conversation with Nolan about her son's genius, she did not think it appropriate to bring up the fact that Daniel's grades had slipped dramatically this year. She did not share her mother's paranoia about Daniel becoming a mountain man, but she had no doubt that his obsession with Hemlock Knob was affecting him academically and socially.

Moving to Philadelphia will be hard on Daniel, she thought, *but I've got to look at the long-term picture. Especially after what Nolan told me. I think he needs to get out of the woods, for now.* The fact that Daniel had missed supper again in spite of his promise to be home finalized her plans.

Then she thought of her grandfather. Abigail could not sleep now. As she lay there in the dark, she rethought her answer to Nolan's question. She was a young woman when her grandmother died, but Nolan's query resurrected memories of that sad event.

Tom and Annie Reilly had lived in a nice neighborhood in Uniontown, Pennsylvania, a city located ten miles west of Lick Hollow. Their large brick house stood tall and proud, shoulder to shoulder with other homes of similar fashion, built in the early 1900s by a rising middle class. Tom and Annie had eloped before they were twenty years old, much to the concern of both sets of parents. Tom worked at what employment he could find, but the couple was so poor that they lived for a

Wooden Spoons

short, agitated period with Annie's parents. Ten months later, shortly after Janice was born, Tom was fortunate to be accepted as a member of the Uniontown Fire Department. At the time of Annie's death he had served the department with distinction for forty years.

The evening after the funeral, family and friends crowded the big house and were loud in the kitchen. Abigail saw her grandfather slip down the hall, away from the crowd. She waited a few minutes and then followed him. It was summer and windows were open wide in all directions. She could hear the broadcast of a Pittsburgh Pirates baseball game from some distant radio.

When Abigail walked into the dim living room, her grandfather was beside his own radio, a glass of sherry in hand. Tom smiled, but it looked to her as if he had been crying. The room served the purpose a den would have for another man, since it never had become a living room for his family. He was the only one who consistently used it. This might have been because it was a bit formal in its furnishings and decor. The room had become a showcase for the finer pieces of furniture the family accumulated as their monetary situation improved. In truth, it never was a comfortable room to live in. Another reason was the large and inviting kitchen, which naturally became the place to congregate. There was a congregation there tonight. Laughter and conversation reverberated down the hall.

Abigail remembered that her grandfather began to question her in a teasing way about her new boyfriend, Allen Whaley. He more than anyone found it appropriate that she would meet a man attending Temple University in Philadelphia, who had grown up in Uniontown. Tom had met Allen the day before and liked the young man immediately.

Dennis Ruane

As they talked, Abigail glanced about the room until her gaze stopped at a framed photograph of her Uncle Tom, Tom Reilly, Jr., in his uniform, a proud smile on his face. She turned to see that her grandfather had followed her gaze. Abigail was at a momentary loss for words, finally asking a question that she thought was appropriate. "Paw, do you think that Uncle Tom and Grandma are together tonight?"

Her grandfather continued to stare at the photograph as he answered. "No dear, I don't. My comfort on this day is that your poor grandmother's suffering is over. She no longer has to bear the pain of her cancer or the grief over the death of her son."

"Then you don't believe in a heaven or maybe some sort of an afterlife?"

He sighed and looked at her. "Abigail, I never prayed so hard when my son went off to that damn war. I prayed for his safety, I prayed for his return. Since that awful moment when I learned of Tommy's death, I have never prayed again."

-5-

As he drove along Main Street, Lick Hollow seemed smaller then Daniel Whaley remembered it. He drove a blue Jeep presented to him three months before as a graduation present from his grandparents. He was meandering toward The University of Wisconsin in Madison, where he would begin graduate studies toward a Doctor of Philosophy degree in biochemistry. He was making the journey itself a short vacation. Daniel had told his great-grandfather about the trip to Wisconsin in a letter, and had informed him that the itinerary included a stop at Mountain Farm.

After his family moved to Philadelphia, Daniel's life changed dramatically. Contrary to what he advised, Nolan Whaley did tell a number of people about Daniel's extraordinary test scores, and so did Daniel's mother. One of the last to hear, but the one who took the information and acted upon it, was Daniel's grandmother. By the time he arrived in Philadelphia, Penn Academy was waiting for him and the academic pace of his life accelerated. Daniel exceeded all expectations while at the Academy, and then again at Villanova University.

Earlier in the spring, he graduated with highest honors from Villanova University, his grandfather Kelly's Alma Mater.

Dennis Ruane

Although Janice Kelly was disappointed that he did not pursue a medical career, she was glad that her husband was able to get Daniel into a prestigious graduate program in the field of his choice. Tom Kelly had a good friend at Villanova, a professor of Nutrition who had done his graduate studies at the University of Wisconsin. This friend still had many contacts there, most significantly a former housemate who was now a professor of biochemistry. It took only a half-dozen phone calls back and forth, and Daniel was admitted to the graduate program with a full research-assistantship. For his part, Daniel knew little about the school or even much about the state of Wisconsin.

Soon he was creeping up Hemlock Road, maneuvering over ruts and washouts, joyfully reacquainting himself with the sights and scents of this mountain he once knew so well. Daniel had been to Mountain Farm for only two hasty visits since his family moved to Philadelphia. Only Tom's sporadic letters kept him informed of such matters as the health of the sugar bush, or the condition of the road.

When his progress was blocked by a fallen tree, he joyfully pulled a new axe from the back seat, a tool he had purchased for this opportunity. Although he had not swung an axe since his early teens, the competence he had achieved then came back to him quickly. Daniel deftly removed the smaller limbs, or *bucked* the log, as Tom would say, and then chopped the main trunk into smaller sections that could be rolled out of the way. To his delight, he had to repeat this operation on another large maple branch before reaching the log house.

As the house came into view, Daniel was not surprised to see his great-grandfather behind the sawhorse. Emma was sitting at attention on the porch. Tom only looked up once as the jeep drove down Reilly lane, and he did not acknowledge

Wooden Spoons

his great-grandson's presence until Daniel had stepped from the vehicle. Daniel had let his hair grow long at Villanova and it hung down to his shoulders in uneven strands. He was an inch taller than Tom now.

"Don't they have barber shops in Philadelphia?" Tom said, finally turning, a mischievous smile on his face. "Come inside and I'll get you ready for school with my hair shears."

Daniel laughed. Then his great-grandfather surprised him with a firm handshake accompanied by a strong pat on the shoulder. His wrinkled face bore such a joyful smile that Daniel never felt so welcome anywhere, before or after. Emma was hovering over his feet, and he stooped to pet her affectionately. Then Tom touched him on the back and motioned toward the house.

For an hour, they sat on the front porch drinking tea and talking. Daniel told his great-grandfather the family news and the current events in the world, just as he always had. Afterwards, Tom and his great-grandson went on the customary tour of the homestead with Tom talking and instructing as usual. Like Lick Hollow, Tom seemed smaller than Daniel remembered him. His great-grandfather's health appeared good but, unlike before, he felt uneasy about his aged ancestor living alone on the mountain.

When they passed through the woodshed, Daniel noticed that there were less than five cords of firewood and it was nearly autumn. Later, he convinced Tom that he had been looking forward to cutting firewood as part of his vacation. They passed some mirthful hours at the sawhorse that afternoon, and although Daniel's shoulders and arms began to ache, he cut until dark.

That night, he slept upstairs in what had been the bedroom of Tom's sisters, Helen and June. They were born

Dennis Ruane

nearly ten years before Tom and were both dead now. Helen, the oldest, had married a man from West Virginia. She and her husband raised a large family near Bluefield and their descendants were still concentrated in that area. Daniel knew little about them.

June Reilly married Michael Campbell, a man from Lick Hollow. She and her family had lived at the end of Bennington Road, less than a mile from where Daniel grew up. He had visited her eight years ago with his mother, and could still picture her kind face, smiling at him as she patted his hand and softly laughed. At the time, her husband had been dead for a decade and she had but one more year to live. He remembered that June was very feeble and while she didn't say much, she seemed delighted that he had come to visit. In a tinny, weak voice she said that he reminded her of her father.

Daniel welcomed sleep after such a strenuous evening of work. He lay in the darkness listening to the curious night noises: chirping frogs, whirring and clicking insects and the thrashing of leaves as they captured the wind. Then came the forlorn hoot of a barred owl. A sense of peacefulness and security lulled him to sleep.

The next morning as they ate a breakfast of oatmeal and raisins topped with maple syrup, Tom looked up at Daniel. "You still have that jackknife?"

"Sure do, Paw," Daniel replied, pulling it from his pocket.

"Let me see it."

Daniel handed the knife to him and Tom held it close to the window, examining the blade carefully.

"Pretty nice edge. Could take a little honing."

Daniel chuckled.

Wooden Spoons

Tom got up and went to his room. He returned with a canvas roll and placed it on the table in front of his great-grandson. "Here's your graduation present."

Daniel swallowed the oatmeal in his mouth and put his spoon down. Undoing the leather straps, he unrolled the canvas to find the woodcarving tools that had once belonged to Adam Reilly.

Tom cleared his throat and then spoke with unusual seriousness. "I gave carving one more good try but I don't have the patience anymore. I'm ninety now and I think I've run out of time. I sometimes feel that I hung onto the tools longer than I should have. You know, Daniel, of all the things I have, I cherish these tools most. But they were made to be used, to create works of art, not to sit on a shelf. Pap gave them to me hoping I would use them. I guess it just isn't in me or I would have found the time. So I'm passing them along to you now and I hope that you'll use them, or at least pass them along into the right hands someday."

"I, I'll use them, Paw."

"Well, I hope so. I hope so. That would be the best that could come of it."

"I mean it, Paw. I'm going to use them. I promise."

Tom nodded and smiled. "You know, Daniel, if you are ever inclined, my opinion is that making wooden spoons for a livelihood would be a fine profession and could make a man an honest living."

Daniel expected to hear his great-grandfather clear his throat and smile but he didn't. Instead Tom was looking at him with a very serious expression. "I, I think I'm going to be a scientist, Paw."

"Well maybe you will be, and maybe you won't. I thought once that I was a fireman." Tom leaned on his elbows and was

Dennis Ruane

quiet for a moment. Then he softly spoke. "Follow your dreams, Daniel. Find an occupation you enjoy and one you believe in. Everything changes and passes away sooner or later. You can never depend on any person to always be there for you, or any happy era to go on forever. You must always have your own plan, one that will keep you moving when the trials of life begin."

This made sense to Daniel, but it was unusual for him to hear such advice from Tom. His great-grandfather typically advised him on more concrete subjects, such as the proper length of a red oak shingle or the quantity of sugar water required to produce a gallon of maple syrup. Daniel nodded but remained silent.

Tom continued with a look of concern. "Whatever you do, never let the pursuit of money distract you from life's real goals. Money is a necessary commodity in our present state of society, a means to an end. But it will distort your judgment and suck the marrow right out of life, if you let it become the end in itself."

Daniel nodded again.

Tom stopped, and finally smiled. "Now on the more practical side of the matter, I will give you some advice my father gave me. Never get into debt, especially to a friend, and when you are able, squirrel away enough cash to see you through at least one year of infirmity or unemployment. And I mean cash that no bank or government is aware of." Tom stopped again and smiled. He felt that he had said enough.

Daniel watched as his great-grandfather slowly stood and searched his pockets.

"Here's something to aid your transport," Tom said, plopping a wad of bills on the table.

Daniel picked it up and unfolded five one-hundred dollar

Wooden Spoons

bills. He looked up. "Paw, I can't take . . ."

"Oh yes, you can. I've got more than I need now. This is my pleasure, to help you a little along your path. Get yourself some clothes, or some good tools, a haircut, whatever you need."

Daniel laughed.

At midmorning, they returned to the sawhorse and resumed cutting firewood. There were several large beech logs nearby that Tom had dragged there with his truck. Daniel and his aged relative used the two-man crosscut saw to cut them to firewood-length pieces. Daniel split these into wedges, the size he knew his great-grandfather preferred for the wood stove. They did not stop working until there were six cords of firewood stacked in the shed. While Tom did not expect this service, he was noticeably grateful.

That afternoon, Daniel took leave of Tom and Mountain Farm. Once again he was rewarded by a hearty handshake and a warm pat on the shoulder. Emma sat beside her master, old and stiff herself, watching as the young man drove off toward the east. Although Tom jokingly warned against it, Daniel was determined to go through to Furnace Road. Tom even pointed out that Wisconsin was in the opposite direction, although he knew that fact was irrelevant to this young man, so happy and full of life.

With his ax beside him and his jeep beneath him, Daniel Whaley was determined to make it through to Furnace Road and out into the world. He laughed and carelessly sped up. A hundred yards down the road, at the first bend, he stopped and waved to his great-grandfather. Tom raised a hand in return, confident that he had done the right thing in giving Daniel the woodcarving tools. He was also well aware of the fact that he would probably never see his great-grandson again.

-6-

Daniel was greeted at the apartment door by his wife, who was carrying their one-year-old son. She gave him a kiss and handed him the baby.

"Please take over while I finish dinner, O.K.?"

Daniel nodded and smiled. Ken settled comfortably into his father's arms.

"How did it go today?" Debbie asked over her shoulder as she hurried to the kitchen.

"Good. We're starting to get some interesting results. I talked with Doctor Henry this morning and he seemed pleased. He even mentioned that I should start thinking seriously about my PhD proposal."

"Wow, that's good news."

"How was your day?" Daniel asked, moving to the kitchen doorway.

"Great. That job on Gorham Street was a piece of cake, and I picked up another from a neighbor who saw me there." She looked up and smiled as she chopped a salad. "I grabbed a rotisserie chicken at the store before I picked up Ken, so it won't be long."

"Sounds good to me," Daniel replied, smiling back.

"You know, I'm seriously considering hiring help."

Daniel raised his eyebrows. "Help with your cleaning?"

"Of course with the cleaning," she answered, laughing. "I think that there is really a demand in Madison for what I do. Not just cleaning houses, there's a demand for that everywhere. I mean the way I do it, fast and hard, and on a moment's notice. And the pay keeps getting better."

"Then it will be like a real business."

"Yeah, Dan, like a real business." She noticed furrows forming on his forehead, so she did not elaborate on her plans. Debbie also decided to wait to tell him that she was considering not returning to school. Fortunately, she remembered a good reason to change the subject. "Oh, there's a letter on the counter from your mother."

He looked at her blankly for a moment, adjusting to the sudden turn in the conversation. He carried the envelope and Ken into the living room. Daniel placed his son on the floor and piled an assortment of toys around him. It seemed odd that his mother would write to him now when she was expected for a visit in less than two weeks. He read quickly, while out of the corner of his eye, he watched Ken dismiss one toy after another. When Debbie entered the room to announce that dinner was ready, she knew that something was wrong.

"What is it, Dan?"

He continued to read and didn't answer.

"Daniel, what is it," she said, moving her face close to his.

He looked up at her. "Paw died."

"Paw?"

"Paw, my great-grandfather."

"Oh, oh yes. I'm sorry. How did he die?"

He was engrossed in the letter again and did not answer.

"Daniel, how did he die?" This time, when her husband looked up, Debbie saw that his eyes were tearing.

"Old age, I guess. He was ninety-two."

Dennis Ruane

"Ninety-two," she repeated in a tone of disbelief. "Well, was your mother there?"

"No, nobody was there," he said, his voice choking. "They found him by the sawhorse, the spot where he always cut firewood. They guess he may have died late last fall."

Debbie's mouth opened wide but she said nothing. She knew that her husband was very fond of his great-grandfather. Over the years, she had listened politely to the stories he told without much comment, but having grown up in Chicago, she couldn't help but share Grandmother Kelly's opinion of Tom Reilly's lifestyle.

Daniel got up, went to the hall closet and rummaged around impatiently. He brought down a canvas roll from the top shelf and carried it to the living room. Debbie was puzzled at first, but remembered the woodcarving tools when Daniel unrolled the canvas on the coffee table.

"That's right. Your great-grandfather gave you these."

Daniel nodded. "I think he wanted to pass them along to the right person in the family, or in my case, maybe the best option. These tools belonged to his father, Adam, who was a woodcarver. Paw always meant to continue his father's craft but he didn't. He felt I might, for some reason."

"Why didn't he?"

"It just wasn't meant to be, I guess," Daniel replied with a shrug, suddenly not wanting to answer any more questions. "He was too busy. He had a family and he was a fireman for many years."

"Did you ever use the tools?"

"Ah, no, I never really used them. Not yet. Maybe it isn't meant to be for me either."

"When was the last time you saw your great-grandfather?"

"Uh, right before I moved here." Then, he quickly related

additional information from the letter in an attempt to redirect his wife. "Hey, Mom's still coming to visit, she and Bob."

"Really? It'll be interesting, to meet Bob."

"Bob's all right. We're not too much alike, but he's all right. Hey Deb, I'm not so hungry right now. Go ahead and eat without me."

"O.K. I'm sorry about Paw," she said as she leaned over and kissed him on the cheek. Debbie took Ken to the kitchen, realizing that her husband wanted to be alone.

Daniel leaned forward, with elbows on his knees and stared at the woodcarving tools.

Abigail and Robert Whyel arrived in Madison ten days later. Determined to experience the city from within, they had rented a suite at the newly refurbished Washington Hotel, located only a block from the State Capital Building. In comparison to Philadelphia, Madison seemed more like a large town than a city and for that reason they were captivated by it. The city center is situated on an isthmus between Lake Monona to the south, and the larger Lake Mendota to the north. The majestic, granite Capital Building stands on a hill in the center, and Madison emanates from it in all directions. It was only a short and entertaining stroll on State Street, the cultural heart of the city, to the University of Wisconsin, which spread to the west along Lake Mendota.

For two days they explored Madison, toured the university campus and ate out, leisurely adjusting their plans around Daniel and Debbie's busy schedules. On the third afternoon, they wanted to relax and talk before heading west to visit Robert's son in Arizona. They met Daniel and Debbie on the Memorial Union Terrace, a popular leisure spot on campus which overlooked the lake. When Debbie excused herself to pick up Ken at the daycare center and Robert went for a cigarette stroll, Abigail and her son were finally alone.

"Did you get the letter from Simon Joseph?" she asked.

"No, I haven't," he replied, with an apprehensive expression. Simon Joseph was the family attorney and a longtime friend.

"Don't worry. You're not in trouble. It's good news. Paw had written a will of which none of us were aware. That's what Simon will be contacting you about."

"Do you know what's in the will?"

His mother nodded. "It contained only three requests. First, Paw wished to be buried in the little family cemetery behind the log house."

Daniel had known that his great-grandfather wanted this and nodded.

"Second, he wished that the contents of the log house and the other buildings go to John Campbell, Jr." This too was not a surprise to Daniel, aware that Paw and his great-nephew had been close. John Campbell and his wife, Nora, owned and operated the Lick Hollow Mercantile, a general store located at the eastern end of Lick Hollow. This was where Tom Reilly's maple syrup had been sold, and was where he had bought all of his supplies.

"How are John and Nora?"

"They're good, Daniel, tough as always. They handled Tom's death well and made the funeral arrangements. They're like him in many ways."

Daniel started to ask another question, but his mother interrupted impatiently.

"Wait, Daniel. The last item in Paw's will is that he wished to leave the family property on Hemlock Knob to his great-grandson, Daniel Whaley."

This statement came as a total surprise to Daniel. On a much larger scale, it reminded him of when he was presented with the carving tools. "What about Grandma?" he asked.

"Well, your grandmother was not too surprised to be left out, considering the relationship she has had with Paw over the years. She was not really counting on Mountain Farm as part of her retirement plan, anyway. She and your grandfather are very well off. Actually it's the rest of the family, uncles, aunts, and cousins, that are grumbling a bit. But the fact is, this was not a last minute decision. Paw's will was written up twelve years ago."

Daniel counted back and realized that this was during the period when he began visiting Mountain Farm alone. "Why didn't you tell me this before, Mom?"

Abigail cleared her throat, nervously. "I didn't have a chance to be alone with you. It's not that I'm trying to be sneaky, but Paw left the property to you and I wanted you to know first. That's all."

Daniel didn't know exactly what this answer meant. Bob rejoined them at this point.

"What will I do with Mountain Farm?" Daniel asked, naively.

"Just sit on it for now," Bob interrupted, obviously aware of what they were talking about. "It's not worth a great deal of money as property goes, especially to people in that area. There's money headed that way, though."

Robert Whyel was an executive vice president of Milton Bank in Philadelphia, and he offered his opinion on financial matters freely. Although Daniel had only met him a few times before, his impression of his mother's new husband was good.

"An interstate is in the planning stage that will connect

39

Dennis Ruane

Pittsburgh to Baltimore and Washington D.C. Hemlock Knob is somewhere in between. People in the cities have always looked for places in the mountains to escape to for a vacation or to build a second home. They haven't looked as far as your mountain yet, but with an interstate and easy access, it's only a matter of time before they do."

Daniel listened politely. This was easy advice to take, since he would never consider selling his great-grandfather's home.

"We stopped in Lick Hollow on the way here," Abigail said. "John Campbell readily volunteered to look after Mountain Farm until you decide what you want to do. He said that he goes up there often and that he could recruit some of the local hunters to keep an eye on it. I gave him your address and phone number."

The topic changed at this point when Debbie arrived with Ken. Bob questioned her about the cleaning business and then listened intently to her answers, some of which Daniel hadn't yet heard. Bob was quickly impressed with Debbie's basic business instinct.

While they talked, Abigail turned to her son and spoke softly. "How is your work going? You have settled on biochemistry as a major, right?"

Daniel nodded but was still listening to the ongoing conversation.

"Absolutely," Bob exclaimed. "That is the key to any business, find a niche where there's a need and move into it aggressively."

"You enjoy it, don't you?" Abigail asked, trying to get his full attention.

The question surprised him. Daniel tried to answer thoughtfully. "I don't enjoy science like I did at Villanova when my studies were more general. The thing is, the further along you go in a particular field, the more specialized it becomes and, well, that's what's happening now. But it's a job too; I have a family to support. When the work starts to get to me, I remind myself of that."

Abigail paused with this remark, and looked at her daughter-in-law and her husband, who were still engaged in conversation. She smiled. "Poor Bob, spending all this time with only me to talk to. He's starved for conversation about business with somebody."

Daniel grinned while thinking to himself that the same statement might also apply to Debbie.

"What about the future? What do you want to do after the PhD?"

"I'm fairly certain that I want to stay in academics, but in what capacity, I don't know at this point."

"Bob said that there would be a lot more money working as a scientist for a large corporation," Abigail added with an mischievous smile.

Daniel smiled back, not the least surprised that Bob would have that opinion. "Well, I like to think that I can apply my knowledge and skills in a direction that might do some good for the world, even if it's in a small way."

"Just so you are happy, Daniel. Time passes quickly, and the pace accelerates as you get older. No one can afford to spend too many years doing something they don't enjoy."

That night as she lay in bed, Abigail stared out the window. As far as Daniel's domestic situation was concerned, she liked Debbie but wondered how her son had fallen in love with someone so different from himself. Several years ago

Dennis Ruane

when she had last spoken to her brother-in-law, Nolan, concerning Daniel, his opinion was that his nephew had been pushed in the direction of a science career. Abigail sighed. Once her mother got the wheels rolling, it was difficult to slow things down. Daniel seemed so stiff and cautious now. It was hard for his mother to imagine that he was the same free-spirited boy who worried her so much with his solitary forays on Hemlock Knob.

-7-

The professor awoke in a large leather recliner to a discordant metallic clanging noise. It was distant and yet strangely familiar. He was not certain how long he had slept, for he had no idea when he had fallen asleep. On a table beside the chair was a glass with a thick film at the bottom. Daniel Whaley did not feel well and had no desire to get up.

Professor Whaley and his wife Debbie lived in a beautiful Tudor-style home on Lake Mendota Drive. It was conveniently located two miles from the campus of the University of Wisconsin, where he was a Professor of Biochemistry. Strategically situated on a two-acre lot that bordered land owned by the university, it was an exceptional piece of property in an already exclusive neighborhood.

Suddenly, there was the noise again. It was coming from behind the garage. "Damn it," he muttered, lurching forward out of the recliner. Daniel was wearing a burgundy-colored robe from some Christmas past that covered gray sweat-pants and a white tee shirt. Again came the noise. He guessed what it was now, but could not understand how it was possible that he was hearing it.

As the clanging continued, the professor plodded to the kitchen and threw open a closet door. Impatiently, he put on a green trench coat, wound a scarf around his neck, pulled a stocking hat over his head, and donned a pair of garden boots. Daniel stumbled out into the cold, a picture of dishevelment. When he glanced to his left and saw his son's car parked beside the house, his irritation grew. Rounding the corner of the garage, he found Ken slumped inside the raised hood of an old jeep, which was parked in a cluster of small trees and bushes. Daniel startled him as he stalked up from behind.

"Hey Dad. What's up?" Ken blurted, looking guilty. Ken was four inches shorter than his father. He was handsome, with pale-green, nervous eyes. His hair was neat and like his clothing, stylish for the times. "Didn't expect to see you here in the middle of the day."

"Yes. Hi, Ken. I, uh, I didn't go in today. Head's bothering me. I've been having headaches again, I mean."

He did not have to explain. Ken knew that some variation of the problem his father had been experiencing during the past year had reoccurred. Although a headache was only one of the symptoms, 'headache' was the term his father always used to describe his ailment.

"That's too bad." Ken said quickly. " Say, the reason I . . ."

"No work today, Ken?" Daniel interrupted.

"I walked out on that idiot. He didn't know what the hell he was doing. I know more about cars than he does, and I only worked there six months. Besides, I was sick of the way he jerked me around with my hours. Nobody jerks me around like that, not anymore."

Daniel stared in the direction of his son but was only half-listening. He had heard variations of this diatribe before.

Recognizing the vacant look on his father's face, Ken raised his voice and continued. "Listen, Dad, I have a plan now. A good plan. That's the reason I stopped by. Lenny and I are going into business . . ."

Wooden Spoons

"Your cousin Leonard?"

Ken shrugged. He knew that his plan lost some credibility with the mention of his partner's name. "Yeah, yeah, Dad, that Lenny. We're going to open our own garage, an independent business. We found a building just outside of Waunakee. Well, actually, Lenny's brother-in-law owns it so all we have to do is fix it up a little."

Daniel was no longer listening to his son and his blood pressure was rising. When Ken sensed that he was losing his audience, he moved closer and spoke even louder. "Wait Dad, don't shut me off, damn it. You never take my ideas seriously."

Daniel fixed his blue eyes on Ken, but said nothing.

"All I'm asking for is a little help, a small loan, to get the ball rolling, then we'll be on our own, an independent business, like Mom's, with no idiots calling the shots."

"What's with the jeep?"

"The jeep, uh, this old thing? Well, until we realize a little cash-flow and can buy a wrecker, I thought we could use this to tow. What the hell, it's better than nothing."

"Better than nothing, is it?" Daniel asked, coolly. The notoriously mild-mannered, biochemistry professor found himself struggling to control his temper. He looked past his son at the jeep and then spoke in a calm but firm voice. "Well, Ken, I'm not in a position right now to finance your business venture, but I wish you and Leonard the best of luck."

It was so uncharacteristic of his father to respond this way that Ken did not know how to react at first. He had not expected an immediate *yes*. He figured that it would take a little work. Yet he fully expected to get the money as well as the jeep. His surprise turned into anger, and then careless words. "Well I didn't expect a loan from you. Mom's the breadwinner here, isn't she? She isn't a professor but she

45

Dennis Ruane

knows business. She lives in the real world, like me."

Daniel cleared his throat. "If your mother wants to lend you money, that's her choice, but I won't lend you a cent toward this business venture with Leonard. I've been through this before with you. And, leave the jeep alone."

"Well, hell with the jeep, this piece of junk. I thought I'd do you a favor and get the eyesore out of here so Mom doesn't have to be embarrassed about it anymore."

Daniel Whaley was a passive man. The temper he inherited from his mother's side of the family never surfaced in his quiet academic world. This morning his son was pressing him at a bad time and in the wrong way. Daniel was tall with a large frame, and was actually quite strong. Yet, standing there in his odd wardrobe, he must have seemed weak to his son.

Ken moved a step closer and began to shout. "I didn't expect to get a helping hand from my Dad." He signed air quotation marks with his fingers as he said 'Dad'.

Daniel hated air quotes.

"I'll leave your precious jeep alone and you can go back to your cave and sleep for a few more days."

Ken had gone too far. Daniel's right hand shot out and grabbed his son by the jacket just under his chin. Ken stopped talking abruptly. It was then that he realized, as if for the first time, that his father was larger than he. Ken was also aware that the grip which held him was deliberate and powerful. Daniel pulled Ken slightly forward and with a somewhat wavering but terse voice, spoke plainly. "I don't want to hear another word from you."

Ken was silent as his father held him for a few seconds.

"Not another word," Daniel repeated as he shoved his son backward.

Ken was thunderstruck. He had never been physically

threatened by his father, nor had his father ever spoken to him in such a manner. Ken had made much worse statements over the years and never provoked this reaction. Usually, Daniel stormed away to the study and then simply did not speak to him for two or three weeks. Ken hesitated, but eventually turned from his father's gaze and walked down the driveway. Beside his car, he pointed a shaking finger at Daniel, who had followed him around the garage.

"You'll see, you'll see," he stammered. Ken started to say more, but stopped and got in the car first. As he backed up to turn the vehicle, he rolled down the window quickly. "Alcoholic," he shouted, with a weird, strained grin on his face.

The car raced down the driveway never stopping at the road. With tires squealing, it turned right and sped away. Professor Whaley stood looking after his son, equally surprised at what had happened. At age twenty-eight, Ken was a great disappointment to his father. Although regret was already seeping into Daniel's cooling conscience, many events over the last decade had set the stage for this scene.

It was in high school that problems first surfaced. Ken had done well during his early school years. Daniel and Debbie were stunned when informed at the midpoint of their son's junior year that he was failing several courses. When confronted with this information Ken assured them that he had been through a rough spell but now was doing well again. The Whaleys were stunned all over again when Ken did indeed fail these courses. Ken dared try to convince his parents again until they finally held the grades in his face. He paused for a moment and then became hostile. He blamed his failure on them, especially on his father

That introductory incident was over a decade ago. Many others followed as Ken developed a pattern of missteps, nonchalant lying and belligerence. This particular event would hardly stand out, except for the way it had ended. Daniel continued to stand, staring down the driveway, growing cold and listless.

He walked back to look at the jeep, half-claimed by the hedge row. Despite the circumstances, it had sounded good to hear the engine turn over again. It was this vehicle that had transported him to Wisconsin nearly three decades before. Debbie and he went on their first date in the jeep, and for several years after their marriage, it was the means of transportation for their new family.

Debbie urged him many times to get rid of it after they had moved to Lake Mendota Drive. For some years Daniel demonstrated its usefulness by hauling the balled hemlock trees, which he had planted obsessively on their property. When Debbie finally halted this activity, claiming that she did not want their entire acreage turned into a forest, the jeep sat idly for long periods of time. She was then able to convince him to at least park it out of sight. Thereafter, when Daniel had time for a yard project, he would tinker with the engine and eventually rattle and squeak away to the building supply store or garden shop. While Debbie often wished the jeep would die once and for all, she admitted that her husband was happiest after these outings. She joked that it was the hillbilly in him. It had been more than two years now since Daniel had driven his jeep.

As the sun slid through a billow of clouds, the cold was amplified. Daniel turned back toward the house and the comfort of his study. In the kitchen he poured a cup of cold coffee, leftover in the percolator by his wife. He heated it in the microwave. Back in the study, he returned to the leather chair and thought about the remarks that Ken had made, particularly the one in which he called the study a cave. Daniel had not heard that reference made in many years, and then it was in a humorous, teasing way. It was a nickname Debbie had coined to describe the experience of sitting in the big leather recliner in the dim study while gazing out the windows into the light.

-8-

Once again, Professor Whaley had no idea how long he had slept. He did know that his head felt thick and his throat was sore. He vaguely recalled a dull lunch sometime earlier in the day, followed with brandy. It was dark outside. Memory fragments of something that happened with his son were piecing together in his sluggish brain. Daniel grew warm and uncomfortable as he recalled the encounter. Detecting a faint aroma of cigarette smoke, he realized that his wife was home. He also knew that she was aware of the incident with Ken.

Deborah Bradley had been a sophomore at the University of Wisconsin, working toward a degree in nutrition, when she met Daniel. He had just entered the PhD program in the Biochemistry Department and she was a friend of the laboratory technician who worked in his lab. Although one could hardly imagine a more unlikely couple, their attraction to each other was immediate.

Debbie was from Chicago, tough, assertive and gregarious. She loved a party. Daniel grew up in a small town of nine hundred inhabitants and was quiet and conservative. Although known to be polite and friendly, he was uncomfortable in a crowd. She found this amusing and even charming in the beginning. He found Debbie to be irresistible.

Wooden Spoons

They rented an apartment together and passed the months laughing at their differences. Daniel did things he had never done before such as play softball, go to rock concerts, dance and make love.

When Debbie became pregnant, it seemed to be a mere speed-bump in the fun. The young couple hesitated, talked it over, impulsively got married, and named the baby Ken. Debbie withdrew from school at the end of the semester. Her intention was to stay at home with the baby and then work part-time to supplement the meager income that came from Daniel's research assistantship. She cleaned houses. The hours were flexible and the money was good. Dependable and willing to work on short notice, Debbie soon had as many jobs as she could manage.

Meanwhile, Daniel advanced at a rapid pace, setting the upper end of the curve for the rest of the students in his classes. He received his PhD in four years, then became an associate professor two years after that. It was obvious at this stage that Professor Henry, who was nearing retirement, was grooming Daniel to succeed him.

Debbie never returned to school. She continued cleaning houses and slowly turned the part time work into a sound little business. By the time Ken was in school and her husband had received his PhD, she had hired an employee and owned a secondhand van, which proudly bore the name *Bradley Maid*. Debbie was a natural businesswoman and when she realized the demand for a fast, dependable, cleaning service that would respond on short notice, she aggressively moved to answer it. By the time Daniel was a tenured professor she had two new vans and five employees.

Daniel stood up, palmed his empty glass and lumbered down the hall to the kitchen doorway. There he faced his wife,

Dennis Ruane

sitting at the table, cigarette in hand, poised and waiting. Some years ago after new evidence of the adverse effects of second-hand smoke were announced, Debbie had proclaimed that she would no longer smoke in the house. She had abided by that statement ever since. The fact that she was casually ignoring it now, was the reason Daniel knew that Ken had already spoken to her.

When Daniel first met Deborah Bradley, she had been sitting at a table smoking a cigarette. With her trim figure, pretty face, and long black hair, he thought she looked like a movie starlet. Sadly, as he stood there now, in his old robe and sweat pants with hair protruding from his head in all directions around a profound bald spot, he still thought that Debbie looked like a movie starlet.

"Well, Professor Whaley, you handled that well."

"Now Debbie, I . . ."

"Wait," she interrupted, pointing a finger at him. "Did you actually grab him by the throat?"

"No. Of course I didn't. I grabbed his jacket, near his throat, not his throat. I did it because I had a point to make."

"I know, that he's an idiot. Subtle point."

"No, wait, Deb, I did not say that." He paused, struggling to sort out the facts before he said more. "I came home early, I had a headache . . ."

"Ah," she said, loudly, "you and your headaches. I'm sick of your headaches. You are suffering from some kind of depression. You need help and you won't face up to it."

"So you think I should have gone along with another of Ken's wild ideas," Daniel asked, steering the conversation away from the point she was making.

"It is not a wild idea and you don't have to go along with it. I'm going to lend him the money."

Wooden Spoons

At first his expression was of anger. Then it became a vacant stare. She knew the look well and hated it because it signaled the end of their discourse. She called it *the stoneface*. Daniel never argued about Ken for long before it appeared. He did not say it this time, but Debbie knew that her husband believed she had spoiled Ken, particularly so after her financial situation improved.

Daniel did not speak, but walked over to an oak dry sink that served as a liquor cabinet. He had bought it for Debbie on the occasion of her thirtieth birthday. Daniel knew that his wife felt he had always expected too much of Ken and could not accept their son for what he was. The professor also knew, too well, that he couldn't win an argument with Debbie. He briskly opened the cabinet door and removed a bottle which was more empty than full. Rather than fill his glass, he decided to take the bottle with him. Daniel did not look back as he shuffled down the hall.

"End of discussion, eh, Dan?" she called after him.

He did not turn but raised the bottle above his shoulder as an apparent affirmation.

Back in the study, Daniel eased himself into the leather chair and filled his glass. Daniel Whaley *was* suffering from some sort of depression, as his wife had said, and he *was* somewhat of an alcoholic, as his son had said. He was fifty-five years old and few things in his life had turned out the way he had hoped.

When he was a boy, Daniel would sit on the highest rock at Point Lookout, gazing down on Lick Hollow, Pennsylvania, his hometown. He often thought about the grand things he might accomplish one day. These were typically such feats as beating up a bully that was ruining Lick Hollow or of one day becoming so famous that he could share his wealth with everybody in town. The inability to fulfill these childish daydreams did not trouble him now. Instead he found amusement in remembering them. It was a failure to achieve the typical desires of adulthood such as a happy marriage, a loving family or a rewarding career that caused him to question the course of his life. This was the reason he sat alone in his study, drinking brandy and neglecting his academic duties.

Life isn't fair. Working hard and trying to be a good person doesn't guarantee that you will have a happy or a prosperous life. I did what I was supposed to. I did my job well. I wanted to do something good for the world and I tried to do what was right for my family. Look at me now.

For many years, the success of his career buffered him against the domestic shortfalls. As a scientist, he was contributing to human knowledge, improving the lot of mankind, changing the world. As he grew older and more cynical, that rationale failed to muster the same charge in him. The fact was, he spent his days taking slow, measured steps toward scientific details, while the world changed rapidly, not affected by or even aware of his efforts.

And what about Dad? He worked so hard at his coal business, supported all of us, went to church every Sunday, and then he suffered and died at an early age. He took a long, hard drink. Daniel attempted to steer his thoughts in another direction, seeking distraction, trying to find some happy parcel of life to start pinning hope around. Naturally, he thought of his daughter.

Jeannie was born seven years after Ken, much to the surprise of friends and family who had grown accustomed to the idea that the Whaleys had stopped after one child. Both Daniel and Deborah seemed so engrossed in their careers at this point that no one guessed they were ready to make the sacrifice of time that a child demanded. Daniel was also surprised by his wife's decision to have another baby. When she was born, Jeannie became the joy of her father's life. She was a delightful baby and a happy child. As she grew to be a young adult, it was obvious that she took after her father in most ways. She did inherit her mother's attractive features and, fortunately, a measure of assertiveness to compliment an otherwise quiet, intellectual personality.

After high school, Jeannie attended the University of California at Berkeley only to withdraw after her freshman year. She remained in Berkeley and worked so that she could travel in Europe the following year. When she returned to the United States, she settled in Santa Fe and worked in a bookstore to raise funds for a trip to Alaska. Last year, Jeannie began working toward an art degree at the Academy of Fine Arts in Amsterdam, a city she fell in love with during her travels in the Netherlands. That is where her father currently corresponded with her. They both preferred handwritten letters and the receiving of hers were scarce bright moments in a dull existence.

Interestingly, for a person whose career began like a well-oiled machine on a track, Daniel never questioned the winding path his daughter traveled. He listened to her stories with pleasure, answered her questions, and helped financially on the rare occasion that she asked. He missed her very much. "Thank goodness she got away," Daniel said, raising his glass in a toast.

-9-

Another two days passed in dull routine, sleeping, drinking, eating occasionally and rarely leaving the study. Professor Whaley drank brandy and purchased it in large bottles. This morning his stomach was particularly raw, which was not surprising considering that the evening before, he had only eaten thick slices of cheese and a bratwurst. His head had a dense, swollen feeling and the back of his throat was sore as if he had snored all night.

He was alone in the house. Debbie loved their home and she preferred to work out of it at least part of each day, but as soon as her husband's illness would resurface, she planned her schedule to avoid him. He forced toast and coffee while making a great effort to keep the memories of the preceding days at a mental distance until he was ready for them. Daniel entertained no thought of going to the Biochemistry Building.

Moments later, as he struggled to pull on a change of clothing, he heard the sound of a vehicle coming up the driveway. "Oh no," he murmured, quickly putting his robe back on.

Creeping to the kitchen window, he recognized the car of Victor DiAngelo, chairman of the biochemistry department. "Damn it," he exclaimed, ducking out of sight.

Victor DiAngelo and he were friends. They had entered

the department at about the same time, Daniel as a graduate student and Victor, ten years his senior, as an associate professor. For a few nervous seconds, Daniel considered simply returning to his study with the hope that Victor would believe he was not at home, but he could not do that to Victor. As chairman of the department, it was Victor who heard the concerns raised over Daniel's erratic behavior and neglect of duty. He did not know what he would say to his friend, but he owed him an audience at least.

Answering the door, Daniel greeted Victor who was wearing only a tweed jacket over a turtleneck shirt against the bitter cold. As usual, he was smiling. Victor was of average height with a stocky, powerful build. He was good-looking, dark complexioned with brown eyes and a deep dimple on his chin. His curly, silver hair had been tossed in all directions by the wind. Outgoing and charismatic, Professor DiAngelo was well liked, and perfectly suited to his position as department chairman.

"Morning, Daniel. Can I come in?"

"Sure, sure Victor, I was just, uh . . . Would you like a cup of coffee?"

"Hey, that would be great."

Daniel rattled two mugs from the cabinet and poured a jittery stream of coffee into each.

"Nothing like hot coffee on a cold morning," Victor said cheerfully.

They each took a few sips in an uncomfortable silence until Daniel felt compelled to speak.

"Victor, I know that this is . . ."

Professor DiAngelo held up his hand. "Wait. I didn't come for an explanation, just to talk. Please let me say something first."

Dennis Ruane

Daniel nodded and lowered his eyes, embarrassed that he had put their friendship in this awkward position.

Victor cleared his throat. "I want you to know that I have some insight into what you are going through right now, and it's because I had a similar experience about ten years ago." He had Daniel's full attention with that statement. "It seemed to me that after years of climbing up the academic ladder, I was running out of steam and could no longer find a reason to keep going. Fame, duty, the thrill of discovery, none of these old rallying cries could get me on track again. Indifference set in toward my work, and eventually toward life in general. At the age of fifty-three, I started to question if I had even chosen the right occupation."

"Victor, I had no idea," Daniel said, shaking his head.

"Well, you were too young and busy then. Besides, I'm better at hiding things than you are," he said, grinning.

"You seem to me to be someone who fits their job well. I thought that you were born to be a scientist."

Victor laughed. "I started out an English major, wanted to be a writer, actually. An undergraduate advisor suggested that I add some science courses to my curriculum to strengthen my resume. I liked them and did well. Forty years later, here I am."

They both chuckled.

"Let's save that story for another time, Daniel," Victor said, becoming serious again.

"The point I want to share with you is that when the trouble started, I would not accept that I had a problem, especially a mental problem. I wouldn't get help at first. I tried to keep working and thought that I would get through it. But I didn't. My life eventually came to a grinding halt."

"You've obviously come out of it well, Victor," Daniel said

cautiously, now very interested in his colleague's story.

"Well, first and foremost, I got good help, a psychiatrist who listened with an experienced ear. I learned from him that this sort of thing can be a hazard of our profession. John Medford at the Enzyme Institute, a very similar case a while back."

"Really? I never would have guessed that. Professor Medford has always struck me as the epitome of self-confidence and stability."

"Not always, Daniel, not always. In fact he recommended the doc that finally got me back in gear. Depression, that's what it is, as simple as that and as devastating as that."

"I understand what you are saying, but I think there's something else wrong. I have such bad headaches too, sharp and painful. I can point to the spot where they're coming from. And now I hear a strange rumbling sound. I hear it inside my head, and other times, it seems to be coming from outside my body. I'm not always sure if it's a noise or a vibration."

Victor nodded as if none of this surprised him. "I have heard of physical symptoms, too, although different from what you describe. I was also experiencing bad headaches, a while back. I was sure I had a brain tumor and went to see Dr. Barten over at McCardle Labs. You know Willy Barten, don't you?"

Daniel nodded.

"He ran me through a battery of tests and found nothing."

Daniel was certainly impressed with what Victor was telling him, but not totally convinced that his own problem was the same.

"Daniel, I didn't come here to tell you what to do, only to tell you what I did. Think it over. If you want to give him a try, the psychiatrist's name is Paul Taylor, number is in the book.

59

Dennis Ruane

A nice guy, really down to earth."

"I never dreamed that something like this would happen to me."

"Nor did I, but I got through it and Bob Medford got through it and you will too. It's not easy by any means and will take time, but you'll get through it. One point that Doctor Taylor insisted on was that I take up a hobby, a hands-on activity that was very different from my profession, something such as gardening or woodworking or running. Something basic but most importantly, an activity that gives steady, measured results. So, I bought myself some tools, set up a woodworking shop in the basement, filled the house with dust, and threw myself into furniture making. And it did the trick. I started out with simple things, towel racks, bird houses, then moved along to book shelves and eventually to some pieces of furniture."

"I had no idea you were a woodworker, Victor."

"I'm not. I haven't touched the tools in years now," he said, laughing. "But that era served its purpose. It was a very introspective period during which I realized I had come to enjoy the administrative side of science as much as the research. I began shifting in that direction, eventually vying for the chairmanship position. Had I not gone into science, I think now that politics might have been a possibility."

They both laughed and then Victor became serious again. "Come in half-days for a while. Take it one step at a time. We do need to talk about academics. There are new graduate students coming and class schedules to decide, etcetera, etcetera. I know you don't need this right now, but many of these things are out of my hands to control or even slow down for long." Daniel nodded, knowing that Victor wanted to help him but also aware that as chairman, he had a general responsibility to the biochemistry department.

"Gotta run, Daniel," Victor said suddenly, tapping his colleague on the shoulder with a fist. "Come in and talk to me. We'll work this out."

As he neared the door, he turned back. "Hey, if you think the furniture-making idea has potential, I've got the tools. I'm serious. Besides, my wife would love to get them out of the basement." He grinned and hurried out the door.

Daniel smiled and stared after his friend. Victor DiAngelo had stood by him throughout this erratic year, addressing the critics, patiently waiting, hoping in his optimistic way that this problem would work itself out. The fact that he felt compelled to come here today suggested to Daniel that Victor was running out of room to maneuver.

Victor DiAngelo drove slowly back to campus, a bit subdued. He had taken a chance and spoke with Daniel on a personal level. What Victor told Daniel concerning his own problem was basically true, but his bout with depression was never as severe as he had implied. He had talked to Paul Taylor but once, and it was the psychiatrist who felt that Victor simply needed to slow down and take a break from science, perhaps take up a hobby. His problem with headaches occurred several years before this.

He exaggerated to convince Daniel that there was nothing to be ashamed of, that the problem could be worked out. Victor felt that his message was well-received, but he was disheartened by his friend's appearance and demeanor. He noticed the tremor in Daniel's hand as he poured coffee. Alcohol was never part of the equation in his own case.

Daniel was correct in assuming that Victor was running

Dennis Ruane

out of maneuverability. There were some in the Biochemistry Department who felt that it was time for the chairman to take action regarding Professor Whaley's errant behavior. One associate professor, who coveted Daniel's position, was openly stating that it was time for the professor to step down.

-10-

Daniel sat in his dim world, sipping purposefully on a glass of brandy. He had been trying to keep the discussion with Victor DiAngelo out of his thoughts, not wanting his colleague's words to apply to his particular case. He had to admit a parallel between Victor's bout with depression and his own problems, but he still felt that what was happening to him was different. As hopeful as Victor's advice sounded, Daniel was not sure he wanted to make the effort to get back on track.

The alcohol eventually soothed his mental turbulence to the extent that he was able amuse himself with the thought of his friend's short woodworking experience. Then he recalled Victor's offer of the tools. Since he was a young man, Daniel had thought that furniture-making would be an enjoyable hobby. Borrowing Victor's tools would make it easy to give it a try, or at least it seemed so at the moment.

With sudden motivation and his glass in hand, Daniel stood up and staggered down the hall to the kitchen. He refreshed his drink and hastily donned his odd assortment of outdoor clothing. Professor Whaley launched himself out the back door in the direction of the garage, the ends of his coat and scarf flapping in the cold breeze.

The garage was a large building which could easily

accommodate two vehicles. Inside, Daniel steadied himself against a wall and assessed the possibilities for workshop space. His Grand Prix was parked there, but because Debbie never parked her Lexus in the garage, there was ample room for the woodworking tools.

Daniel fantasized. He imagined the space, warm and well-lit, and then pictured himself amidst the woodworking tools, carefully pushing a board of some hardwood along a table saw fence. He would show his critics. He would reveal another dimension of himself, creating fine pieces of furniture, works of art. Just when it seemed he was down and out, that his career was floundering, he would rise again. Daniel Whaley would be known as the professor-craftsman, scientist by day, artist by night. Debbie would be impressed again, this time with his skill and artistry like she once was with his intellect.

But the vision grew fuzzy. His head drooped. What if he didn't see it through? What if in the end, he really didn't like it, which is what happened fifteen years ago when he took up hunting? Or worse, it could end in frustration, as did a more recent attempt at golf. After three years of effort, he quit because he was so inept at the game. What if instead of the professor-craftsman he was just the same old, stuffy professor off on another tangent? Rather than being impressed with the fine pieces of furniture he was creating, Debbie would be angry with him because he had filled the garage with tools and dust. He jerked his head up and shook it from side to side. *No, dammit. This will work. It has to work.*

Then he looked toward the ceiling. The garage had an upstairs, and while not a practical choice for a woodworking shop, it was a much more appealing space. The second floor was accessed by a stairway at the back of the building. It had

Wooden Spoons

been originally designed to be a guest apartment, but from the first owners to the Whaleys, it had been used for storage. Daniel had not been up there since the previous summer, and Debbie had not climbed the stairs in well over a year. It was this abandonment that suddenly made the second floor appealing to him. It could be a secret workshop. With renewed enthusiasm, Daniel exited at the side door and went behind the garage.

As he started up the stairs, he stopped and gazed back along the tree row that bordered the property. Daniel focused his eyes on the vehicle merged with the foliage. The jeep was a sad relic of what had been the happiest era of his life. That was why it was still parked there. *Maybe it would have been better to have gotten rid of it years ago, as Deb wanted me to,* he thought. *That would have at least prevented the latest trouble with Ken.*

Daniel turned, stepping carefully to avoid the remnants of ice on the stairs that the sun had not yet melted. At the top, he entered the unlocked door. Winded and light-headed, the professor immediately sat down on a dusty chair that had a back rung broken out. With windows on all sides, the room was well lit. Daniel gazed upon an assortment of objects: furniture, a baby carriage, two bicycles, books and labeled cardboard boxes. It was a family archive of items whose era had passed. As Daniel stared, nostalgia distracted him from his mission. The brandy was having a sedative effect and his head began to nod forward. But he resisted, straightened himself and forced his eyes open.

Then his gaze fell upon a narrow bookshelf in the far right corner of the room. It had been purchased as unfinished pine furniture nearly three decades ago by Daniel and his wife. Along with it, they had bought an *antiquing* kit and did their best to turn a cheap piece of furniture into an antique reproduction. It was one of the first items to be taken to the garage when they moved to the new house, and over the years it had become Daniel's personal storage area.

He could see the backpack and sleeping bag that he had received for Christmas many years ago. There was the canvas hunting jacket that he liked, but had hardly used, and of course, the golf clubs, lying on the top shelf. Daniel was captivated now and after struggling to his feet, worked his way across the room for closer inspection.

He stared at a coffee can situated on the first shelf. He knew that it contained a coin collection from his early graduate student days. In a corner to the right of the shelves was the axe he had bought shortly before departing for Wisconsin. On the next shelf was a collection of literature on the subject of homesteading and self-sufficient living, an idea that had begun and ended with the books.

Then Daniel's eyes wandered to the bottom shelf and a wooden box, which was locked by a small brass padlock. He pulled it out, stared for a few seconds, and then reached for a key that was hanging behind the shelves. When he attempted to open the lock, his hand was shaking and he realized he had no feeling in his fingers. Instinct prodded him to return to the house. Daniel held the box tightly against his chest and shivered convulsively as he picked his way down the stairs.

Back in the study, he placed the box on his desk and switched on the lamp. In spite of fingers that were tingling as they adjusted to the blunt warmth of the room, Daniel anxiously undid the lock. There were several objects inside. One was a three-fifty-seven magnum pistol. He looked at the gun indifferently and placed it on top of his desk. He reacted similarly to a box of cartridges. The last item was a canvas roll, which contained his great-great-grandfather's woodcarving tools. Reverently, he laid it upon his lap and undid the straps.

When he unrolled the canvas and saw the old tools, Daniel smiled. He had not looked at them for several years, and his immediate impression now was of just how beautiful the collection was. He was captivated by the muted, earthy tones, which accentuated the timeworn appearance of the tools. Daniel admired the picturesque arrangement on the canvas roll; it seemed to be a work of art. He rubbed his fingers over the words embroidered in the corner. They were written in Gaelic, the native language of his ancestors.

Daniel could clearly recall the day that his great-grandfather gave him the tools. As he drove away from Mountain Farm, with the canvas roll on the seat beside him, he was glowing with happiness. The fact that his great-grandfather entrusted him with such a family heirloom infused Daniel with confidence and self-respect. As Daniel admired the tools now, it was hard for him to understand how they had been relegated to a low shelf in the upper floor of the garage for twenty years.

As his early academic career gained momentum, fueled by awards and degrees, the occasional guilt Daniel felt about the woodcarving tools began to fade. He had his career to attend to and a family to support. Many items, which seemed more relevant to his life, accumulated around the canvas roll. It eventually seemed out of place in his study, a space Daniel designed for scientific inquiry. At the least, the tools were a distraction to him. They made their way to the family archive about the same time the jeep was backed into the hedge row.

Daniel picked up the mallet along with a gouge and mimicked the motion his great-grandfather had demonstrated over thirty years before. The tools felt good in his hands and he

Dennis Ruane

had a sudden desire to use them. Daniel stood up and went to the kitchen. A brandy bottle, which was nearly empty, was on the counter above the dishwasher. He put it away in the dry sink. The bout with the cold had sobered him somewhat, and he started a pot of coffee to further the cause. Standing at the counter as the coffee brewed, he looked down at a stoneware crock, which was filled with cooking utensils. He spotted a wooden spoon, purchased by Debbie at an art fair. He knew that the wood it was made from was cherry.

Thirty minutes later, he was climbing the stairs of the garage, this time dressed in work clothes, a blue jean jacket and a stocking cap. He had a cup of coffee in his right hand, the tools under his left arm and the cherry spoon in his left hand. His ascent of the stairs was considerably steadier this time and he entered the upstairs with new stamina.

Rummaging about, he found an ancient electric space heater and plugged it into an outlet next to the door. Coils chattered noisily and then glowed red, while the heater gave off a pungent aroma of burning dust that Daniel thought was pleasant. Then he dragged a maple desk across the room and situated it directly over the heater.

Upon the desk he unfurled the canvas roll and sat on the chair with the broken rung to examine the tools. Picking up a gouge that was curved at the tip, he ran it along the bowl of the spoon. This was the spoon gouge that his great-grandfather had pointed out to him many years before, and it was obviously well-designed for its purpose. Now he needed wood.

Daniel stood up and glanced across the room, remembering that there was a table somewhere in the attic that was made of cherry. Upon locating it, he impatiently removed books that were stacked on top. It was an antique table, which he and Debbie had bought at a yard-sale decades

Wooden Spoons

ago. Their plan had been to refinish it for eventual use in the kitchen. Here the table had stood since the mid-seventies, the drop leaves removed and leaning against a wall behind it. A light area on top, where some of the varnish had been removed, was evidence that the refinishing had at least begun, but it was safe to say that this project would never see completion. Without sentiment, Daniel carried one of the leaves to the desk.

Grasping the mallet and gouge firmly, he chipped out a divot of wood. The table leaf jumped and slid at the assault, prompting Daniel to search for a clamp. When the board was secured firmly to the desk, he traced an oval shape around the indentation he had made, using the cherry spoon as a pattern. Daniel soon learned that by gouging out chips from both ends of the tracing, a crude bowl would eventually form. Then, with a coping saw, he painstakingly cut around the outline, resulting in a crude, two-dimensional, spoon-like object. Guided by the model from the kitchen, employing gouges, a wood rasp and various grits of sandpaper, the professor slowly shaped his creation into a spoon.

Daniel turned it over and over in his hands. He felt a sense of accomplishment that he had not experienced in many years. Although this spoon was plain and heavy compared to the one he had used for a model, no one would guess that it was the work of a beginner.

He stopped at this point, returning to the house to eat a hasty dinner, actually hungry for a change. Then he returned to the garage to begin the spoon-making process again. By late evening, he had another piece completed. This spoon was lighter and more stylish than the first with the handle gently curved to one side. Daniel wanted to continue, but it was getting late and he made himself stop. Earlier in the evening, he had decided to talk with Professor DiAngelo the next morning.

After cleaning up wood chips and sawdust, Daniel carefully rolled up the tools and placed the bundle back on the pine shelves. He put the two spoons in an empty shoebox and placed that beside the tools. Daniel approached the house in the dark, aware that Debbie was home. An hour earlier, he had seen the light from her car headlights shine on the trees behind the garage.

When he entered the kitchen, his wife was sitting at the kitchen table doing book work for *Bradley Maid*. Debbie was startled by his back-door appearance, assuming that he had been in the study. She knew that there would be no more discussion of the driveway incident. The stony silence of the past two days would run its course, eventually dissolving with the necessity of basic communication.

"How did your work go today, Deb?" Daniel asked, surprising her, asking a direct question days before protocol would have normally allowed.

"Ah, good, Dan," she answered, hesitantly, slowly looking up at him. "Too good in some ways. We've picked up more clients and I'm stretched thin again. It's forced some decisions on me. How was your day?" she asked, cautiously.

"It wasn't bad, Debbie. I think I'm beginning to get a grip on this problem now. Tomorrow I'm going to have a talk with Victor, and hopefully he and I can work out some sort of schedule to get me back on track."

Debbie smiled, but she had a weary, doubtful look on her face.

As courteous as this discourse seemed, Daniel did not linger to continue a conversation. He kept moving in a circle around her until he was in the hallway. He paused, looking back, feeling he should say something more. He wanted to let her know that in spite of his odd ways and his recent problems, he still liked being with her. He still loved her after all these years. Perhaps he should say he was sorry for the way he interacted with Ken. He could even tell her about what he had been doing this evening.

"Well, I'm certain you will work everything out with your business, Deb," he said.

She bobbed her head and forced another smile.

He shuffled his feet nervously and stepped toward the study.

Debbie stared after him, not optimistic over her husband's plan to get back to work. She had been around this cycle with him before, and with each relapse his condition worsened. Debbie did notice that Daniel seemed more alert than he had in many days. His eyes were clear and his face lacked that strange, confused expression that characterized the bad spells.

-11-

"So Daniel, sounds like we're ready to rock and roll again," Victor said jovially. He was sitting on the corner of his desk with arms crossed. "And you're making wooden spoons? I can't wait to see them. Whatever it takes, something totally unrelated to this." He waved his hand back and forth at the surroundings.

Daniel sat stiffly in a chair across the room. He shrugged and nodded.

To observe these two men in the same room was a study in contrast. Where Victor was tastefully dressed, neat and casual, Daniel was awkward and uncomfortable in his trademark blue suit. The chairman was eloquent, charismatic and known for his wit, while his colleague was formal, aloof, and serious. Yet they had liked each other from their first meeting, decades before. Daniel admired the many social qualities in his friend and respected his leadership ability. From the outset, Victor knew that Daniel was a good person, a man with integrity. Before long, he recognized that Daniel's intellect exceeded his own as well as that of any professor in the department.

"Now look, I want you to take it easy. Come back up to speed gradually. Just do the necessary paperwork. You are only scheduled to teach your course on fat-soluble vitamins this spring. I want you to take on one new graduate student,

Wooden Spoons

two at the most."

Daniel agreed to these terms, thanked Victor, and shook his hand warmly.

"I can keep the wolves at bay a bit longer," the chairman said with a nod.

Over the next several weeks, Professor Whaley eased back into his responsibilities and by early March was back in his scientific stride. With his keen intellect and phenomenal memory, Daniel's comments on any biochemistry-related topic were always respected. With regards to his specialty, vitamin E, his opinion was the final word in any lecture hall. Victor observed his colleague's progress with satisfaction. He was soon convinced that Daniel had outflanked the crisis, which had been threatening to halt his academic career.

While Professor Whaley seemed to be back on track, his attitude toward the job had changed in a significant way. Now, the scientific details of the day and the politics of the department remained at the Biochemistry building. When he left campus, his thoughts were focused on woodcarving and his evenings were passed in the simple workshop above the garage. The shoebox was replaced by a larger wooden box, and this was filling with spoons.

Daniel elaborated on the basic spoon shapes he had started with. The bowls became thinner and lighter while the handles evolved into an artistic array of sweeps and tapers. For a finish, he used a mixture of olive oil and beeswax, heated together and applied while still hot. He learned of this concoction on the web site of a wooden spoon maker in North Carolina. Daniel found it intriguing that someone actually made wooden spoons for a living. The finished spoons now had a smooth, satin surface, the result of several applications of the North Carolina recipe combined with light sanding between each coating.

"My God, you're an artist," Victor proclaimed several weeks later when Daniel took a selection of spoons to show his friend. Victor was studying five cherry spoons which varied in length from eight to thirteen inches. Two were straight and perfectly tapered while the others had gentle curves worked into the handles.

"Oh, come on, Victor. They're just spoons."

"No, I'm serious. In just a matter of weeks you've gone far beyond anything I did in over a year of woodworking. I just followed directions, like a technician. You are creating these with your imagination. That's art."

"Is that what art is, Victor?" Daniel asked, smiling mischievously.

"Sure, of course it is," Victor responded, laughing.

Daniel laughed with him.

Victor was glad to see that his colleague's sense of humor was returning. "You look good," he said. "I think you've gotten past it."

"Thanks. I feel good. Still the occasional headache, but I ignore them now and keep working."

"I believe they'll pass, give it time. The main thing is that you're back in your groove, and when you're there, my friend, you're the best."

Daniel smiled and nodded, a little embarrassed but grateful for the support and confidence that he received from Victor. Sometimes he wondered how he deserved such unconditional loyalty from his colleague, or how he might ever make it up to him.

That evening, Daniel awoke in his chair, having slept for about half an hour. A strange, disjointed dream was fresh in

Wooden Spoons

his mind. The setting had been the log house on Hemlock Knob. His great-great-grandparents were present, along with other people he did not recognize. Daniel himself was in the dream, but was not seated at the table with the others. He stood near the door, as if he had recently entered but had gone unnoticed. Daniel had once seen a photograph of Adam and Sadie Reilly, and at that time it was half a century after their deaths. However, his great-great-grandparents were very much alive and animated in his dream.

Daniel was aware that it was a celebration, the occasion of Adam's birthday. Earthenware mugs were filled with apple cider, a potent brew that Adam fermented on the homestead. At this point, the crowd seemed to expect a toast from Adam and he acquiesced, standing slowly, and raising his mug. He was a tall, lean man with broad shoulders and a full brown beard. Adam was humble in appearance, and yet he possessed an air of authority and strength such that when he began to speak, the crowd grew quiet.

"To all that is good on this green earth," he proclaimed.

"Here, here," chanted an appreciative audience. They raised their mugs toward the ceiling, and then took a hearty drink.

Another man to Adam's right stood. "May your glass be ever full. May the roof over your head be always strong. And may you be in heaven half an hour before the devil knows you're dead."

The crowd yelled and raised their mugs. It was a traditional Irish saying. Daniel had heard it before.

Several more toasts were offered to the mirthful audience. Then Adam looked at his wife while once again raising his mug. "Art is a good idea," he shouted.

Sadie laughed and blushed, nudging Adam in the back.

Dennis Ruane

The audience paused at first over this verse, obviously not in the popular repertoire. Shortly, one of the men echoed it and then all raised their mugs. It was at this point that Daniel awoke.

Art is a good idea. Such a strange dream, he thought as he stared out the window. *Where did that come from?*

It was true that during the many hours he spent carving, he often reminisced about Mountain Farm, and since he was using the old woodcarving tools, he thought about his great-great-grandfather, Adam, more than he ever had before. Daniel concluded that this was the cause of the dream. The final toast puzzled him a while longer, until he remembered his conversation with Victor earlier in the day. Their short discussion about art would seem to be the basis for Adam's toast. Daniel was content that he had traced the origins of his dream, but that made it no less strange.

Wide awake now, he decided to venture out to his workshop. The weather had warmed somewhat; winter was losing its edge. Soon Daniel was situated at his workbench, the cranky little heater grinding and clicking beneath him.

Art is a good idea. A funny statement, ambiguous but true either way one might take it. It could be a reference to the inspiration behind a single work of art or a statement about art in general.

Daniel felt like working now. He selected one of the last spoons he had completed and turned it over in his hand, studying the handle carefully. His craftsmanship was obviously improving, evidenced by the fact that Debbie's spoon, which had served as his model, was now mediocre by comparison.

There were only a few significant pieces of the antique cherry table left, and he clamped one of them firmly to the

Wooden Spoons

workbench. With a nonchalant skill he gouged out a bowl-shape, and then with a turning saw, recently purchased from an antique store, he cut a ten-inch spoon from the board. He worked this into the shape of the spoon he had just examined. Then, using a small gouge followed by the round edge of a wood rasp, he carved the handle into a gentle spiral. Slow and deliberate sanding revealed the beautiful grain of cherry. While still adhering to the ancient, utilitarian design, this wooden spoon had become a minor work of art.

Thirty minutes later, back in his study, Daniel sipped a glass of brandy while he examined the spiraled spoon. He thought about the dream and smiled. "Art is a good idea," he whispered.

-12-

The immediate benefit Debbie gained from her husband's recovery was solitude in her home. Now she could enjoy her coffee in the morning and begin the day at her favorite workplace, the kitchen table. This was where her business started, while she raised the children and while her professor-husband spent his life at the laboratory. She had grown to like the arrangement. Now of course, with a fleet of vans and a growing army of employees, she had to be present at the Washington Street office the greater part of each day. But she preferred to reserve these morning hours to work here, alone.

Debbie had loved their house from the time she first saw it, on a Sunday drive with Daniel shortly after they were married. The couple had purchased it five years later when he became a full professor. Debbie reworked the inside down to the smallest details while Daniel quietly consented. She did, however, allow a room for his study and for the most part, gave him a free hand with the yard.

When Daniel was ill, shuffling between his study and the kitchen, drinking too much, looking at her woefully, the ambiance was disrupted, to say the least. In fact, when he was down with a *headache* again, she planned her schedule to avoid the house.

Wooden Spoons

If Debbie had thought that her husband would eventually pull out of the depression he suffered from, she never would have guessed that it could occur so quickly. He had seemingly recovered at other times only to relapse, and often with more pronounced symptoms. But she sensed something different this time. It was not Daniel returning to his old self, but a new person emerging from the wreck of the old. It was someone she was not entirely familiar with. He actually seemed cheerful and confident at times, particularly in the evenings. Sometimes she wondered if she knew what Daniel Whaley was really like.

The thing that puzzled her the most was the fact that this man still loved her after all these years. She knew he did now, as surely as she knew it when they first met. That this mattered to her would seem to be a contradiction, for although she and Daniel had remained together for thirty years, they were now little more than housemates. It had been more than three years since they had shared a bed and four times that number since they had made love. But it still did matter to her.

Debbie was midway through her sophomore year and had only been seeing the tall, bashful graduate student from Pennsylvania for three months when she learned that she was pregnant. Daniel Whaley had known that he wanted to marry Deborah Bradley since shortly after they met, before he had even kissed her. When he learned of her pregnancy, he seemed more certain of his desire. His intention did not waver despite her honest admission that the child was possibly not his.

For several years, as they raised the baby and took the first steps along their respective careers, it seemed that they had made the right decision. But by the time they observed their fifth wedding anniversary, their personalities were maturing. Debbie's love of business and her drive toward

Dennis Ruane

financial success stood in stark contrast to her husband's passive, intellectual withdrawal from the world. A persistent respect she felt for him, his undying love for her and the momentum from the years already behind them kept the relationship moving forward.

Then, Jeannie was born and everything changed. Daniel blossomed in newfound fatherhood. While he and his wife continued to drift apart and Ken developed into Ken, Daniel found a new reason to believe in the life he led. There was no doubt that *she* was his child. The physical resemblance was noticeable and the similarity in personality was unmistakable.

Debbie sighed, shaking her head. She worried about her husband, but she no longer loved him. Often, when she grew impatient with their domestic arrangement, she wished that he would just leave one day. If not for the big house that she loved so well, she would probably have left instead. When at home, she focused on her business or watched television in the spacious master bedroom. He spent most of his time in the study. While not exactly the arrangement a marriage counselor might recommend, they remained together and did so in relative peace.

Debbie stopped working suddenly. She thought about the recent change in this routine, especially noticeable on weekends. Daniel had been spending a large amount of time in the garage. She had even noticed the upstairs lights on late some evenings. Occasionally he would go off on a tangent of reorganization, discarding items that were not being used and regrouping what remained according to some new system he had devised. This seemed unlikely now, since that behavior usually resulted in him becoming irritable over all the things they had accumulated. He seemed happy now. Her curiosity became aroused to the extent that she decided to investigate.

Wooden Spoons

Debbie rarely went to the garage and had not been to the upstairs of the building in more than a year. She poured herself a cup of coffee, tightened her robe and walked across the yard. It was mid April and although cold at this early hour, the morning held all the promise of a classic spring day.

As she went around the garage, she looked to her right, across the yard with its handsome stand of hemlock trees. They were nearly thirty feet tall now and formed a green canopy over the clusters of mountain laurel that Daniel had planted. Although Debbie had teased her husband about his compulsion to convert their yard into a forest, she would readily admit that what he had created was beautiful. This was particularly true on a morning such as this with sunlight filtering through at a low angle.

The scene was accentuated by fieldstone walls that Daniel had constructed. One ran along the entire length of their back border and another wall separated the remaining lawn from the hemlock trees. He had worked on them for years, relentlessly scavenging stones from the woods and meticulously placing each one.

Debbie climbed the back stairs of the garage and cautiously opened the door. Just inside she found the maple desk that was once in Ken's bedroom. On top of it were several clamps and some sort of saw. There were also scraps of wood and sawdust scattered on the floor. Most of the room's contents had been moved to the back and were covered with sheets. This was apparently for protection from the fine dust that coated everything. In the center of the room she examined what appeared to be the remains of a table, now only four disconnected legs and a few boards.

Looking back toward the desk she noticed two wooden boxes on the floor to the right of it. Debbie remembered that

Dennis Ruane

Daniel had bought them at a flea-market years ago. At the time, he had excitedly pointed out to her that they had been made entirely by hand. She was sure that she had last seen them in his study.

She moved toward the boxes and opened the larger of them to find it was nearly full of wooden spoons. Turning to look at the table parts in the center of the room, she guessed that the table had been the source of wood. In the other box, Debbie found the canvas roll containing the old tools which Daniel had shown her years before. She knew that they were the woodcarving tools his great-grandfather had given him. While sitting down to look at the tools, her foot hit the space heater under the table. It was the one from the apartment Daniel was renting when they first met. Debbie turned away from it quickly, not wanting her thoughts to drift back into that era.

She looked over the tools and then at the spoon in her hand. *I don't believe it*, she thought, *he's using the old tools to make these spoons. That's what he's been doing, sitting here and making wooden spoons.* Debbie seldom cooked anymore, but she was a good cook. She could appreciate well-made wooden spoons. Debbie was impressed with her husband's skill and craftsmanship. It was as if another window into his personality had suddenly opened after all these years.

But why wouldn't he tell me? She answered her own question. *Why would he? We never tell each other anything that matters.* She looked out the window at the tree-covered bank behind the garage and pictured her husband, Professor Daniel Whaley, sitting at this window, with his old heater warming him, carving wooden spoons.

He seems happy again. Maybe this is what he should have done all along, something like this, something simple with his

Wooden Spoons

hands, instead of wearing out his brain on science.

Maybe he still can. Why couldn't he do something like this? We are in a good position financially and with my business experience . . . Debbie stopped as reality seeped back into her thinking. The era when she and Daniel had happily lived together ended long ago and there was no chance of going back.

Besides, there was another reality which was forcing her in the opposite direction, compelling her to soon end their marriage. She shut her eyes, nested her face in cupped hands and tried to keep from crying. Tears would confirm an underlying despair that she did not want to acknowledge. "Damn it all. He has always treated me with respect and has been kind to me no matter how bad things got," she said ruefully.

When Daniel had asked her to marry him, Debbie was flattered and amazed and scared. She knew that it was taking a chance even then, when they were young and in love. She opened her eyes and stared out the window. Once again she imagined her oddball husband sitting here, happily carving wooden spoons, turning an old table into small works of art. *Maybe this is what he should have done, something like this, and maybe I should have just left the poor man alone in the first place.* Debbie began to weep and covered her eyes. *I swore that no matter what happened, I would never cheat on him. Damn it all. What am I going to do?*

Then she wiped away tears and steadied herself. Debbie was cold, but continued to sit. She stared out the window. "At least I gave him Jeannie," she whispered.

-13-

Victor had been right. Daniel's new hobby of carving wooden spoons pulled him out of the gully he had steered into. He was back on track again. As it had been for Victor, this recovery period was a time of introspection for Daniel. However, he did not come out of it with the belief that a change in focus for his career was the solution. He came to realize that his career was just that, *a career,* not who he was, not his life. Unlike Victor, he did not abandon his hobby when he was well again. In fact, Daniel began to live a double life, dividing his time between science and woodcarving.

Despite this shift in priorities, he was easily able to fulfill his basic professorial duties after so many years of academic routine. He attended only to the essentials as Victor had directed, and was careful to not allow the details of the profession to monopolize his life again. This lack of intensity did not go unnoticed by his critics, but Daniel was a tenured professor with a prestigious record and Professor DiAngelo, chairman of the Biochemistry Department, was squarely behind him. While no one could deny that he was back at his post, it would take time before doubts about Daniel's mental stability were erased. The course of a semester with its myriad demands and pressured deadlines would be the test.

Five weeks after resuming his position, Daniel sat at his

Wooden Spoons

desk, and the office door was open. He was reviewing research data that had been submitted by one of his graduate students. He had capable students under him, who with minimal oversight, were able to work independently on their research projects. Professor Whaley fostered this ethic in all his students from the day they entered his laboratory. It had served this particular group well during the previous troublesome year.

Daniel was in a good mood, happy in the conviction that he had finally struck a balance between science and his personal life. There was no better illustration of this than the wooden spoon which lay on his desk next to the latest edition of *The Journal of Nutrition*. The spoon resulted from a good carving session of the previous evening, during which he once again carved spoons with spiraled handles. This particular spoon was ten inches long and the turn of the spiral was evenly spaced along the handle. It appeared to have been held at both ends and twisted one and a half turns.

Daniel often brought a favorite piece to campus with him, a distraction from science and a reminder of his other occupation. A more direct reminder came from an index card that was leaning against a book behind the spoon. On it was printed the phrase 'Art is a good idea'. The toast offered by Adam Reilly in the dream had become a slogan of sorts for Daniel.

He had finished his assessment of the data and was beginning to write notes of suggestion when there was a knock on the door.

Bruce Planter, one of Daniel's graduate students, stood in the doorway. "Hello, Doctor Whaley," he said, somewhat sheepishly. "Do you have a minute?"

"Sure. Come in Bruce, have a chair. We haven't talked in a

while." Daniel leaned back in his chair and removed his glasses.

Daniel had liked this young man since their first interview two years before, when Bruce had entered the lab. Bruce Planter was not one of the most ambitious students to come under his professorship. There was no doubt that he was intelligent, but his motivation toward science seemed to change with the seasons. Yet Daniel appreciated Bruce's sense of humor and found discussion with this student to be a refreshing break from the usual lab conversation. Bruce's personality reminded him of his daughter Jeannie, which only added to Daniel's fondness for the young man. Moreover, Professor Whaley was confident that the motivation Bruce lacked would come, and so he was patient with him.

"Well, Bruce, how is your work going?"

"Um, Doctor Whaley, that's sort of why I wanted to talk to you."

Daniel turned his head in an inquisitive way, fully expecting a discussion of a technical or theoretical science problem.

"Doctor Whaley, I've been doing a lot of thinking and I've decided that I don't want to continue with my graduate work."

Daniel's expression changed to one of surprise. He put his glasses back on and leaned forward. "Is it your project? It's still relatively early, and if you're not sure of the direction . . ."

"No, it's not the project. It's me. I don't want to continue in this direction as a career."

It was obvious to Daniel that the young man was nervous. He leaned closer across the desk and spoke with a tone of concern. "Is there something wrong Bruce, some problem that I can help with?"

"Oh no. Everything is fine. I've just come to the conclusion that this is the wrong direction for me in life. I tried, but I'm just not a scientist."

Daniel was silent for a short, uncomfortable moment. "Are you sure?" he asked, weakly.

"Yes, very sure."

Daniel paused again. He wanted to know more but didn't really know what to ask. Finally, he nodded and assumed a professional demeanor. "Well, if that is your decision, I will get the paperwork started at this end. You will need to inform the graduate school office, and they will tell you how to proceed with this."

Bruce Planter liked Daniel. He was flattered by the concern that the professor voiced upon hearing his decision. He was also glad that it was accepted without resentment.

Daniel removed his glasses once more and leaned back in his chair. "So, Bruce, do you have specific plans, any other career possibilities in mind."

"Well, I . . . No, not really. Travel some. That will give me time to think about what I want to do."

Then Bruce began to speak quickly, feeling a need to demonstrate that he was not making an impulsive decision. "I was taking college courses when I was a senior in high school and then I went straight through with my undergraduate work. I even went every summer, graduating in three years. I did well and enjoyed the challenge. Then I came here without a break, to start all over again at a more intense level. But the old drive just isn't there any more. I know it's because I don't really know what I want to do. I've been trying to push myself forward just because I've already come this far, not because I want to."

Daniel was listening to the young man's testimony much more intently than Bruce could have imagined.

Dennis Ruane

"But you're doing well, Bruce. Not setting any school records, but certainly well enough to get your degree," Daniel said automatically, although it was beside the point that the young man was making.

"Well Dr. Whaley, I think I could get a PhD if I hang around, but why give up any more years just for the sake of a degree, when I could be out there finding out what I really want to do?" Bruce nodded toward the window to emphasize *out there*, and when he glanced across the desktop, his gaze stopped at the wooden spoon.

Daniel was still looking at Bruce, but his thoughts were drifting. He was thinking back to when he was Bruce's age, and a radical choice such as leaving school was never an option.

"Did you make that, Dr. Whaley?"

"Oh that, yes. Yes I did make that, yesterday evening as a matter of fact." Daniel picked up the spoon and handed it to his student.

"Where did you learn to do this?"

"Just picked it up as a hobby. It was something to help with the problem I was having."

Bruce nodded. He knew about the problem. "I think this is incredible. I want to try things like this, too."

Daniel was flattered. "I want you to have it then, Bruce, a going away present."

Bruce looked up and began to speak, but the phone rang.

"Excuse me," Daniel said, picking up the receiver. "Hello, Will. No, I haven't forgotten. Well yes, something has come up, but I was still planning to come over. Uh huh. Is there a chance that we could discuss it over the phone later? No? OK, I'll be there, then. Thanks, Will. Bye."

"I have to run, Bruce," Daniel said, glancing up at the

clock on the wall. "Another doctor appointment, but I think it's the last."

"You seem to be doing well, Dr. Whaley."

"I am well now, just an occasional headache. But when you're in a social circle which includes so many doctors, no symptom goes unexamined."

"Thanks for this," Bruce said, holding up the spoon. "It means a lot to me."

Daniel shrugged. "It's not a gold watch. A wooden spoon is the best you get under the circumstances." They walked to the door where Daniel shook his student's hand and wished him good luck.

As Daniel shut the office door, his thoughts began to spin. This had never happened, a graduate student who was doing relatively well, choosing to withdraw from school. When he was Bruce's age, he didn't allow himself to question his career. He had a family to support. Eventually the diplomas and awards that began to cover the office walls dispersed what doubt he had. Since Jeannie left home, some uncertainty had resurfaced, but he never thought about quitting. In spite of mental problems, alcoholism, and a dreary domestic situation, he still did not consider the possibility of a career change. It was true that woodcarving was now the focus of his life, but he couldn't leave his profession, not now. Daniel felt that the balance he had struck between his career and his hobby was the only reasonable option.

He looked up at the clock and became agitated. He did not want to go to this appointment, he wanted to go home, to his study. Daniel wanted to hide. He felt a measure of guilt that as Bruce Planter's major professor, he had let the young man down. Perhaps if he had been here consistently throughout this past year, he might have influenced his student to

Dennis Ruane

continue toward a PhD. Underlying this was a greater guilt that he should have questioned his own career choice when he was Bruce's age.

He had to go. He was already late. As Daniel plodded down the halls and stairwells, his head was low, his shoulders sagged and he did not make eye contact with people. The professor had an uncertain and confused expression on his face.

A quarter mile away, on Observatory Hill, Bruce Planter was sitting in the sun and peering out over Lake Mendota. He was relieved that he had finally told Professor Whaley of his decision. A careless breeze was blowing across the lake, fluttering the ends of the young man's hair. He had let it grow long again. Bruce looked down at the wooden spoon in his hand, still surprised to have received such a gift. Although he would never say it to this man for whom he held great respect, his observation of the professor's *problem* was a major factor in the decision to quit. Bruce knew that science was the wrong career for him. He had decided, instead, to wander out into the world to find an occupation that suited him.

-14-

Daniel opened his eyes and noticed the sun's rays slanting through the windows from the west at a shallow angle, and so he knew it was late afternoon. Before dozing off again, he heard the scraping sound of a snow plow accompanied by the chatter of chains, and he realized that there had been a late spring snow. The next day at mid morning, the phone rang, and he listened apathetically to Victor DiAngelo's voice as a message was recorded. It was the day after this, that he awoke to noise in the kitchen and the distinct aroma of cigarette smoke. He recognized the voices of his wife and son immediately, and the other talker he eventually identified as Debbie's sister, Cathy.

Daniel's face bore a strange, blank look as he lay back in the leather recliner. He was motionless, listening to the voices, picturing the faces associated with them. Daniel and Cathy Savage had always been friendly with each other, but they were uncomfortably different and rarely conversed for long. Since his illness had started, he suspected from the way she looked at him, that his sister-in-law thought he was somewhat crazy.

Daniel did not want people here now, especially these people. He started to feel warm and angry. The noise from the kitchen was becoming unbearable and the smoke, suffocating.

Dennis Ruane

His impression that this trio had come together especially to annoy him was true to some extent. Two days before, when Debbie realized that Daniel's illness had returned, she decided that she could not live with him any longer. Coincidentally, a week earlier, she and Tom Stringer had agreed that they wanted to be together on a permanent basis. They wanted to come out in the open with their relationship, face whatever consequence society might bestow, and then move on with their lives, together.

It was with this decision in mind that Debbie planned her response to Daniel's relapse. She had invited her sister and her son over this morning for breakfast in spite of Daniel's presence. It was her house too, and she was tired of it becoming a convalescent home. If he was unable to tolerate the intrusion, then *he* could leave. That would certainly make her life easier. However, realizing that this plan might provoke an unpleasant scene, she had chosen her guests carefully.

Daniel could not hear their conversation, but he could not block out the noise of their voices either. Most irritating was their laughter. He was wide awake now, sick in his stomach, head aching, throat sore, an unpleasant dryness to his mouth. On the floor was an empty brandy bottle lying on its side, another half-empty bottle stood upright on the desk, and an empty glass nested in a sticky area of his robe.

Debbie laughed loudly and then she made a comment, causing them all to cackle. They were happy, thoroughly enjoying this impromptu breakfast. They had momentarily forgotten the man in the room. It was a business breakfast of sorts. Recently divorced, Cathy was in the process of moving from Chicago to Madison where she would manage part of her sister's business. They were scheduled to meet with the rest of the company's management team at ten o'clock when Cathy was to be introduced. Afterwards, Debbie was planning to accompany Cathy to Chicago to help her pack, visit their parents and keep an important dinner date.

In the gloom of his study, Daniel remained inanimate and not entirely sober. He was struggling to control his temper. Then he remembered an idea that had come to him the day before. It was a plan that would solve this immediate problem and all the others. He stood up awkwardly and put on his topcoat over stale clothes. He opened the bottom drawer of the filing cabinet and removed the three-fifty-seven magnum pistol that had been brought in from the garage six weeks earlier.

The gun had belonged to his father, and had been given to Daniel fifteen years before by his mother. Allen Whaley had acquired it from a man who owed him money. Allen had occasionally used it for target practice, but locked the gun away when the first child was born. Daniel was visiting his mother just before she and Bob moved to Seattle, and the gun had resurfaced in the course of their packing. Abigail was not fond of guns, and this one had long ago lost what sentimental value it might have held. She was startled that her quiet, scholarly son received it without hesitation. He disclosed his acquisition to no one, not even his wife, and locked the gun in the box with the carving tools.

With trembling hands, Daniel loaded the weapon and nestled it in his coat pocket. He hesitated at the door, listening to the talk and laughter, waiting for his wife's voice to come around again. Then he thrust himself into the hall, much to everyone's surprise.

However Debbie had prepared herself or had prompted her guests for this possibility, all became silent when Daniel appeared in the kitchen doorway. He was unsteady and pale,

Dennis Ruane

bearing a cold, indifferent expression. The professor said nothing and looked only at his wife as he crossed the room. His shocking appearance and penetrating gaze caused Debbie to uncharacteristically avert her eyes. He stopped when he was next to her and waited for her to look up.

Daniel stared at Debbie as if he wanted to tell her something, but no words were spoken. He turned away, walked unsteadily to the door and stepped out into the driveway. Remaining seated for a few seconds, Debbie got up and went to the kitchen window. She watched her husband walk with an agitated gait to the back corner of the property. At an opening in the stone wall he stumbled in among the trees. She knew that there was a path through the woods that led to a large cornfield, which belonged to the University of Wisconsin.

Ken finally broke the silence. "Whew, I think he's finally gone off the deep end this time."

"Shut up," his mother responded, sharply, without turning.

The look on Daniel's face troubled Debbie. She knew her husband wanted to tell her something. Cathy nervously began to clear dishes from the table, knowing that she and her sister had to be downtown soon. Ken decided that this would be a good time for him to leave. He was hardly affected by his mother's curt response, knowing that he must have made a mistake to receive such a rebuke. Besides, he was in no position to be too proud. He had accepted this breakfast invitation partly because he was hoping to borrow money from his mother.

The business venture with his cousin went badly when they accidentally ignited a gasoline tank while welding a muffler. The ensuing fire destroyed much of their equipment and did considerable damage to the building owned by Lenny's brother-in-law. While dragging legal and financial vestiges of this enterprise along with him, Ken's entrepreneurial spirit remained unflappable. He had a friend in Stoughton who made kayak helmets for a hobby, and now wanted to turn it into a full-time business. Ken had leaped at the opportunity to learn the trade and become a partner. They were short on start-up capital, however, so Ken could eat a little humble pie with his breakfast.

When Ken left, Cathy approached Debbie, who was still staring out the window. Her sister looked so sad and worried that Cathy became angry with Daniel. "I've never seen him this bad. Do you feel safe here with him?"

"Daniel would never hurt me," Debbie answered listlessly, still looking at the spot where her husband disappeared. "He would never hurt me no matter how badly I hurt him."

"Well he scares me." Cathy said, glancing toward the woods.

Debbie turned toward her. "Something has changed. I, I don't know. Somehow, the way he looked at me, I think Daniel knows about Tom and I."

Having known about her sister's affair for a year, Cathy shrugged her shoulders. "So what the hell, you want him to know now."

"Yes, but I should tell him, I owe him that at least. I don't love him and I can't live like this any more, but he has always respected me and I at least owe him respect too."

"But why do you think he knows? He just seemed out of it to me. He didn't say anything."

"That was it, because he didn't say anything and especially because of that strange look he gave me. And where is he going?" She nodded nervously toward the woods.

Dennis Ruane

Cathy knew that her sister was upset, but realized that they had to depart soon if they were to make the meeting on time. She started to clean up again and Debbie attempted to help, although she was obviously distracted. After the food was put away and some of the dishes removed from the table, she took off her apron and tossed it over a chair.

"Let's get out of here, Cath," she said impatiently.

-15-

Daniel emerged from the trees into a cornfield and turned to the east. The ground was lined with the humped rows of corn stumps and other debris from the autumn harvest. Situated on gently rolling hills and thickly bordered by trees and brush, the field was part of an old farm, which had been absorbed by the University of Wisconsin. Daniel was familiar with this property because of the many hours spent walking the family dog here years before. The eighty-acre plot was nearly landlocked, with private property surrounding it on all sides. The University had access through one drive that passed along the perimeter of the graduate student housing tract, and this was on the side of the field opposite the Whaley residence. For these reasons, it was a private space in a relatively populated area.

At the east end of the field, where it bordered Lake Mendota, stood a cluster of trees that surrounded a large mound of stones. It was toward this mound that Daniel was walking. The stones had been piled there as they were removed from the field, and over many decades of farming, the mound grew to its present circumference of one hundred feet. Its stony presence had discouraged plowing, thus permitting seedlings to root at the perimeter. Some of these seedlings had grown into the hardy stand of trees that now surrounded it.

Dennis Ruane

The combination of the stones and trees formed a sort of amphitheater, which was best appreciated if one stood at the peak of the mound. Daniel had stood there often in the past.

He had admired the collection of stones since he first discovered it, appreciating the fact that the mound represented a time when removing stones from a field simply meant picking them up and piling them on this spot. Eventually the pile became so large from this simple, repetitive act that it had never been worth anyone's time or money since, to move it.

Spring was beginning to take hold so that the professor's feet would alternately crackle on ice or sink in mud. A crow sounded warning as Daniel approached the stones. Others joined in until the air was filled with their raspy scolding. Because of the undulation of the land, he could see no houses or roads from the mound. It was isolation on the edge of the city, and it was where he wanted to perform this final act.

Daniel was sick in his stomach, his head ached and he was scared. He fingered the gun inside his topcoat. He wanted to get to the mound and do this quickly. A nervous smile came to the professor's face as he thought about it. One simple movement of his finger would eliminate all the problems.

Upon reaching the trees, Daniel started up the five-foot mound and immediately stumbled to his knees on the loose stones. Using his hands, the professor crawled to the top. He stood and turned a slow circle, reacquainting himself with the scenery. It had been nearly two years since he had been in the amphitheater.

Daniel jerked the gun from his robe and pushed the end of the barrel firmly against his right temple. But he could not squeeze the trigger, not yet. The loneliness of the setting and the fact that his life was about to end caused him to think of his great-grandfather, and of how he had died alone on Hemlock Knob. Not that direct comparisons could be drawn to his own wretched situation. Tom Reilly died high on a mountain, bravely facing down his mortality. His great-grandson would leave the world by his own hand, on a rock pile in a cornfield. Then Daniel thought about Mountain Farm and recalled the wonderful sight of the log house coming into view as he walked along Hemlock Road. His arm drooped until the gun hung at his side.

The professor felt unsteady on his legs and sagged to his knees. Thoughts of the past could not help now, only distract him. He knew that it was necessary to focus on the present and finish this. He was ashamed of what he was doing, but he had come to the conclusion that suicide was his best option. Then tears formed and though he struggled to control himself, he was soon sobbing bitterly. "In the end, I'm nothing but a coward and a failure. I've wasted my life."

"Damn it," he shouted, suddenly kneeling upright. He closed his eyes and placed the gun barrel firmly against his head. Gritting his teeth, he struggled to pull the trigger. Then Daniel heard an unfamiliar noise, which startled him and caused him to turn. He expected to see somebody coming from behind but only saw the empty cornfield. The strange noise continued. He jerked his head upward and saw a flock of geese passing over, thirty feet above him. He often saw Canada geese here but never so low. There were more than forty birds in their customary V-shaped pattern, and the lead bird passed over Daniel, just as he looked up. They were so near that he could see features of individual birds. As the flock passed, the geese made no vocal sound, yet they were so close he could hear their wings dragging through the morning air.

It was such an unexpected and stirring sight that he stood

Dennis Ruane

to watch them fly away toward the southeast. Daniel stared until the flock disappeared on the distant horizon. Then he looked down at the revolver hanging at his side. He had stopped crying. Daniel knew that it was time to go.

-16-

Debbie drove impatiently through evening traffic to the restaurant where she was meeting Tom Stringer. These rendezvous in Chicago had begun two years ago, after an encounter with Tom in Madison. A diamond wholesaler by profession, Tom was introduced to her by a wealthy client of *Bradley Maid* who owned a chain of motels in the Madison area. At the time, the fact that Tom and Debbie were both from Chicago was all that they really had in common, but that was enough.

When Debbie entered the restaurant, she was recognized by the maitre d' who escorted her to a table deep in a corner of the main room. It was far from the window where she and Tom usually sat. The man sitting there stood when he saw her. He took her two hands and kissed her on the mouth, lightly but passionately. Debbie knew instantly that something was wrong.

Tom Stringer was a handsome man. His somewhat boyish features had charmed many throughout his life, and had only become more distinguished in his fifties. He had dark brown eyes, a dimple on his chin, and thinning brown hair, which was brushed straight back and tucked neatly behind his ears. Always impeccably dressed, Tom had a James Bond aura about him and usually exuded the same sort of confidence.

Dennis Ruane

That confidence was not there this evening. He managed a smile as the waiter brought drinks but Debbie thought that he looked sad.

"Tom, what is it?" she asked, putting her hands into his.

He fondled them, slowly, nervously, and finally looked directly into her eyes. "My wife knows of our relationship." He felt her grasp tighten, but observing no dramatic change in her expression, he continued. "Myra hired a private investigator four months ago, and apparently he has been watching and documenting our meetings ever since. She also said, quite definitely, that she was going to contact your husband and share her information with him."

Debbie felt her face flush and her scalp tingle. "When did this happen?" she asked in a weak voice.

"Yesterday evening."

"Then Daniel already knows," she said, grasping her glass. She was silent while she took long sips of her Manhattan.

As usual, Tom had reserved a suite at the Hotel DeWalsh, where they usually spent the weekend together. After another drink they were determined to continue with that plan in spite of the sea change in their lives. Emboldened by a third Manhattan, they agreed that it was for the better. It forced their relationship into the open. In spite of the immediate unpleasantness, they would soon be able to begin their life together.

By the following afternoon, Debbie was driving mechanically up Interstate 90 toward Madison. As the blush of her new freedom faded and she considered the details of the *unpleasantness* that would soon unfold, she could no longer deny her conscience. For all that he wasn't and could never be in her eyes, Daniel Whaley was a good man who had treated her well and, in his own formal way, always loved her. As much as she wished to end their marriage, she never wanted to hurt him like this. For some reason that Debbie could not understand, she did not want Daniel to hate her after all these years. She thought about that strange look he had given her the morning before she had left for Chicago and wondered if that was, finally, hate in his eyes.

It was after dark when she pulled up the drive. There were no lights on in the house, but she never doubted that her husband was home. Debbie had steeled herself for this moment. She intended to apologize to Daniel, and to some extent explain her behavior, but she would press for the dissolution of their marriage regardless of how her husband reacted. Debbie forced herself through the door. When she switched on the light, it struck her that the kitchen was just as she and Cathy had left it when they rushed to the meeting. The dishwasher was open and half-loaded, the bread knife was on the cutting board, the sweet rolls were untouched and her apron still hung on the back of the chair where she had tossed it. Debbie moved slowly to the hallway and stared at the study door, but she could not bring herself to try the knob or knock.

At that moment she heard the sound of a vehicle moving up the driveway. Debbie rushed to the kitchen window, surprised that Daniel had gone out so late. She grew tense, but prepped herself again for what had to be said. Then Ken's old Honda Civic pulled into the glare of the outside lights.

He soon burst through the door with a grin on his face. "Hey, Mom. Cut your trip short, huh? I was buzzin' by and saw your car."

"Hi Ken," she replied. She motioned for him to step back outside the door and closed it behind them. Debbie spoke in a hushed voice. "Have you seen your father lately?"

"Huh uh. Not since the morning you left. He's not in his

room?"

"I don't think so."

Her son looked puzzled at first, but quickly deduced that his parents were fighting about something. He was happy to become involved if this were the case. "I'll see," he said enthusiastically. His mother started to stop him but then let him go.

Ken entered the house, hurried down the hall and wrapped sharply on the study door. "Dad, hey, Dad." He looked at his mother and shrugged his shoulders. Ken knocked again before turning the knob and opening the door to a dark room. He switched on a nearby table lamp, which cut through the darkness enough to reveal that his father was not there.

"Not here, Mom," he reported to Debbie, who was now standing in the study doorway. "Maybe he just went somewhere for a change. Did you check to see if his car was here?"

Debbie shook her head. She had a weary expression on her face. Ken bounded for the door, now totally absorbed in the hunt for his father. Debbie went to the kitchen door and watched Ken approach the garage. He shouted back that the car was there. She turned and walked slowly back to the study. Leaning against the doorway, she peered inside her husband's little world.

Two high bookcases darkened one side of the room, filled with books that Daniel had accumulated over the course of his scientific career. These were the seeds of his destruction, as far as Debbie was concerned. The most interesting feature of the room was the leather recliner that she had bought him shortly after they moved to the house. Daniel had liked the chair from the moment he received it. Now he passed a large portion of his life in it. She thought back to an instance, years ago, when she

Wooden Spoons

had surprised him by bursting into the study and sitting on his lap in that chair. Ken heard the laughter and toddled into the room. He climbed aboard and they all laughed together like a normal, happy family. That particular event was so prominent in her memory because not too many years passed before such scenes never occurred. Now it was hard even to imagine, since she and her husband never touched and Daniel rarely laughed.

With a growing sense of unease, she moved to the window and looked toward the garage. Debbie saw that Ken had widened his search, because the second floor light was on. When she turned from the window, she saw that there were messages on Daniel's phone and she automatically pushed the play button. It was Victor DiAngelo's voice. The first message, which had been recorded before she left for Chicago, was simply an inquiry as to Daniel's whereabouts and health. The second was a plea for Daniel to contact him, stating that they needed to talk immediately, that he could no longer keep the wolves at bay. The final message featured the drollest incarnation of Victor's voice that Debbie had ever heard in all the years she had known him. It begged Daniel once more for contact and then sadly informed him that the faculty oversight committee was convening the next day to discuss his case.

Debbie had to sit down. She was fatigued and baffled. As her eyes wandered over her husband's desk, she noticed a wooden spoon. The desk top was unusually empty and the spoon was placed directly in the center on top of a folded piece of paper. The spoon was about ten inches long, and its gently tapered handle was thin and delicate. A heart was carved at the end. When she picked it up, Debbie saw that her name was written on the paper. Upon unfolding it she found a simple message:

Dennis Ruane

By the time you read this I will be gone. Considering the circumstances, I feel this is best for both of us.

As always, I wish you the best in life.

Love,
Daniel

Disbelief gave way to tears. Then her eyes opened wide. "My God, no. Surely not that," she exclaimed as his words conjured up the possibility of suicide. She read the note again, her hands trembling. Then she heard Ken briskly shut the kitchen door.

"Mom, hey mom," he hollered, coming down the hall rapidly.

Debbie was frozen with dread. Ken entered the doorway, out of breath.

"What is it?" she whispered.

"The jeep's gone," he gasped.

She looked up at him blankly.

"The jeep, Dad's old jeep, it's gone."

-17-

He returned to Mountain Farm from the direction he last departed it, from the east, off Furnace Road. The jeep had experienced mechanical difficulties most of the journey but never failed. Along the road, Daniel met many mechanics in small garages or gas stations who were sympathetic to his old vehicle. He traveled mostly minor highways and always by day, hating interstates and disliking travel at night on any road. This proved to be a prudent plan, for as one mechanic pointed out, the registration and inspection were three years behind and two back lights were not functioning.

Nonetheless, he was slowly approaching the summit of Hemlock Knob, two days after leaving Madison. When the flock of geese flew over him that day in the cornfield, he thought of Hemlock Knob. He had never experienced such an event on the mountain, but the emotion that coursed through him reminded Daniel of similar wild scenes he had witnessed there as a boy. He suddenly wanted to see the old home place one last time, and so he decided to postpone his suicide.

The jeep performed surprisingly well at this juncture, grinding out the last few miles of the journey, negotiating Hemlock Road without hesitation. The vehicle was not so loaded as one might expect for such an exodus. When Daniel returned to the house that morning, he established a simple parameter for packing. He would take nothing along that pertained to his life in Madison, a life that ended in the cornfield. The jeep was the first and easy choice. Next were the woodcarving tools and the spoons he had made. Daniel also took the axe that had accompanied him to Wisconsin three decades before.

As for clothing, Daniel packed work clothes and hunting apparel. A decade before, under the influence of a neighbor, he had briefly taken up pheasant hunting. The sport never did appeal to him as much as the clothing. The blue suits and all vestiges of formality were left behind. It was a pair of khaki hunting pants, a heavy flannel shirt and high-top leather boots he chose for his departure. Upon his head was an odd-looking hat, which he described as an English-hunting cap, but Debbie had always called it *Dan's Sherlock Holmes hat*. Daniel had also packed the loaded pistol.

Two days before, as he drove along Lake Mendota Drive for the last time, he was an odd sight to any neighbor who witnessed his passage, but now, as he drove up Hemlock Road, he did not appear out of place. He hadn't shaven in a week and his hair was in wild disarray. Daniel's face was pale and expressionless.

For two days his effort had been focused on getting to Mountain Farm. He slept in the jeep when and where it was possible; he ate when he had to and whatever was convenient. As the jeep passed the spot where he had turned and waved goodbye to his great-grandfather thirty-five years ago, Daniel slowed the vehicle to a walking pace. He grew apprehensive now that he was confronted with the reality of being here. Communications with John Campbell had dwindled to about a letter or phone call every two years, so he had only fragmentary knowledge of the condition of Mountain Farm. What he did know gave him reason to expect the worst.

Decades ago, with Daniel's approval, John had enacted a plan to preserve the farm by allowing people to live there rent-free, but with the responsibility of maintaining the buildings. The offer appealed to men, and typically to those who were familiar with the demands of such living conditions. This arrangement had worked to some extent for the first twenty years after Tom Reilly's death. No great improvements were made on the farm, but the buildings remained intact.

The third decade started with some bad tenants who abused the house for two years until they were ordered to move out. They left, took the wood stove with them and threatened to file a complaint about the primitive and unsanitary conditions of the rental property. They were followed by two young men who used the log house as a base for their belongings, staying there only sporadically, usually in the hunting season. When John learned that during a wild party, the porch railing was broken apart and burned in a bonfire, he evicted them and decided to lock the house. He hoped that with the help of hunters who utilized the property, he might at least forestall the inevitable vandalism. John made this effort because of loyalty to his great-uncle, Tom Reilly, not because he felt any obligation to his distant cousin Daniel Whaley, the absentee-owner who seemed to not care what happened to Mountain Farm.

As he drove down Reilly Lane, Daniel was elated to see that the old log building was still standing, sturdy and proud, in defiance of the years. Trees and brush had encroached from all sides such that the house appeared to have moved closer to the woods. When he walked up to it, he could see that it had been well vandalized and anything that could be removed from the building had been. All the windows were missing and most were boarded over. Surprisingly, the front door was locked. Scars from the many hasps that had been replaced on the door were evidence that an effort had been made to keep it locked.

The back door, however, was wide open, the jamb splintered from some recent invasion, and Daniel was able to step into The Great Room. The interior of the house was bare and dark with piles of debris, leaves, beer cans and furniture parts littering the floor. Damp areas were evidence that the roof was leaking.

Daniel could not help but to be disheartened. *What did I expect, Paw waiting for me with a pot of rabbit stew? It's my fault. Mountain Farm was given to me, and I let this happen.* Fortunately, his memories of the house enabled him to overlook the conditions and momentarily put aside his guilt so that he could reacquaint himself with the old building. Slowly and methodically he explored each room, picturing them as they once were. In The Great Room he pushed some of the debris into piles with his foot and then carried several armload of wood scraps out the back door, piling them on the ground just beyond the porch steps.

Next, Daniel walked to the woodshed. As with the log house, he found the basic structure intact while all doors and windows were broken or missing. To his amazement, the massive old workbench was still there, lying on its side. The great weight of the bench had apparently discouraged theft. On close inspection he saw that it was scarred with initials and had obviously been chopped with an ax on some occasion. Daniel stooped and fondly ran his hand across the top edge. Then he knelt down, gripped the thick planks of the top side with both hands and righted the heavy bench with a mighty heave. Winded by this impulsive effort, he leaned against the wall, took deep breaths of the shed's musty aroma and lapsed into a daydream. *How nice it would be to see this place as it was, the old tools on the back wall and six cords of firewood stacked by the doorway.* He lingered with that thought a few minutes, and then forced himself out the door.

Daniel visited the forge, the spring house, Tom's boiler shed, and finally the outhouse. He found all four structures to be in a similar state of disrepair and yet, all were standing. Eventually, he climbed the gentle slope behind the house to the cemetery. The graves of his ancestors came into view beyond foliage which intertwined the fence, and guilt started to gnaw at his conscience.

The weeds and brush were relatively thin among the five headstones because of the large maple trees that blocked the sun. Some of the trees were growing there when the first grave was dug in 1871. This was for Michael Reilly, the first born of Adam and Sadie. Michael had died at the age of three from cholera. The tombstone was scarcely readable now, but Daniel remembered the oral history of Mountain Farm.

Twenty years later, Daniel's great-great uncle Jack, younger brother of Adam, was buried on the hill. He lived at Mountain Farm for only a year before he died. Jack had emigrated from Ireland five years after his brother. He was a professional boxer for a number of years with some success in the ring, and then worked in the coal mines when his boxing days ended. Jack never married, got sick one day, and turned to his brother when he was down for the count. Adam and Sadie took Jack into their home and eventually buried him alongside his nephew. Daniel stared at the weathered headstone and saw that his ancestor was fifty-one years old when he died. *That's four years younger than I am,* he thought, shaking his head.

Dennis Ruane

Tom had told Daniel that Jack was a nice man who sat by the fire, wrapped in a blanket, smoking his pipe and telling stories. It was Jack Reilly who had brought the carving tools to America and delivered them to his brother. They had been in the possession of their grandfather, who decided that Adam should have them.

Sadie Reilly died in 1926. Daniel recalled that she was considered somewhat odd and superstitious. She died suddenly one spring morning at the age of eighty-two. According to the story that had been handed down to Daniel's mother, Sadie had just informed Adam that she had read the signs and that it was time to plant the garden.

Adam was laid beside his wife three years later. Daniel remembered his grandmother Kelly, making the remark that her father got his stubbornness from his own father, Adam. She said that Adam refused to leave Hemlock Knob in the final year of his life, although he was very ill and in pain.

Daniel recalled a story his great-grandfather told him concerning Adam's death. Tom had helped as much as possible as the end approached, and was at his father's bedside when he died. Tom said that Adam slipped in and out of consciousness during the final hours. After he had been quiet for some time and was breathing almost imperceptibly, it seemed that the end had come. But suddenly, his father called out. "Tommy, Tommy, are you here?" he asked, without opening his eyes.

"Yes, Pap, I'm here," Tom answered, going to the bed and placing a hand on his father's shoulder.

"Tommy, is that doe standing at the edge of the meadow, among the apple trees?"

Tom told Daniel that he looked out the window and there was a deer at the far side of the field, in the orchard that Adam

Wooden Spoons

had planted many years before.

"Yeah Pap, it's there," he answered, returning to the bedside. He said that his father smiled and spoke no more. Adam died within the hour.

The grave of Tom Reilly still stood out from the others as more recent, although it was now three decades ago that it had been filled. It was here that Daniel sat, next to Paw. He looked down at the little homestead with its sturdy log and stone buildings and from a distance it appeared much the same as it had three decades ago. It was quiet and still on this warm spring day, with only the occasional cawing of a crow interrupting the calm. Daniel felt at home in this scene. He felt like he belonged here.

What was it all worth? All those years of work and worry, doing what I was supposed to. What is it all worth now? Questions such as these did not ease the nagging guilt over the condition of Mountain Farm. He looked around himself at the clutter of limbs in the cemetery, the rusted fence with its sagging gate, and the inscriptions on the headstones, fading into obscurity.

Why did Paw trust the care of Mountain Farm to me? Before he considered the answer to this question, Daniel stood and hurried down the slope to the jeep. He returned with a bottle of brandy and then drank from it determinedly. He knew that the brandy would reign in his conscience. *There's nothing I can do now about the choices I've made.* He took another drink as he peered over Mountain Farm. Then he looked back at the graves. *What a peaceful place to be buried. Maybe I should request to be buried here in my suicide note.*

When he considered this idea for a moment, he shook his head. *I don't deserve to be buried here with them. I abandoned Mountain Farm. I let this happen to the family home. I let my* ancestors down. *Paw was wrong about me.* He took another drink. *The least I can do for Paw is to clean up around here a little. Why not?*

"After all, I don't have anything else to do," he said aloud. Daniel looked up into the canopy of maple leaves and sighed at the absurd truth of this statement. Taking another drink, he leaned back against one of the massive old trees, closed his eyes, and allowed his thoughts to drift with the scents and sounds of spring. He soon fell asleep.

An hour passed before he awoke to the sound of an approaching engine. A pick-up truck came into view, moving fast along Hemlock Road. As it reached Reilly Lane, Daniel could hear music and voices. He stood and instinctively hurried down the hill as the vehicle approached the house.

Coming around the cabin, he encountered three men who appeared to be in their early twenties. They had food and beer with them and apparently planned on spending some time at the log house. They had been looking toward the jeep, discussing its presence among themselves when Daniel appeared.

"Can I help you, gentlemen?" he asked in a professorial voice.

The trio looked back and forth at each other. One of them, a lanky man with short, blond hair, looked at Daniel and answered sheepishly.

"Well, ah, we were going to hang out here today. That's all."

Daniel could not help but be amused by the confusion on their faces. He spoke to them in a calm but definite tone. "I'd prefer that you didn't. I've just arrived, and I'm tired. I have a lot of work to do tomorrow."

They stared at this tall disheveled, stranger with doubtful

expressions.

"Do you own this property?" their spokesman asked.

"Yes, I do."

The young men shuffled back and forth, glancing at each other and then over at the jeep. They were certain that this could not be true, but being squatters of a sort, themselves, they were not in a position to argue. They shuffled and glanced a while longer and then turned toward their vehicle. The men made no more eye contact with the stranger and did not speak to him again. When they climbed into the truck, Daniel could see that a very animated conversation ensued.

-18-

Daniel awoke on the floor of his great-grandfather's bedroom. He lay on his back for a few minutes, orienting himself to the unfamiliar surroundings. His makeshift bed of blankets and clothing had served him well. With the accumulated weariness of his two-day sojourn, he had slept soundly through the night.

When he stepped onto the front porch, he was struck by the dramatic quiet of Mountain Farm. It was cool with a heavy, wet fog. Daniel could see the other buildings and some of the meadow beyond, but then, just a white cloud. The scene had a dreamlike quality that seemed appropriate to his situation.

Along the road he had bought a strange mixture of foods, depending on his mood or his location. He ate a breakfast of raisins, nuts, and a pepperoni roll. After breakfast, he went to the spring house and with cupped hands, pulled the cold mountain water across his face. The sensation was exhilarating, and he felt more alert and energetic than he had in days. Sun rays were beginning to slant through the mist, and the fog was dispersing. Daniel was anxious to start.

He began by removing the boards that covered the windows of his great-grandfather's bedroom. Then he transferred his possessions to the room and arranged them in an orderly fashion. He passed the rest of the morning opening the other boarded windows and clearing the house of debris. After a meager lunch, which was similar to his breakfast, Daniel walked up the hill to the cemetery. He stood beside Tom's grave and gazed down at Mountain Farm. He had lost no enthusiasm for his decision to clean up the property. On the contrary, his plans had expanded as the day wore on. Daniel now wanted to do some basic repair work on the buildings. Fully aware that it would be an impossible task for him to return the farm to its original condition, he was determined to accomplish as much as he could while he was here and able to work.

Daniel remembered the homesteading skills that his great-grandfather had taught him and knew how to utilize the forest for raw materials. However, he needed tools and some basic items such as glass and hardware. Since he planned to live in the log house, he also wanted some furniture. A trip down to Lick Hollow was necessary. That was something he had not wanted to do, and, in fact, had planned the route of his arrival to avoid it. Tomorrow he would descend to his hometown, but today, he wanted to be alone on the mountain.

The only tool in his possession relevant to his plans was the axe that had returned to Mountain Farm with him. Daniel began cutting back the brush and trees that were encroaching on the house. As he worked, he instinctively saved whatever was suitable for firewood, bearing in mind his great-grandfather's guidelines concerning the fuel supply. Daniel realized that he had a tremendous amount of cutting to do if he were to have six cords by winter. At first, he swung his axe with careful, measured strokes, reacquainting himself with the tool, but before long, he worked like a man possessed, a man making up for lost time. Sometimes, for the challenge, he swung wildly, cleaving a sapling with one mighty swipe.

Dennis Ruane

As they commonly do, the locust trees had won the competition for the open area. This suited Daniel, for he knew well that they yielded excellent firewood. After cutting a tree down, he sliced off the limbs and chopped the main trunk into six-foot logs. His plan was to cut these into eighteen-inch firewood lengths, after purchasing a saw.

Daniel was about two hours into his work when he heard a vehicle driving on Hemlock Road. He turned to see a pick-up truck, approaching rapidly. During all of his youthful excursions on the mountain, he encountered few vehicles, and this was already the second in as many days. Despite the fact that he had lived in a city for many years, surrounded by traffic noise, it was an intrusive sound to him here.

As the blue Ford turned down Reilly Lane, Daniel stopped cutting, leaned on his ax and placed his right foot atop one of the locust logs. The truck jerked to a halt within fifteen feet of him. Daniel could see the reddened face of an older man, wearing a green plastic visor, wire-rimmed glasses, and a deliberate scowl. The man got out of the truck quickly, revealing that he was of small stature and was bald. He had a white shirt on and baggy khaki pants, which were upheld by blue suspenders.

"Can I help you, fella? Do you have permission to cut here?" the man asked, with obvious displeasure.

Despite the many years which had passed since he last saw him, Daniel recognized his cousin, John Campbell.

"I think you can help me. I own this property. I inherited it from my great-grandfather, Tom Reilly."

The man in the visor had expected any answer but this one. He just stared at this unusual-looking man while he struggled to comprehend what he had just heard.

"Hello John. I'm Daniel Whaley and I drove in from

Wooden Spoons

Wisconsin yesterday," Daniel said, walking toward him with an outstretched hand.

The name was familiar, but this tall man with his scraggly beard and odd hat did not even remotely match the mental image John Campbell carried of his relative, Professor Daniel Whaley. John squinted at Daniel as they shook hands. "I'm sorry," he said. "You're not the person I expected." John's face began to change dramatically as recognition dawned on him. The red faded and the scowl transformed into a smile. "Pardon me, Daniel. My goodness. I can scarcely believe it. How is it that you suddenly turned up here to hack away at the trees after all these years?"

"That is a long, strange story."

John nodded. "Well then, may I ask, what are your plans? Are you staying?"

Daniel hesitated before he answered. "I'm staying for a while. Can't really say how long. I'm hoping to stay long enough to fix up the place a little"

John Campbell's head bobbed up. "Really? Splendid. Splendid. That's the best news I've heard in some time. You are thinking of living here on Hemlock Knob?"

Daniel nodded.

"That's splendid. As you can see, I've been fighting a losing-battle here, trying to maintain the old place."

"How did you know I was here?"

John Campbell looked up at his tall cousin. "Everybody in Lick Hollow knows that you're up here."

Daniel was at first surprised at this remark, but then he remembered the young men he had encountered the day before.

"I can't run up here all the time like I used to, but when I heard there was a stranger with an out-of-state license plate,

119

claiming to own the place, I thought I had better take a look. As you know, I promised Uncle Tom that I would look after the farm until you returned."

Daniel was confused. "You mean to say that Paw was expecting me to come and live here all along?"

"I don't know, now. That was the impression I got from him back then. As the years passed, I didn't know what to think. But keeping an eye on the place wasn't any bother either. It was sport for me in some ways. It's just that as time passed and I got older, it became more difficult. I worried that you might never come. I thought that I might have to just give up and let the place go the way of the world."

Glancing hastily at his watch, John announced that he had to get back down the mountain. "Nora will be fixing lunch and I'm expecting a client at one o'clock. I allowed myself exactly one hour to drive off the squatter and get back down on time. Would you care to join us for lunch?"

"Thank you, but another time, soon. I need a day at least to adjust to the sudden change of scenery. I'll be down. I'm going to need some things."

John nodded and turned to go, but then stopped. "Oh, I have the tools, you know," he said, facing Daniel again.

Daniel was surprised and didn't reply.

"The old woodworking tools that belong to the farm here."

"Yes, I knew that Paw left them to you."

"Well, that was the most convenient way to handle it at the time. Uncle Tom knew that he would need them right until the end, and afterwards he wanted them to stay together. He asked me to keep them until you needed them. Anyway, gotta go," John said, turning back toward his truck "Stop in. The Mercantile is in the same spot. We'll be there." John Campbell climbed into his truck and drove away.

-19-

The next day dawned clear and cool; Daniel awoke, stiff and sore. As he lay on the bedroom floor, familiarizing himself once again to the new surroundings, he decided to go down to Lick Hollow that morning. Daniel wanted to buy more substantial food and the construction supplies that he needed. The fact John Campbell had the old tools was additional motivation to go soon.

An hour later he was creeping down Hemlock Road toward the village, excited and apprehensive at the same time. Daniel rolled both front windows down so that he was able to absorb the cool spring aroma. It had been over thirty years since he traveled this route but it was still familiar to him and he relished the scene that unfolded with every turn in the road. Just past The Bend, a ninety-degree angle in the road where it was frequently washed out during heavy rains, a large, rectangular rock sat against the bank on the left side. About four times the size of the jeep, it was well embedded in thick mountain laurel. Daniel stopped, got out, walked up to the rock and placed his hand on it. He smiled. Nearly fifty years before, he and his brother had done the same thing. They were on their first hike on Hemlock Knob with their father and had been amazed by what was the largest rock they had ever seen.

When he had traveled about a mile, Daniel came upon the

Dennis Ruane

first house, one that had been built since he last came this way. Before he reached Buttermilk Lane, at the end of Hemlock Road, he saw several dozen unfamiliar houses, and for some reason, this bothered him.

The Lick Hollow Mercantile was situated on the corner of Main Street and Buttermilk Lane. It was a one-story frame building with additions jutting out from two sides, making it much larger than Daniel remembered it. It had a wood-shingled roof and was sided with rough-cut hemlock wood, with bark still on the edges. The graveled parking area was three times the size it had been, and the row of maple trees that once covered the front was gone. It was now flanked by several large blue spruce that framed it perfectly. As different as the building was from his recollection, Daniel still thought the store was charming and inviting.

John's parents had opened the Mercantile eighty years before, and for many decades it was the principal grocery and supply store in the village. Over time, the business adapted to the changes in travel patterns so that by 1965, when John and Nora took over, the Mercantile was catering to a burgeoning tourist trade. Now as it entered the twenty-first century, it could be described as a deluxe convenience store with a homespun twist. To the credit of the proprietors, the store had not become a souvenir shop. Although the Lick Hollow Mercantile had broadened and modernized its inventory over the years, it still remained a general supply store.

John and Nora's home was located seventy-five yards behind, nestled into a hollow that was bound by forest. Along with the neat, two-story frame house were a small barn and an old stone spring house. Lick Hollow Creek, now swollen with spring rain, bisected the property. A stone arch bridge spanned the water and completed the picturesque Campbell homestead.

Wooden Spoons

John also dealt in antiques and was an avid collector of Americana. It was the barn that housed this alternate business along with his personal collections.

When Daniel walked through the door of the Mercantile, he was greeted by an elderly black man who was drinking coffee alone at a table near the front window. "Well, hello there. Are you Daniel Whaley?" the man asked.

"Yes, I am," Daniel answered with his usual reserve.

The man approached, smiling. He was of average height with an athletic build. He had a kind face and a confident, casual air about him. Dressed in worn but neat blue jeans and a flannel shirt, he appeared to be a man who regularly did physical work. A distinguishing feature of his wardrobe was the squarish blue cap that was tilted to one side on his head.

"My name is George Haynes. I knew your father way back when, and I met you once when you were but an infant," he said and softly laughed. It was a cheerful sound that quickly put Daniel at ease. "Hear you're gonna fix up the old home place."

Although that was basically his intention, it was strange for Daniel to hear his plan to work on Mountain Farm described in this way. He liked the way it sounded and nodded.

"Glad to hear it. Glad to hear it. Say, I know a little bit about everything when it comes to working on places, got lots of old building materials. Let me know if I can help out."

Daniel was shaking George's hand and thanking him when John Campbell appeared from a back room. John always walked quickly, regardless of the task or degree of urgency. He often whistled as he walked and usually at the same tempo as his gait. To Daniel, he looked much more comfortable in this setting, wearing a denim apron and a pencil behind his ear.

"Daniel," he said, as he crossed the room.

Dennis Ruane

"Hello, John."

John Campbell turned quickly toward the sales counter. "Nora, this is Daniel, our relative and Uncle Tom's great-grandson."

Nora Campbell had been standing behind the counter all the while, slowly wiping the glass cases, but only looked up now. Like her husband, she was a small person. She had long, coarse, white hair that framed a somewhat mournful face. Nora glanced at Daniel and nodded and then continued to wipe.

George Haynes moved close to Daniel, hid his mouth with his hand and spoke in a whisper. "She doesn't warm to new people quickly, but when she does, she would defend you against an army, and win."

Daniel smiled, but he did not need that explanation. Although he had never met Nora he had heard about her peculiarities from his mother.

"Come along, Daniel," John said excitedly. "Let's go look at those tools. Pull the jeep over the bridge and up to the barn, and I'll meet you there."

"Well, I have to be moving along, back to work," George said leisurely. He nodded to John and Nora before turning to Daniel. "Nice to meet you, Daniel. If I can be of any service to you, just let me know." Daniel shook hands with George Haynes and thanked him again.

The barn was a stately building standing on a neat fieldstone foundation and sided with weathered hemlock boards, nailed vertically to a log frame. It predated the house by fifty years, a remnant of the original settlement on the property. Daniel walked through the large barn door into a rustic gallery of antiques. Mostly furniture, the inventory was neatly arranged into groups of related items and divided by narrow lanes.

Daniel inhaled the musty aroma that he fondly associated with old wood "You have an impressive collection here, John," he said as he turned a circle, shifting his gaze up and down.

John Campbell grinned. "It's what I do, Daniel. It's what I do." John hurried him to the back and into a smaller room that served as an office. Arranged on the far wall were the old tools. Daniel remembered them well. He would have been thrilled just to see them again, and it was beyond any expectation he might have had, that they would be his to use.

John watched with curiosity as Daniel examined the tools, rubbing the edge of a saw blade or testing the fit of an adze handle. He looked at them differently than anyone else had over the many years they had decorated the office wall. It was obvious that his relative loved these tools like Tom Reilly had. He was looking at them with use in mind.

There was a scuffling of feet in the show room and John looked over his shoulder. "Got to go to work, Daniel. Take your time. There are some other items from the log house in that trunk in the corner. Whatever you need. You can pull the jeep through the grass to the back here." He nodded toward a door to the right of the tools.

After Daniel loaded the tools, John was no longer in the barn so he pulled the jeep to the front of the store. When he entered, he could hear talking in the back room. Daniel wandered the aisles, picking up items he needed, and stopped when he saw a wide-brimmed felt hat. Most of the headwear on display was of a western style and did not appeal to him. This hat did. It had a rounded crown, a down-turned soft brim, and a narrow leather band. He took off his English hunting cap and tried the hat on. It fit perfectly.

"It's you, Daniel," John said, as he emerged from the back.

Dennis Ruane

"I'll sell that to you for half price. That style never did catch on, and we've had that last one forever."

Daniel left it on his head.

"What about furniture?"

Daniel shrugged his shoulders.

"Most of the original furniture from the log house is in the Lick Hollow Folk Museum, which is located on the second floor of the library. Have you ever been there?"

Daniel shook his head.

"Well no, of course not. It has only been in existence about twenty years. That's where the furniture is. You should visit the museum. Your great-great grandfather, Adam Reilly, created the finest handmade furniture ever to come out of this area, and his spinning wheels and looms are true works of art. He also did some wonderful woodcarving."

"Then I want all that to stay there, of course. I just want the basics, something to use temporarily," Daniel said, realizing the point his cousin was attempting to make.

"No problem, then. Splendid, splendid. George and I will fix you up. I've got lots of pieces here that will never be antiques soon enough to help my cause. George has quite a collection of his own and a good truck for hauling. He'll get you some sort of a wood stove too. George is a good man. We go way back. Knowing him, he's probably already gathering your things together."

After Daniel loaded the final box of necessities into the jeep, he paid Nora with two one-hundred dollar bills that he unwrapped from a roll in his coat pocket.

"Say Daniel, do you still have the old carving tools?" John asked.

Daniel turned slowly to face his relative and nodded.

"Do you use them?"

Wooden Spoons

"I didn't until recently. Now I carve wooden spoons with them."

John's face showed obvious surprise. "I'll be darned," he said. Then he shook his head and grinned.

John stood on the porch as the jeep backed away. "Look for George Haynes in two or three days."

"The museum is located above the library?" Daniel asked through the open window.

"Yes, first right as you go in the main door, up the stairs. Robert Cranston is the librarian. Tell him who you are."

As the jeep drove away, Nora came to the door. "He's a sad man," she said.

-20-

Daniel was anxious to begin working on Mountain Farm but he wanted to see the Lick Hollow Folk Museum and the work of his great-great-grandfather, so he turned west out of the parking lot. Driving down the Main Street of his hometown, he was not impressed. Daniel saw little of the charm that he held in his memory. Interspersed among typical small-town businesses he saw littered, empty lots, dilapidated and vacant buildings with sagging signs, thrift shops and second hand stores. Even the hardware store, the restaurant, and gas station appeared run-down and struggling.

Daniel's impression did not improve when he passed the large stone building known as the Martin House, where he grew up. The building was in obvious disrepair, but that was a minor affront compared to the total denuding of the yard. The three grand maple trees that once faced Walnut Road were gone, and so was the tall mulberry hedge that his father had painstakingly cultivated to frame their half-acre yard. There was a large, sloppy mobile home, roosting at the rear of the property, flanked by a pair of weather-beaten commercial, outbuildings. Daniel nearly drove off the road, he was so distracted.

The Lick Hollow Library was an old two-story brick building located one block off Main street. Built as a private residence at the turn of the century, it had been purchased by the town fifty years after, during a more prosperous era. It was a handsome building, large for a private home, but somewhat small for a public library. After his disappointing tour of Main Street, Daniel was pleasantly surprised with the library and its well-tended gardens.

Entering the lobby, Daniel saw a sign at the base of a stairway that read: *Lick Hollow Folk Museum*. As he turned to begin his ascent, he noticed that a man behind a tall wooden desk in the main room glanced in his direction. Daniel had only reached the landing where the stairs switched back when a voice from behind startled him.

"Can I be of any assistance?" asked the same man he had seen at the desk.

"Oh, no, I was just . . . Well, actually, I learned from my cousin, John Campbell, that one of my relatives has some pieces in the folk museum."

"Really? I can certainly help you then. I'm Robert Cranston, head librarian and curator of the museum," he said with a measure of pride and a smile. He extended his hand. "Not to mention head gardener and groundskeeper."

R. Cranston, as he was commonly known, was a thin, small-framed man of average height. He had an elfish face, thinning black hair that was slicked to one side, and most noticeably, disproportionately large, heavy-framed glasses. The thick lenses distorted the appearance of his eyes. He wore a white dress shirt, a thin dark tie and gray pants that were too high above his dark leather loafers.

"Daniel Whaley," Daniel said, taking his hand.

The librarian turned his head with a curious expression on his face, recognizing the local name but clueless as to whom this tall rough-looking stranger might be. "Ah, yes, Whaley.

Dennis Ruane

What is the name of the family member whom we represent?"

"Adam Reilly."

"Adam Reilly? My goodness. You certainly have come to the right place then. And how are you related to Mr. Reilly?" R. Cranston asked, moving onto the landing.

Daniel found it difficult to discern the man's age, particularly in the dim light of the stairway. He seemed to be anywhere between forty and sixty. Actually, it was right in between. R. Cranston walked with a cane that seemed too tall for its purpose, but neither that nor his limp slowed a rapid, excited gait.

"I'm his great-great grandson. I'm originally from Lick Hollow. Tom Reilly was my great-grandfather."

Suddenly R. Cranston realized exactly to whom he was speaking and his mouth partially opened with an expression of disbelief. "Daniel Whaley? Professor Daniel Whaley? You own the property on Hemlock Knob, right?"

"Y-yes, that's correct."

"Well follow me then, Professor Whaley," R. Cranston said enthusiastically, continuing up the stairs, his cane thumping on each step.

The second floor consisted of one large open room with a high vaulted ceiling. It had once served as a ballroom. The paint was dull and stained in places, especially near the bottoms of the tall arched windows, and the room possessed the musty aroma of old wood. R. Cranston led Daniel into the midst of it with obvious pride. Many objects relevant to the history and culture of Lick Hollow were displayed on tables and shelves or within glass cases around the room. As Daniel listened to background information on the museum, he glanced from object to object with fascination.

"There were some of us," R. Cranston said, "John

Wooden Spoons

Campbell among them, who realized the town was beginning to change. The young people were moving away and leaving an aging population from another era behind. Invaluable information was being lost every year to death and senility while historical artifacts were being casually discarded or hoarded by antique dealers."

They had reached the far side of the room when R. Cranston stopped and turned toward Daniel. "We were eventually able to procure this space to house the museum, and Mr. Campbell's donations became the nucleus of our collection." He turned and swept his arm across the area behind him. "These are the artifacts from Adam Reilly that I'm honored to show you."

Daniel moved past the librarian; drawn to what he saw. The piece that caught his attention first was a human figure about thirty inches tall, a mountain man carved from black walnut. It was a very detailed piece, capturing the folds in the clothing, features of the face and even individual fingers on the hands.

Sensing that Daniel might want to be alone, R. Cranston glanced at his watch and grinned. "Oh my, I can get carried away. I must get back down before chaos breaks out on the main floor." He hurried away as if he believed it could happen.

Daniel smiled and listened to the descending thump of the cane. Then he returned his attention to the walnut carving. The man depicted in the woodcarving had a wide-brimmed hat, similar to the one that Daniel now wore. The figure was turned such that he appeared to be looking back at something as he walked away. He had a duffel bag slung by a strap over his right shoulder. Daniel bent down to peer at the face of the man and he saw a grim, haunted expression that reminded him of his own image in the jeep mirror.

131

Dennis Ruane

Close beside it was a smaller piece carved in cherry, an elderly woman seated in a rocking chair. This was also very detailed, even to the rendition of hands folded on her lap and to the individual rungs of the chair. The figure appeared to be relaxed and Daniel could imagine that the chair might actually rock. When he touched it, it did. He was in awe. His forefather was an accomplished woodcarver well beyond Daniel's expectations.

On the wall behind these two pieces was an assortment of bowls and spoons which were particularly interesting to Daniel because of his own woodcarving efforts. He looked at each piece closely, studying the lines and deciding which chisel or gouge had been used to create them. Then he turned to see two of Adam Reilly's renowned spinning wheels along with a child's cradle fashioned from walnut. The high level of craftsmanship and the painstaking attention to detail made his great-great-grandfather's work easy to recognize. Daniel was inspired and now anxious to carve again.

At the bottom of the stairs, he nodded to R. Cranston, who was attending to a woman at the counter with an armload of books. The librarian hesitated, nodded, then continued with what he was doing. Duty came first, no matter how much he wished to talk with Adam Reilly's great-great-grandson.

As he left the building, Daniel saw a sheriff's car parked behind the jeep. There was a man sitting in the front seat, reading a newspaper. As Daniel neared the jeep, the sheriff laid down the paper, put on his hat and stepped out of the vehicle.

Harry Pinto was a large man, overweight but firm. He had a dark complexion, with thick wavy hair and a rugged, weather-beaten face. He always wore dark sunglasses. Harry was in his mid sixties and had been a Fayette County sheriff for twenty years. He had some American Indian in him, everyone knew that. Harry had wanted to be sheriff since he was a boy. He grew up tough in a tough home, worked hard and achieved his dream. He took the job as sheriff very seriously, and while some laughed behind his back for this reason, no one ever laughed to Harry's face, for any reason. He was slow to anger but if provoked, could erupt like a volcano. Harry Pinto was basically a fair and honest man, but always wary of strangers.

"This your vehicle?" Sheriff Pinto asked.

"Yes it is," Daniel answered, turning.

"Show me your driver's license, please."

Daniel nervously fumbled for his wallet until he found the license and handed it to the Sheriff.

"Looks good. No problem here. Got problems with the vehicle though. Registration and plates expired three years ago. Were you aware of that?"

Daniel looked at the jeep and then turned back to the Sheriff. "Honestly, yes. I didn't plan on this trip, officer. I've had some problems come my way and I got in the old jeep and drove away from them."

Harry nodded. He could relate to that. "You're staying in the old log house on Hemlock Knob, right?"

"That's right," Daniel answered, realizing that John Campbell had not exaggerated when he said that everyone in town knew he was on the mountain. "I inherited Mountain Farm from my great-grandfather, Tom Reilly. I've lived in Wisconsin for many years and never made it back until now."

Harry looked at the driver's license again. "Whaley. I know Whaleys. You from here?"

Dennis Ruane

Daniel nodded. "I grew up on Main Street, in the Martin House," Daniel said nodding to his left.

"There by the bank?" the Sheriff asked, somewhat intrigued.

Daniel nodded. "But the bank wasn't there then. I saw it for the first time today. It was where Charlie and Mary Dawson lived when I was growing up."

Harry Pinto almost smiled at that. He remembered Charlie Dawson, a happy old veteran of the coal mines, a tough-nut, a die-hard Pittsburgh Pirate fan. He looked at the license again before he handed it back. He felt no threat from this stranger.

"Well, Mr. Whaley, you seem to be on the up and up, but you got to legitimize this here vehicle. Can't let you drive around like this. Won't cost you much, fill out a few forms. Give you two weeks, uh, or month or so, to get it straightened out. All right?" Harry was rarely so lenient.

Daniel nodded and thanked him.

The sheriff got in his car and drove away. Harry's great-grandfather was Dutch, and his great-grandmother, Shawnee. They struggled to raise five children on an overworked little farm they had purchased two miles south of Lick Hollow. Their oldest child, Josiah, became Harry's grandfather. His conversation with Daniel Whaley caused him to recall a story his grandfather had told him. It involved Adam Reilly, whom Harry knew was the man who built the house on Hemlock Knob.

In the story Josiah was a young man and had been sent by his father to buy corn seed at the general store on Main Street, located at the time directly across from the Lick Hollow Tavern. He had loaded two sacks of seed onto his mule and would have begun his trek home except that two local men stumbled from the tavern in his direction. They knew who Josiah was and they didn't like him. This was partly because he was Dutch but mostly because he was Indian. They began by asking him demeaning questions in an exaggerated accent of what they presumed his language might be. One then began to tell a story of how his own great-grandfather had dealt with some troublesome Indians while the other nonchalantly untied the rope that bound the seed bags. They aimed to provoke him into a fight, and when the bags fell to the ground they had nearly succeeded.

"What's the trouble here?" came the stern voice of a man who was coming toward them from across the street.

The two men from the tavern looked back in surprise.

"N-no trouble Adam. We're just getting acquainted with our new neighbor, that's all," the stocky one replied.

Harry remembered that his grandfather laughed at this point of the narration. "Suddenly, these two tough men were not so tough," Josiah had said.

But then the leaner man, who didn't really know Adam Reilly, grew bold. "If you ask me, it's none of your business, mister."

Adam stepped to within an arms length of the man. He stared at him with penetrating, blue eyes, saying nothing at first.

The man shifted nervously and averted his gaze as Adam spoke. "I did not ask you, sir," he said in a low, restrained voice. "So I'll thank you to spare me your opinion." It was not so much what he said, as how he said it that was intimidating. Then he turned his back on the two men.

"Adam Reilly, he said to me, as he shook my hand," Josiah Pinto had told his grandson, proudly. "Then he helped me tie my seed bags back on the mule. From that day on, I was never

Dennis Ruane

bothered in town again. Nor was anyone in the family."

The Sheriff remembered his grandfather's description of Adam Reilly. It fit the man he had just spoken to. W*hat goes around, comes around, I guess,* thought Harry Pinto.

-21-

As he maneuvered the jeep up Hemlock Road, Daniel reflected on the events of the morning. What he had seen and learned in Lick Hollow bolstered his desire to restore Mountain Farm, the plans growing more lofty with each bend in the road. By the final turn onto Reilly Lane, he had a clear vision of what he wished to accomplish. Daniel wanted the homestead to be like it was when he was a boy, a place where a person could experience the same sense of wonder he once felt.

Daniel drove past the house, turned, and backed up to the door of the woodshed. For the next hour he returned the tools to their proper place on the back wall. The shelf and the iron pins upon which they originally rested were still in place, and to the best of his memory, Daniel arranged the tools in their former positions. He stepped back to view them from a distance. With so much to do on this poor neglected homestead, his forefather's woodworking tools, hanging in place again, were an inspiring sight.

Churning with nervous energy, anxious to begin, Daniel made a quick meal at the house and then hurried to cut firewood. While it would not seem to be the most pressing need, so early in the spring, it was psychologically the logical start of his venture.

You can never have enough firewood. Winter is always

coming. He remembered his great-grandfather's words and smiled. Armed with the felling axe and buck saw, tools that Tom had used right until the time of his death, Daniel quadrupled his fuel supply in a matter of hours. He stacked the wood neatly in the woodshed and his confidence grew with each tier he added to the pile. He decided that each day on the mountain would begin with the cutting of firewood. Even if he was not present this winter to burn it, the meditative and inspirational value in the effort was reason enough.

When Daniel turned his attention to the buildings, restoration of the outhouse to working order was a priority. Like all the structures on Mountain Farm, it was built square and solid of hemlock logs and stone. The outhouse was a more substantial structure than one commonly associates with the name. This was no small, rough plank building with a crescent moon cut into the door. The two-holed white oak seat was still in place, but rough and cracked from rain that reached it through the rotted roof. The seat covered a large, rectangular box, built of stone. This was filled to within a foot of the openings with excrement, which had long ago neutralized itself.

Daniel was familiar with the building, having used it as a boy. He also learned from his great-grandfather that it had been built on a mound of earth so that it could be shoveled out when necessary, through the opening behind it. This obviously had not been done for many years.

There was a small hole at the back of the seat, near the wall. Daniel knew that this was where the venting pipe once exited the stone box and then extended through the roof. On the south wall, which was constructed entirely of stone, there was a chimney flue. In cold weather, a fire in the small wood stove that was once there would heat the building during the day and the subsequent radiant heat from the logs and stone would make the outhouse fairly comfortable during the night.

Daniel walked to the woodshed and returned with a spade. Before digging, he surveyed the building for a few more minutes. It was a simple design, built for utility and comfort. At the same time it was aesthetically pleasing; it bore the stamp of Adam Reilly's hand. Daniel decided that any work he did on Mountain Farm must measure up to these same criteria. Then he began to dig with enthusiasm.

The next day, Daniel moved from one building to the next, determining what needed done to render them functional, or at least to protect against further decay.

The homestead spring house was another stone and log structure built against the side of a hill where a spring emerged from the rock face. The spring water flowed directly into a stone and concrete box. The remnants of an iron pipe, which once directed water to the house, dangled from one side. The box had an indented lip at the opposite end, directing the overflow into a long trough, also made of stone and concrete.

Daniel remembered the mysterious stoneware crocks with slate lids standing in the trough, half-immersed in the flowing water. It was in the crocks that his great-grandfather kept food chilled. Daniel would have preferred to use similar containers, but for the present, five-gallon plastic buckets with snap-on lids, purchased at the Mercantile, would serve his purpose Daniel only had to clear the box and trough of debris, and the spring house was ready for use. Vegetables and fruit he simply suspended from the rafters in plastic bags.

The forge required only a tarp to cover a hole in the roof. It was the most simple of the outbuildings with three-inch gaps between the hemlock planks to vent the intense heat. It still held an aroma of smoke, although a fire had not been lit for

Dennis Ruane

several decades.

Like the forge, the boiler house required no immediate attention. These two structures were stone and hemlock shells now, whose functions were once defined by the equipment they had housed. Daniel would forge no iron nor boil any sugar water during his stay on the mountain. As much as he would have liked to, he had no practical reason to reequip the buildings.

Finally, Daniel turned his attention to the log house. This would be his major project. If he finished nothing else, he wanted to return this old building to its original condition. Besides the obvious damage from vandals, there were leaks in the roof. Daniel knew that aside from fire, water was the most serious threat to a wooden structure. He covered the decayed areas of the roof with a tarp and decided to start making wooden shingles that afternoon.

It was while he searched for a suitable red oak to begin this project that Daniel noticed a half-fallen tree at the forest edge. Examining its exposed roots, he could see that it had grown directly over a large, flat rock and so had never developed a supportive root system. The tree had no bark and apparently had been dead for years. Daniel was delighted when a swipe of his ax proved it to be cherry. The upper limbs had tangled with other trees as it came down, so the cherry tree had remained off the ground. This allowed for a slow, steady drying, preventing the decay which would have surely ensued if it had lain upon the forest floor.

As excited as Daniel was about restoring Mountain Farm, he had lost none of his enthusiasm for carving wooden spoons. In fact, after viewing his great-great-grandfather's work in the museum, he was even more inspired to see what he was capable of creating. With the discovery of this tree Daniel now

Wooden Spoons

had the wood he needed to begin.

With a tire chain that was in the back of the jeep Daniel managed to fasten a stout root to the front bumper of the jeep. Then he slowly backed the tree away from the woods until it fell to the ground. Daniel cut off the limbs with the buck saw and then used a one-man crosscut saw to cut the tree into eighteen-inch sections. These he carried into the woodshed. Smaller pieces for spoons could be split from the sections, ahead of his need. As he prepared to saw the last large section of the trunk, he stopped, stepped a few paces away, and then studied the log carefully. There was something about the gentle sweeping curve in the wood that intrigued him. He put the crosscut saw down and paced around the log, studying it from all angles.

Then, he grabbed one end, squared his shoulders, and stood the log on its other end. It was about his own height. Daniel envisioned a human figure in the wood. As he circled the log, he felt a sudden desire to carve the figure.

Shoving it to the ground, he rolled the log to the woodshed. The large side doors of the building, hanging on a rusted iron track, had remained closed for decades. Daniel dug the sod away and eventually slid them open. He struggled with the heavy log but finally moved it through the side doors and onto the floor of the woodshed. Again he heaved it to a vertical position.

Only yards away, the carving tools lay on the workbench. That very morning, Daniel had arranged the tools in the spot where he had first seen them, forty years ago. From the canvas roll he chose the largest gouge and then grasped the mallet with his right hand. Slowly, Daniel began to chip away at the top of the log, delighting in the experience of using the tools on such a large piece of wood. An hour passed before he paused.

Dennis Ruane

Despite the many wood chips scattered on the floor, the log did not look very different at this point. Still, Daniel could see something within it, and he was elated with his progress.

He worked another hour and then forced himself to stop. It would be dark soon and he had not finished clearing the brush from behind the house. Daniel was slightly irritated with himself for becoming distracted so easily. As much as he enjoyed woodcarving, the restoration of the homestead had to come first if he were to have any real chance of achieving his goal.

When Daniel retired to the Log House in the evenings of those first days on the mountain, it was nearly dark. Behind the house, he had constructed a crude fireplace of stone and dirt. He would build a fire and heat water in a five-gallon metal pot. When it reached a boil, dilution with cold spring water resulted in a mixture of a suitable temperature for bathing. Professor Whaley would stand naked near the fire and with a small plastic container, dip water from plastic buckets to pour over himself. He doused thoroughly, lathered with soap and rinsed with the water that remained. He shivered in the cool mountain air as he toweled off.

Eventually, Daniel would settle onto the floor of the Great Room, wrapped in blankets, propped up by clothes and boxes. With a mug of brandy and burning candles beside him, he ended his day writing in a journal. It was something his doctor had recommended and an activity he had come to enjoy. He wrote mostly about the progress of his work on the farm, describing the tools he used and detailing the techniques he employed for specific tasks. At his doctor's suggestion, he would also write about the events and personalities of his life. He wrote about Debbie often. In spite of everything, he missed her and he hoped she would forgive him for leaving like he did.

-22-

George Haynes lived alone in the last house on Pine Creek Road, at the point where the pavement ended. With the Forbes State Forest surrounding him on two sides, he had a quiet home life to offset his public gregariousness. For half his life, George had lived in Uniontown, a considerably larger town located ten miles to the west of Lick Hollow. George had been a jack of all trades his entire working life and a master of each such that he had never been wanting for work or money.

He became familiar with Hemlock Knob through jobs that drew him to Lick Hollow, and he decided when still a young man that he wanted to live close to the mountain some day. His was never a smooth marriage and it came to an abrupt end when, at the age of fifty, he announced that he wanted to move to Lick Hollow. After the divorce George bought a dilapidated old house at the foot of Hemlock Knob, exactly the sort of place a handyman of his caliber dreams of.

He had first done work for the Campbell family half a century before, and so had known John and Nora since they were all in their twenties. After he moved to the neighborhood, they became good friends. John and he soon cornered the growing antique market in the area. They worked potential customers between each other in a charming way that made them both successful.

Today George was steering his truck up the long winding road toward the summit of Hemlock Knob. He was hauling furniture and a heavy cast-iron wood stove. He was familiar with the scenery, having driven or walked this route many times over the years. The old pick-up lurched along slower than was necessary, so that the driver could peer down every hollow and examine each prominent rock or tree. At The Bend he stopped for a break, pouring strong black coffee from an old, dented thermos. George was never in a hurry while on a job, but then again, he never stopped for long. That was one of his secrets to success.

When he pulled onto Reilly Lane, it was obvious to him that Mountain Farm was inhabited now. The claim the forest had been making on the property was being challenged. All the brush and most of the small trees had been cut back from the Log House. George was delighted to see the old place in the open again. The boards were gone from the windows and many of the missing glass panes had been replaced. He knew first-hand the plight of the old building, having assisted John Campbell on numerous occasions, repairing damage and replacing locks. Also, George had been a friend of Tom Reilly, and for this reason it had bothered him to witness the building's steady decline.

He knocked politely on the door frame but did not really expect an indoor response on such a fine day. He went around the house and walked instinctively toward the woodshed. Halfway there, he came upon a pile of red oak, obviously from a large tree. It was cut into logs about two feet long. Although he had not seen such an operation in many years, George knew at a glance that these were the preparations for shingle making. He pushed at one of the logs with his boot and smiled.

Wooden Spoons

Poking his head in the doorway of the woodshed, he noticed that a half-cord of firewood had been stacked neatly in the traditional spot. He chuckled when he realized that it was split small, the way Tom had liked it. "Hello," he called. George stepped inside. The obvious change was the magnificent array of tools on the back wall. *This is truly a going concern now*, he thought. *Who would have guessed it? I was beginning to think that the return of Tom's great grandson was a myth.*

He heard the sound of an engine and walked outside. Daniel Whaley pulled up in the jeep with a load of firewood. "Hello Daniel," George greeted cheerfully.

"Good morning, George," Daniel replied.

"Got you a truck load of goods," George said as he reached for an armload of firewood.

They quickly unloaded the jeep.

"Old Tom would sure be happy to see those tools back in place." George said, as he walked toward them, amazed at how similar the arrangement was to what he remembered. He was also intrigued with the logs positioned around the room. Passing the workbench, he glanced down and saw three wooden spoons, roughly cut from cherry wood. "Well, I'll be. J.C. mentioned that you were making these."

Daniel came up behind him. "Those aren't quite done yet." He hesitated, but then picked up the box which contained the spoons he had made in Madison, and placed it on the workbench.

When its contents were revealed, George's eyes opened wide. "I'll be darned. You're good. Real good. Are you planning to sell these?"

"No. Not really. I just make them to, uh, relax, I guess."

"You shown J.C.?"

Daniel shook his head.

145

"You show him. These will sell. You're good."

Daniel just smiled. He liked George.

"What're you cuttin' there?" George asked, looking at the six-foot log standing on end near the open side doors. While it still looked much like a log, there was no doubt that some sort of work was underway.

"Hmm, not quite sure, yet. I'm just chipping away at it slowly, waiting for something to emerge," Daniel answered, a little embarrassed. George nodded, although he didn't really understand this approach to a project.

Back at the log house, they unloaded George's truck and Daniel was pleased with the selection of furniture. Simple, sturdy pieces, exactly what he had in mind for his stay at Mountain Farm. Finally he and George maneuvered the heavy wood stove off the truck and into the house, using thick wooden planks for a ramp. George had brought stove pipe and quickly connected the stove to the opening in the chimney.

"You'll be needing this sooner than you think," George said with a grin. "Burn your dead limbs and scraps first and let the bigger stuff keep drying until the serious weather comes."

They walked back to the truck and George gazed across the homestead, turning a circle. "Man, what a place. Adam Reilly chose well. You know that the state forest has closed in on Mountain Farm from all sides now. I'm surprised they haven't been at you about buying this property."

"Oh, I received a letter from them every few years, but when I did respond, it was a polite no. The fact is, if they had pushed the issue, a while back, I might have sold. Or, I mean, we might have sold. We needed the money then. That is, my wife and I. We . . ." He stopped, his face reddening slightly.

George nodded. He knew what Daniel was saying.

"There was another man, a Mr. Nicklow who I would get a letter from occasionally."

"Maurice Nicklow?" George asked, with obvious disdain.

"Yes, that's right. Maurice Nicklow. He has wanted to purchase the land for about the last ten years."

"Well, surprise, surprise," George said, shaking his head.

"You know him?"

"Yeah. Everybody knows him. Maurice Nicklow, the small-town lawyer done good, the land developer, the millionaire. Owns half the buildings on Main Street. What did you tell him?"

"I eventually wrote him a letter and stated that I wasn't ready to sell yet. When the next letter arrived from him, a couple years later, it basically asked the same question. It never acknowledged my letter. After that, I just tossed them."

"Well, that's probably the best thing you could have done. The man buys up every farm, homestead, or any other mountain land he can, cuts them up into lots and sells them to folks from Pittsburgh. He's made a bundle. He and his son have a construction business that Maurice started. Most times they get the contracts to build the houses."

"Sounds like a nice little operation."

"Yes, sir. And you could guess he would want this property. It's got everything his customers want: a mountain top with a view and the state forest all around to keep it private. He's cut up and sold some nice property around here, but nothing like this. My advice to you is to steer clear of those two."

"They're trouble, eh?"

"Well, Maurice is pushy and stubborn and usually gets what he wants. If you stand your ground though, he'll leave you alone in time. He's no backstabber. He just is what he is, a

Dennis Ruane

small town boy who made more money than he ever imagined. Trouble is, all he thinks about now is making more. Now Donny, his son, that's another story. He's just plain trouble, big and loud and mean, has been ever since he was a little fellow. When he gets drunk, which is often, he's much worse. Been in lots of trouble. Man works hard when he works, got to give him that, but you don't want to tangle with his bad side."

"The letters I received were professional. I never would have guessed all that you've told me. All I want is to be left alone up here and I have no plans of selling, so taking your advice is easy."

George nodded in approval.

"What do I owe you for all your trouble, George?"

"No trouble, this is what I do. Comes to three hundred dollars."

Daniel's surprise at this low price was obvious.

George chuckled as he reached for the truck door. "J.C. and I are having our spring clearance sale, so you are shopping at the right time." George turned and Daniel approached him with three one-hundred dollar bills in his hand. "Well, thank you," George said, taking the money. "Do you need a receipt?"

Daniel just smiled.

"Good luck, Daniel Whaley." George got in the truck and immediately leaned out the window. "Hey, bring some of those spoons with you next time down."

-23-

"**I** think you have a goldmine here," John Campbell exclaimed as he gazed down at the twenty-five spoons Daniel had brought to the Lick Hollow Mercantile. Daniel picked out items he needed from the shelves, but he was watching John's reaction with interest.

"You do want to sell them, don't you?"

"No, I don't think so. I never really made them to sell, and I don't need the money. You are each welcome to have some spoons, if you wish. I will probably give them all away eventually."

John looked at Daniel as if he were speaking a foreign language. John Campbell had worked the Lick Hollow Mercantile for four decades now, and he knew that these wooden spoons, fashioned by this fourth-generation native son living on Hemlock Knob in the old family home, would cause a frenzy with his clientele from the city. Daniel continued to move along the shelves and John followed, trying to impress him with the opportunity he was passing by.

John scarcely heard Daniel's offer, nor did it really register with George, who was seated at his usual window table. Nora, however, had slipped from behind the counter and was intently looking over the collection of spoons. She finally picked one up that had a long, stout handle. She looked toward

Dennis Ruane

Daniel and when he smiled, Nora took it with her behind the counter.

George had been watching the interaction between the two men with amusement. "When do you find the time to make spoons, Daniel? You already got a full-time job up there."

Daniel turned toward him. "It's the last thing I do in the evenings. I'm tired, but I enjoy it so much that I can keep working. If the sun goes down, I place kerosene lamps and candles in a circle around my work area. It's when I relax and think."

George nodded and smiled. He might have expected such an answer. Years ago, he had learned the practicality of scheduling the most enjoyable task at the end of the long workday.

Moments later, as he was checking out, Daniel noticed two, quart canning jars among his purchases.

"Peppers," Nora said. "I've been needing a long sturdy spoon to work them up with." She made eye contact with Daniel, and he thought that she might have smiled this time.

While Nora was totaling his bill, he glanced to the right and noticed a coffee can with a slot cut in a plastic lid. On the side of the can was a photograph. He squinted and moved closer to see that it was a picture of a man and a woman with a small girl. The man and woman seemed young to Daniel and they had an uncomfortable, uncertain demeanor about them. He assumed that they were married and that the girl was their daughter. The woman was bent down and had her arms around her while the man stood stiffly behind them with one hand on his wife's shoulder. On the side of the can was a hand written note which explained their situation. It read: *Donations for Connie Pavloc's leukemia treatment.*

Daniel stared at the picture again, wanting to learn more

Wooden Spoons

from it. He remembered the name. He knew Pavlocs when he was a boy.

"Poor little thing," Nora said as she was arranging his purchases in a cardboard box.

"You know them?"

"Oh my yes, we've known Johnny and Sue since they were kids. She was a Spaw. You're related to the Spaws on your father's side." She did not look up as she spoke. "Johnny and Sue live down Bennington Road about a mile. They just found out about the little one's cancer this spring. No health insurance." She finished packing and then looked up at Daniel, who was still staring at the photograph on the can with a distant look in his eyes.

He turned away from the picture and walked toward the men who were bent over the spoons. "John. I've changed my mind. I would like to sell the spoons."

"That's splendid, Daniel," John said with surprise, straightening up and rubbing his hands together briskly. He always did this when he was about to engage in a business transaction.

"I'd like to sell the spoons, but give the money to Connie Pavloc's family to help pay for her medical bills."

John stared at him for a moment. He pointed over in the direction of the coffee can as if to be certain he had heard correctly. Daniel nodded. "Well, my goodness. Goodness. That's a marvelous idea. Do you know the Pavlocs? Daniel nodded again.

"They will be grateful. They are in a bad spot and every bit helps. But are you sure you want to give it all? If you kept half for . . ."

"No. I can imagine what they are going through now, and I don't need the money."

Dennis Ruane

"OK then, Daniel, OK, as you wish. We in turn will take no commission."

"Would you price them for me, John? I really have no idea . . ."

"Sure can, Daniel. No problem."

George approached Daniel and extended his hand. "That's mighty kind of you, Daniel." Daniel shook George's hand, somewhat embarrassed. Not usually an impulsive person, he was as surprised as they were at this decision.

When the last of the supplies had been loaded onto the jeep, George followed Daniel out of the building and went to the passenger side of his truck. He removed a brown bag from the seat and transferred it to the jeep through the open window. Daniel watched him with a puzzled expression.

"I was in Uniontown, the other day, and stopped at the East End liquor store to see my cousin who works there." Daniel still looked puzzled.

"Got you a bottle of brandy."

Daniel turned his head. "Why?" he asked, in an amused tone.

"I saw the half-empty bottle at the log house," George said as he walked past Daniel and back up the stairs. "Thought you might need a spare."

Daniel chuckled. "Thanks, George."

"Save me some," George said over his shoulder as he went back into the mercantile.

As the jeep was pulling out of the parking lot, John moved to the window and watched. "He's a funny person, isn't he?"

"He's a good person," Nora answered as she began to wipe the counter.

"That he is," George added, putting on his jacket.

"He's so serious, not much like Uncle Tom." John said.

Wooden Spoons

"He doesn't really take after his father either," George added.

"Maybe he takes after Adam," Nora suggested without looking up.

-24-

A black Cadillac cruised slowly east on Main Street. The driver observed from side to side, scrutinizing buildings and sizing up pedestrians. Maurice Nicklow in his big car was a common sight in Lick Hollow. As he rolled by, there was an occasional nod of recognition from a business associate but no spontaneous smile or friendly gesture. Maurice was an attorney who had served Lick Hollow and the surrounding area for forty years.

The attorney owned many buildings on Main Street, and as he passed these, his eyes narrowed and the car slowed. All his buildings were in need of repair and because of the high rent he charged, only half of them were occupied. This didn't bother Maurice. That was a healthy percentage as far as he was concerned. In truth, he really didn't need to make money on these buildings. To the attorney they were simply a long-term investment and a short-term tax write-off

As the car passed the Lick Hollow Tavern, he slowed to see if his son's truck was in the parking lot. He was relieved to see that it wasn't. Further up the road, Maurice did see Donald's black Dodge parked outside Martin's Restaurant and he pulled in beside it. He walked past the truck wearing a sour expression. It was speckled with mud and the right taillight cover was cracked. "Why the hell does he always have to buy the biggest pick-up on the market?" he grumbled to himself.

Maurice found his son sitting at the counter, leaning on his elbows, holding a cup of coffee with both hands. There was a cigarette smoldering in an ashtray nearby. Maurice Nicklow was a big man, six feet tall and weighing just over two hundred pounds. He dressed well, professionally, always in a suit. He had a big head with large ears and thick, wavy gray hair that was brushed straight back. Maurice's face was long and he held his mouth in such a manner that he seemed to be always gritting his teeth. At sixty-five years of age, he looked good, confident and successful.

Donald Nicklow was of a similar build, but he was larger than his father. His face resembled Maurice's, but unless they were side by side, few would guess that they were father and son. Donald's hair was brown, laced with gray. He wore it long such that when he turned his head, curls brushed his broad shoulders. He was dressed in a gray sweatshirt, blue jeans, and high leather boots. On the back of his stool was a canvas work coat with gloves protruding from a pocket.

"Donald," Maurice said as he positioned himself on the stool next to him.

"Hey Dad, what's up?"

"How are things going over at the Batey farm?"

"Good. Good. Right on schedule. Machine broke this morning but nothing serious. I had other business here in town, so I ran for parts. But, yeah, things are looking good. Any takers on those last two lots?"

"One," Maurice answered. "The other will go quick."

"Coffee?" a waitress asked mechanically. She was already pouring when Maurice looked up and nodded. Donald winked at her; she smiled at him and turned away.

"Say Don, what do you know about the man who lives on

Dennis Ruane

Hemlock Knob in the old Reilly place, Daniel Whaley?"

"The Professor, you mean? That's what they call him. You know he was a college teacher, don't you?"

"Yes, I'm aware of that. But what kind of person is he? Have you ever spoken to him?"

"Nah. See him outside Campbell's store with J.C. and George Haynes. Drives an old beat-up jeep. Looks pretty wild. Don't know much more. J.C. or George Haynes, I'd talk to them. What's up with him, anyway?"

"It's his property. He owns the top of Hemlock Knob, a hundred acres. Nice piece of real estate. I've inquired about purchasing it before, back when he lived in Wisconsin, with the standard letter that I've sent to all the property owners for years. He responded only once, if I remember right, said no. Recently, I've been approached by a man from Pittsburgh, a Mr. Tom Arnold, who wants that piece of property in a big way. Apparently he went hunting there with his father when he was a boy and has never gotten over the place."

"What about some of the other places we have? Some of them are up high with good views."

"I told him about what we have. He wants *that* place, and he's the type of person who gets what he wants. Got lots of money."

"Lots of people got lots of money," Donald replied with slight irritation in his voice.

"Not like this guy. From what I know, he could buy and sell most of the people we have dealt with so far."

Donald took a long drag on his cigarette and exhaled the smoke slowly in the direction of the ceiling, trying to imagine how much money that would take. "How do you figure that after all these years, this Whaley shows up right when this Pittsburgh guy is ready to make a move for the property?"

Maurice shook his head. "Who knows? Happens in business."

"Too bad," Donald said, grinning. "If he hadn't moved in, I could have had somebody burn that old house down. That often helps people let go of the old home place."

Maurice thanked the waitress, who was refreshing his coffee and did not acknowledge his son's remark.

"Well, I'm sure The Professor has his price," Donald stated confidently, lifting his coffee mug. "Hell, there ain't even power or running water up there and he must be using that old log outhouse. The right amount of money should tempt him off the mountain, or maybe just a new house with a flush toilet."

Maurice agreed, but he still wished to gather as much information about Daniel Whaley as possible before he made a move. He took a deliberate drink of his coffee and stood to leave.

"Say Dad, does this Arnold want me to do the building?"

"Yes. He wants the complete package with us, from the legal work to the trim on the windows. It will be worth a bundle now and if we do it right, there will be spin-off business from people like him."

Donald gulped his coffee and followed his father out into the parking lot.

"I think I'll head up to The Mercantile now to talk to those friends of his."

"Need some muscle?" Donald asked, grinning.

"No." Maurice answered, frowning. The attorney pointed to the broken truck taillight as he passed. "Get this fixed. It'll get you in trouble."

Donald shook his head as his father got into the Cadillac. "See ya, Dad," he said after the door snapped shut.

As Maurice continued up Main Street, he was thinking

Dennis Ruane

that his son looked clear-eyed and steady today, which was a relief to the attorney. Donald's notorious drinking binges and consequent reckless behavior had been definite stumbling blocks on an otherwise remarkable road to financial success for Nicklow Developers, Inc.

There was no question that when he was sober, Donald was good at what he did. He worked hard and handled the crew well, such that jobs were completed quickly and with quality work down to the details. Donald was forty-two now, and his father had hoped for many years that he would turn some corner in life and get his drinking under control. That was much of the reason why the project on Hemlock Knob was important to Maurice. It would keep Donald on a job site. Tom Arnold planned to build a small complex of buildings, which included a main house, a guest house, and a stable. This job would keep his son busy and focused for years.

That's what he needs now, Maurice thought as he pulled into the graveled lot at The Mercantile. *The man needs to focus.*

Maurice entered the store, and there seemed to be nobody there. The only sound was the churning of boiling water in a kettle on the pot-bellied stove. His eyes wandered and eventually spied a rack of wooden spoons. There was a sign above the display which read: *Handcarved on Hemlock Knob by Daniel Whaley. All proceeds benefit Connie Pavloc.*

Maurice was impressed by the spoons, although he tried not to be, feeling somehow that it might complicate his business here. However, he knew enough about timber and woodworking to appreciate the individual feat of craftsmanship each of these represented. As he turned a spoon over and over, examining it closely, he could hardly believe it had been done entirely by hand. He understood the last part of

Wooden Spoons

the sign when he saw the coffee can with the picture of the Pavloc family. Now it was on a stand beside the spoons. He remembered that his wife had a cousin who was a Pavloc. Maurice looked at the photograph, but did not let it distract him.

"Can I help you?" came a voice from behind the counter.

Maurice started at the unexpected question and turned. Nora Campbell was looking at him from behind the counter, and he realized that she must have been there all along. Maurice quickly regained his professional composure. "Good day to you, Mrs. Campbell. I'm Attorney Maurice Nicklow, and I was hoping I might speak with your husband if he is available."

"He's not," Nora answered stiffly. She knew who Maurice was.

"Well, then perhaps you can help me. I would like to get in touch with the man who makes these wooden spoons, Daniel Whaley. Do you know how I might do that?"

"You can't get in touch with him."

"Do you expect him to come here anytime soon?"

"Not really, he just shows up from time to time, delivers spoons and buys supplies. Never know when."

"I see. Well, he does live on Hemlock Knob, so I guess I could drive up there," Maurice said, smiling, trying to be as friendly as possible.

"You won't make it in that," Nora said, nodding toward the Cadillac.

"Of course not, I have another vehicle . . ." Maurice stopped. He got the impression that this little white-haired woman was not going to help him. "If I leave a card, would you be so kind as to ask him to contact me the next time he's in town." Nora took his card without a word and did not look at it.

159

He nodded his head, thanked her, and walked out. Maurice did not want to drive to the summit of Hemlock Knob, particularly at this time of year. After he left the Lick Hollow Mercantile, he drove a short distance on Main Street and turned left into Martin's Service Station. Maurice had known Ed Martin since he was a boy. Ed was a quiet and likeable man who seemed perfectly suited to the career he had been born into.

"Hello, Mr. Nicklow," Ed said as he pulled down the brim of his hat.

"Ed. How's business?"

"Been pickin' up lately."

"Family's well, I hope?"

"They're good, real good. Thanks for askin', Mister Nicklow."

"Say, Ed, do you know the man who lives on Hemlock Knob in the old Reilly place?"

"The Professor."

"Yes, him."

"Know him to see him. Bought gas here once. See him over at the Mercantile, mostly. His jeep's easy to spot."

"Well, I need to talk to him. Would you do me a favor and the next time you see him over there, give me a call?" Maurice handed Ed one of his business cards.

"Sure, I can do that for you. What did he do?"

Maurice grinned at that. "He didn't do anything, it's just business." Maurice thanked Ed and started to get back into his car, but then stopped. "Say Ed, while I'm here, how about filling er up?"

-25-

It was August and the days were long and warm. More than two months had passed since Daniel Whaley's unlikely return to Mountain Farm. He had settled into a routine of work which focused on his goal of restoring the log house. Each task was assigned a level of priority, and then time was allocated accordingly. He was impatient. The progress seemed slow to him, although the changes on Mountain farm would have been obvious to any observer who was familiar with the property. There were no observers, however. For the first time in his life, Daniel was entirely alone, and he grew to like the solitude.

He was an unusual-looking character these days. Daniel wore a red paisley kerchief over his head to protect the bald spot from the sun's rays. Brown hair protruded from underneath along the sides of his head, and a course beard was highlighted with gray patches. His meager wardrobe, which he washed by hand and repaired with needle and thread by kerosene lamp, was rough and simple, fitting his character well. From long hours of work, he had a lean and sinewy appearance that suited him and was appropriate to the setting.

As it was for his great-grandfather, the cutting and sawing of firewood became his favored activity. Daniel was

Dennis Ruane

determined to have six cords in the woodshed before the burning season began, especially now that he hoped to live on the mountain at least one winter. He had nearly two cords of wood stacked. Weeks before, Daniel had built a crude sawhorse from small oak logs, squared with the broadaxe. He placed it on the spot where Tom Reilly's had been. Today Daniel was cutting small maple logs into eighteen-inch sections, a size which fit well in the stove. He focused on the work, not allowing his thoughts to drift into the past or to ponder the future. The present was his only real hope.

When Daniel had cut his quota of firewood for the day, he walked to the spring house for a drink. Next he planned to make more shakes for the log house roof. Although there was already a large stack from the previous week's effort, Daniel had calculated that five times this amount would be needed to complete the roof. His great-grandfather had often stressed the importance of maintaining the roofs of the log buildings, warning that once a roof went bad the rest of the building would follow quickly. Consequently, Tom had carefully instructed Daniel in the art of shingle making, from choosing the proper red oak tree to trimming the newly split shakes with a draw knife.

A metal dipper hung from a rafter in the spring house. Daniel dipped it into the water box and took a long drink of the cold water. Then he stopped. He heard something moving in the woods below the meadow, some sort of animal. Having become accustomed to the quiet, predictable background sounds of the mountain top, Daniel was immediately aware of any unusual noise. It was heavier than the hasty rustling of a squirrel, but was not the measured stepping of a deer. He hung the dipper and walked slowly to the edge of the meadow on the west side of the house. Moving as quietly as possible, he stopped at a point where the ground sloped sharply downward into the forest.

Sweeping his vision from right to left, he soon saw the source of the disturbance. It was a dog. The animal was working its way up the hill toward him, looking from side to side and sniffing the air, as if it were searching for something. It had not heard Daniel's approach but soon caught his scent. The dog looked directly at him when it was about forty yards away. It froze and stared with alert eyes, but it did not show fear. Daniel stared back.

The dog had a short, heavy coat of a pale-yellow color and a strong wide head with medium-length ears. It was stocky and muscular with a deep chest. Daniel could not decide what breed it was, but even at this distance he could see that it was an older animal.

Daniel had always been fond of dogs. The last one he owned was a Black Labrador-mix he had claimed on impulse from a litter of puppies put up for adoption in a grocery store parking lot. Debbie and he had just purchased their new home on Lake Mendota Drive and Ken was four years old. Daniel reasoned that it was a natural addition to the family. He named the dog Cody. But Debbie was adamant, Cody could not stay in the house. Daniel placed a kennel beside the garage and built a dog house.

He walked Cody every day after returning from campus. The dog lived for those long walks out into the cornfield and up to the interesting rock mound that they had discovered together. He would run circles around his master and romp about the field joyfully, too simple and happy to question his living conditions. But Daniel always felt some guilt over the confinement, which seemed all the more pathetic as the dog grew old and feeble. When Cody's debilitation advanced to the point that he could no longer walk, Daniel had him put to sleep and did not speak to anyone for a week.

Daniel and the dog watched each other for a minute longer without motion. He decided to return to work and ignore the animal, not encouraging it to linger here. Even if it was a stray, he had no time for pets now. Besides, it would be unfair to the dog, because it would have to be abandoned in the end. Daniel started back across the field, but midway to the cabin, he turned, looking back toward the woods. In spite of his better judgment, he half-hoped the dog would follow him.

Passing through the woodshed, he removed a froe and hickory maul from the back wall and carried them out to the red oak tree. He had previously cut the log into two-foot cross sections. The froe had a long iron blade with a short piece of round wood attached at a right angle for a handle. It was a tool perfectly designed for its function. Grasping the handle, Daniel placed the blade on the end grain of a section of oak. Striking the back of the blade with the ponderous maul, he began splitting off thin sections or *shakes*. Forty-five minutes later, when he paused for water, he saw the dog sitting on the porch of the log house, watching him. The animal was still there an hour after that, when Daniel stopped for lunch.

He cut up some potatoes, which had been boiled earlier in the day, into small cubes and added them to a wooden bowl with cheese and olive oil. Before Daniel ate his simple lunch, he spooned some of it into a smaller bowl that he carried to the porch and placed near the dog. As he ate, he watched the animal slowly walk to the bowl, sniff, and finally eat the offering.

When Daniel approached again, the dog watched him with alert eyes that showed neither fear nor malice. He stroked the back of its head and noticed that it wore no collar. "Where did you come from, boy?" he asked softly. The dog turned its head at the sound of his voice, and Daniel stroked it again.

After returning to work, Daniel would look toward the porch from time to time expecting that the dog would eventually leave. He was glad to see him sitting attentively at the same spot each time he turned. The animal was either watching him work or staring across the meadow toward Hemlock Road. That night, when Daniel retired to the house, the dog slept on the porch.

By the next evening Daniel accepted the fact that the animal was staying, and so he arranged a blanket on the porch for it to sleep on. Over the days that followed, he and the dog were never apart, and eventually he started calling him Cody. This dog was wild and free as he often had wished its namesake could have been. Daniel found the animal's quiet presence reassuring, somehow making him believe that his goals for Mountain Farm could be achieved.

Days passed, weeks passed, life on the homestead fell into an easy rhythm, only interrupted by an occasional vehicle on the road. Daniel soon realized that he could be aware of the approach of a vehicle by observing his canine companion. Thus he came to appreciate the practical basis for the ancient alliance between dogs and humans. Restoration of the homestead progressed. Even Daniel had to admit to the changes as he and Cody gazed down from the little cemetery during a morning coffee break.

Daniel was ready to begin replacing the roof of the log house. He now had a pile of shingles large enough to make a good start. At George's recommendation, they were covered with a tarp to slow the drying. He told Daniel that they would nail down much easier while wet and once fixed rigidly in place, the shingles would dry straight. He needed shingle nails,

Dennis Ruane

however, and he wanted to talk to George once more about the process before he began.

Daniels also needed supplies; dog food for one thing. He enjoyed his forays into the village and had gone down several times since his initial visit.

The next day at mid morning, Daniel pulled away from the log house. A box containing fifty spoons was on the seat beside him. While Cody followed Daniel wherever he went on the mountain, the dog would not get into the jeep. He sat on the porch and watched as the vehicle pulled away. Daniel knew that Cody would be there when he returned. He had grown very fond of this mysterious animal that had wandered into his life.

-26-

John Campbell was waiting at the door of the Mercantile when Daniel stepped onto the porch.

"Hello John," he said, entering the door. He tipped his hat to Nora, who he knew was behind the counter.

She smiled and continued arranging items in a display case.

"I hope you have a delivery for us," John said enthusiastically.

"I do. Fifty this time."

"Splendid. Splendid. I think we may have a tiger by the tail with this spoon business. This is still the slow season, and I can scarcely keep them on the rack. I've raised the prices once, already. The Pavlocs are beside themselves with gratitude. Besides that, word of what you are doing is spreading around town, and it's causing people to loosen their purse strings."

Daniel shuffled a bit, uncertain what to say. However, he was impressed with what John told him, particularly with the fact that other people were moved to help. "Well, that's good. I can bring them regularly now that I'm set up and have some good cherry wood to work with."

He handed John the box and then wandered down an aisle to begin gathering supplies.

Nora walked over as her husband laid the spoons on one of

the tables. Nora and John had been impressed with each batch of spoons that arrived, noting the steady improvement in Daniel's skill, but they were transfixed by what they saw now. They were most impressed with the spoons that had human figures worked into the handles.

George Haynes walked in at this point, and after tipping his cap to Daniel at the rear of the store and to Nora as she passed him on her way back to the counter, he joined John at the impromptu spoon display. Looking over the collection that John had neatly arranged on the table, George shook his head in amazement. "My goodness, J.C., these are masterpieces," he whispered.

John met his gaze and nodded.

"How much would you have to charge for something like this?" George pointed to a long slender spoon with a gently spiraled handle from the bowl to within seven inches from the tip. On the top of the handle was the stylized figure of a woman in a long garment. There was no detail, only suggestions of folded arms, long hair lightly tossed by the breeze, and a face lost in contemplation. He was not a ready admirer of contemporary art, but he found this small figure very appealing.

"Eighty bucks," John answered, businesslike. "Not a penny less, and it will sell at that. But considering how this spoon was made, where it was made, and by whom it was made, the price should be much more." He lifted his head and located Daniel, still selecting merchandise. John looked back at George and in a hushed voice said, "Someday they are going to sell for a great deal more."

"Oh boy," Nora said with irritation in her voice.

When John and George looked up they saw that she was staring out the front window. A black Cadillac pulled up to the

Wooden Spoons

building and stopped next to Daniel's jeep.

George walked back to Daniel. "We didn't get a chance to tell you, but this man coming now, he's the Maurice Nicklow who has written to you in the past about buying your property. He has recently been asking about you here."

Nora looked above the Cadillac and focused her eyes on Martin's service station. She could tell from his stance that it was Ed Martin by the pumps, and he was looking in the direction of the mercantile. She knew why Maurice Nicklow had suddenly appeared. Ed would hear about it, too.

The door creaked open and the attorney stepped in. He quickly nodded to John, George, and Nora, and then turned his attention to the tall stranger who had a bag of dog food under his arm. "Hello sir, Daniel Whaley, I presume. I'm Maurice Nicklow, Attorney at Law," he said with a smile, extending his hand.

Daniel's immediate impression of the man was not good. He nodded his head slightly and returned a weak hello, but did not smile or let go of the dog food.

Maurice lowered his hand. He was surprised at Daniel's appearance in spite of what he had been told. This man did not look like a disheveled street person that from some descriptions he might have imagined, nor did he look like an eminent university professor, which Maurice knew he had been. Actually he bore a resemblance to a framed pencil drawing which hung in the attorney's office. This was a depiction of an early settler of the Allegheny Mountains who also had a beard and wore a wide-brimmed hat. Maurice also saw on Daniel's face that same intense expression that had always intrigued him about the figure in the drawing.

"My good man," Maurice began. "I understand that you own the Reilly property on Hemlock Knob."

Daniel nodded. He was beginning to feel warm and uncomfortable.

"I would like to talk with you today, if possible . . . "

"Look, Mr. Nicklow" Daniel interrupted.

"Call me Maurice, please."

"Mr. Nicklow, I know what you want to discuss. Mountain Farm is my family's home place, and I have no desire to sell it under any circumstances." He shrugged his shoulders as if to signal that the discussion was over.

Maurice's expression changed slightly, his face began to redden, and he remained uncharacteristically silent for a moment. The other occupants of the room did not move. The hissing of the iron kettle on the stove seemed to signal a growing tension. Attorney Nicklow was not accustomed to being cut short in this manner. He didn't win every time, but at the least, he always presented his case.

"Now hear me out. I did not come here empty-handed. I represent a Mr. Thomas J. Arnold from Pittsburgh and he is prepared to pay quite handsomely for the acreage on Hemlock Knob."

"I'm sure your client has good intentions, Mr. Nicklow, but money does not matter to me. I have all I need. I will not sell Mountain Farm to him for any amount."

"Hear me out," Maurice repeated, although he was not exactly sure where his proposal would go after such a rebuttal.

"Mister Nicklow, this discussion is over." Daniel stepped to the side and attempted to move toward the counter.

The attorney could not allow himself to be dismissed so easily, especially in front of an audience. A compulsion to get the situation under control as quickly as possible clouded his judgment. He held his left hand in front of Daniel's chest to physically block his passage and when he turned, Maurice held an index finger close to Daniel's face. The attorney had a crimson hue about him, and he spoke in an impatient tone, emphasizing each word. "Now see here, friend. I came here in good faith to make you an honest proposal. If you ask me, you are reacting rather foolishly in the face of a sound business proposition."

George thought that Daniel looked different, somehow. He seemed to be standing straighter and his face was severe, with blue eyes fixed on Maurice in a penetrating stare. Maurice lowered his hand as Daniel took a step closer.

"I did not ask you, sir," Daniel said in a low, restrained voice. "So I'll thank you to spare me your opinion."

It was not so much what he said as how he said it that was intimidating. Then he turned his back on the attorney and moved to the counter.

The crimson faded from Maurice's face. Daniel's statement was not an open threat, but the attorney felt threatened. He was not typically one to back down from a confrontation, but he was unnerved by this strange man. The attorney looked over at John and George with a stunned look on his face. They looked back with equal surprise but with no sympathy.

The only sound was the hissing of the kettle until Maurice cleared his throat. The attorney did not speak, but walked to the door and then turned toward Daniel. He started to point his finger before he spoke but nervously returned it to his side. He cleared his throat again and spoke in a subdued but professional voice. "You, sir, may hear from me again." Maurice nodded indifferently to the others and walked out the door.

When the grinding of the Cadillac tires on the gravel lot faded away, George walked over to Daniel.

"Daniel, hey, you OK?"

Dennis Ruane

Daniel looked up at George and nodded. Then he turned to John. "I'm sorry," he said and then slowly moved his head from side to side, as if he were loosening his neck. There was weariness in his voice. He nodded toward Hemlock Knob. "I better get back up there."

George and John exchanged glances. John started to say something, but Nora spoke first.

"Do you have all the supplies you need?" she asked, in a scolding manner.

Daniel paused for a moment and then shook his head. John and George, in turn, tried to realign the morning with sudden bursts of conversation, but Daniel remained distracted.

"I shouldn't have been so quick to get angry," he finally said. "It's been a recent problem of mine, this temper. It's just that I've put up with people like him my whole life and I can't tolerate it anymore."

"Maurice Nicklow is an overbearing, pompous ass," Nora said with conviction.

The men turned to see her angry little face behind the counter. John and George nodded in agreement.

"The way you dealt with the man, Daniel, is the way most people have wanted to for years," John added

Daniel began gathering his purchases, anxious to get back to Mountain Farm. "I really just want to be left alone so that I can fix up the farm for Paw. Hopefully, Nicklow and I will just stay out of each other's way from now on." He attempted a smile.

The other men echoed that wish, but they were doubtful.

John suddenly walked back to where the spoons were laid out, actively changing the subject. "Daniel, these are magnificent. They're works of art and I'm going to price them accordingly."

He moved close to Daniel before he spoke again. Perhaps it was because of the same simple clothes that his relative always wore, or the old jeep which sputtered along on borrowed time that John felt an influx of cash to Daniel's economy might be welcome. "Are you sure you don't want a percentage of the sale price? No one could criticize you for that, considering all the time that's gone into these."

Daniel shook his head and spoke as if he was thinking of something else. "No, I'm sure. I don't need money, just time, John, that's all I need now."

John was startled by the sad, haunted look he saw in his cousin's eyes.

Daniel went to the counter, paid his bill, and said little more as the men helped him load. John and George watched as he drove away.

"Man's a puzzle, isn't he?" George said.

John nodded. "I have a feeling that there is a piece of the puzzle that he is holding in his hand."

George turned his head.

"I think that there's something driving Daniel Whaley besides just a desire to restore the old home place," John said.

-27-

By early November there had been considerable rain, but only one snowfall. In Lick Hollow the snow melted soon after it covered the ground. George Haynes was thankful that this winter was slow in coming, for he was not so fond of the season now that he was approaching his seventieth one. As he nosed his truck up Hemlock Road, George saw snow in sheltered spots, under rock overhangs and at the base of laurel thickets. Near the summit of Hemlock Knob, snow covered the ground and clung to the trees.

Since he last made this trip, the scenery had changed considerably and was interesting in a new way. Without the leaf cover, the contours of distant mountains were visible through a web of limbs. George drove slowly, stopping often to study a familiar landmark in the distance. On the floor of the passenger side of the truck sat a brown paper bag from which came a steady clinking of glass on glass.

Daniel paused his sawing when he heard a vehicle approaching. He was expecting the intrusion, because a minute earlier he had noticed Cody, sitting perfectly upright, staring towards the break in the tree line that bordered Hemlock Road.

Hemlock Road is getting to be a damn freeway, he thought as he continued working. Two other vehicles had driven by only yesterday. Daniel did not look up, even when he heard that the driver had pulled onto Reilly Lane. He did look up, however, when he realized that the vehicle had left the roadbed and was coming directly toward him. It was the sight of George Haynes grinning through the windshield that quickly dispersed Daniel's irritation.

"Man, you sure can give somebody the ol' crook eye," George said, as he eased out of the truck.

"A person shouldn't sneak up on a helpless homesteader like that," Daniel quipped back.

"I don't think you're so helpless. We were beginning to wonder if you were still around."

George saw Cody sitting at attention on the porch, watching intently. "So this is the dog, huh?" he asked as he walked toward the porch.

Cody did not seem threatening, but he did not relax and approach George either. George walked slowly over to the dog, talking softly. "Are you a good dog? Yeah, that's a good boy. That's a good boy." He held out his hand to let the animal sniff. When he saw calm in Cody's eyes, he rubbed the dog's head. "Yeah, you're a good dog."

"Ain't seen one of these in a while."

"A dog?" Daniel asked, not really trying to be funny.

George looked back at him and grinned. "You might have a little of old Tom in you after all." He turned back toward Cody. " I see plenty of dogs, but not Mountain Cur anymore."

"A Mountain Cur, that's what he is? That's a breed of dog?"

"Uh huh," George answered as he continued to rub the dog's head. "They say that Curs brought over with the settlers mated with Indian Curs. Got a little hound and herder mixed in along the way to being the true Mountain Cur. Used to be common in these parts in the old days; homesteading family wouldn't be without one. Cur dogs love to please their master and will protect their territory to the death."

Daniel walked over and Cody responded immediately, focusing on him with dark, expressive eyes.

"And Daniel, you are definitely his master," George said. "Old-timers say that a Mountain Cur would hold its ground against a mountain lion or a bear, fight either one, head-on."

Daniel looked down at his dog with new respect to accompany the great affection that he already felt.

"Got some mail for you," George said abruptly, turning toward his truck. Seems like folks have come to think of The Mercantile as where you live."

Daniel followed George and was handed two letters. One looked official. It was from a law firm in Madison, Wisconsin, and he guessed that it originated from his wife. The second was from his daughter Jeannie.

George leaned back into the truck and reached across to the bag on the floor. "Got some medicine for you too," he said as he pulled a bottle of brandy from the bag. He also produced two antique brandy snifters, some of his inventory. George tilted the bottle toward Daniel and raised his eyebrows.

Daniel nodded and smiled.

"Whatcha been making, Daniel? Spoons, I hope. J.C. ran out two days ago. Probably right now he's pacing the floor and looking up here."

Daniel chuckled. "Oh, I have a few for him," he answered as he walked toward the house.

While Daniel poured brandy into the snifters he was watching George. On the table near the front window, the next collection of spoons was laid out. George's mouth opened wide and he pawed his shirt pocket for eyeglasses.

All of the thirty spoons on display had a human figure on

the handle. These were not as detailed as the spoons he had seen last at The Mercantile, and yet he found them more interesting, more animated. Several were depictions of figures which seemed to be in motion, ballet dancers, a mother with long flowing hair, holding a new baby above her head, and a human figure that appeared to be spinning because of a layer of wood that spiraled gently around it.

"Man, you sure got some imagination. This is art!" George exclaimed. "Where do you get these ideas?"

Daniel was smiling as he approached George with the half-filled snifters. They both took a drink before he spoke.

"They just seem to be there. I start to carve and an idea develops." Daniel looked at George with a thoughtful expression. Inspired by the brandy, he chose to elaborate. "I think that a work of art is the result of a series of decisions that need to be made once a piece is begun. Should it be tilted this way or that way, should this be longer or shorter, does it look right this way or that way. An artist makes the right decisions along the way, or at least the more interesting ones. It's that simple."

"Well, I don't know if I see it as simple. You have to admit you have a gift."

Daniel took another sip of brandy. He was enjoying this conversation. "The people that we label *gifted* are individuals who have the genetic predisposition to excel at certain tasks, whether it is sports, science, landscaping, or art," Daniel proclaimed. "I believe that most people are gifted to some degree. It comes down to a question of who is fortunate enough to end up in the right position in life, by chance or by design, such that their particular gift can be expressed."

"If you say so," George said, tilting his head and smiling.

Daniel smiled back. He was glad that George had dropped

Dennis Ruane

in on him, and so he decided to stop bombarding the man with his philosophy.

"What about that cherry log you were working on? Did you make any more decisions about that?" George asked, grinning.

Daniel laughed. He knew that remark was deserved. He nodded as he finished his brandy.

When the glasses were refilled, they walked to the woodshed. The cherry log stood on the spot where George saw it last, but the transformation was remarkable. Only half of the original mass remained, with much of the log scattered on the floor as small pink chips. Although it was still in a crude form, it was obviously a human figure.

"My goodness," George said as he circled the piece. "You did all this with just those carving tools?"

Daniel nodded and smiled. "It's what I do, George, it's what I do."

George chuckled and then became serious. "It's a woman."

Again Daniel nodded.

"A long woman."

Daniel was flattered by the earnestness with which George examined the piece. The log had indeed been sculpted into the likeness of a woman. The woman's arms appeared to be folded across her chest and her legs were positioned such that she seemed to be taking a step forward. While the face had no features at this stage, her head was slightly tilted to one side as if she was lost in contemplation. And, as George observed, the woman was tall. Over the preceding month, Daniel had become obsessed with the sculpture, often working for hours on end and somewhat to the negligence of his restoration plans.

"Well, this will be something to see when it's done," George remarked. "It'll be a masterpiece."

Wooden Spoons

Daniel could not have been more pleased with this first critique of his work. George did not ask about the inspiration behind the sculpture, and Daniel decided to leave it at that.

Back at the house, George lifted his glass toward Daniel as if to propose a toast. "Well, my friend, winter is upon us."

Daniel looked at him, nodded and smiled. Then he crossed the room and opened the door of the stove. Inside was a uniform bed of orange coals with fairylike blue flames skating across the surface. For a few minutes, the men stared in silence.

"You ever get lonesome up here?"

Daniel answered while staring at the fire. "No, George, I don't. I like the solitude." He hesitated before he spoke again, wanting to talk but not sure of how much he wanted to reveal. "Something has happened that has changed everything for me, changed everything forever. Many of the things I once believed in are of no importance to me now. Some things such as titles, awards, degrees, suits, ties . . ." He exhaled a cynical laugh, bowed his head and wagged it from side to side. "Some of the things that I did religiously, now seem downright silly."

"Man's gotta believe in something, Daniel,"

Daniel looked up and smiled. "I believe in art, George. Art is one of the good results of civilization."

George considered this statement and finished his brandy.

When the snifters were refilled, Daniel was feeling good and he raised his glass. "Art is a good idea," he said, loudly.

George chuckled. He looked at Daniel and nodded. "Yes it is, Daniel. Yes it is."

Then Daniel told George about the dream from several months before in which his great-great-grandfather, Adam

Reilly, had proposed that same toast.

"You're his blood. He was telling you something, Daniel." George said with certainty. "Fixin' up the old place here is a good thing, but you're an artist, and maybe you should be spending your time doing art. Maybe you should be working on the long woman instead."

The conversation grew quiet then, each man thinking his own thoughts as they studied the fire.

"I better get down out of here," George said, suddenly. "I got some trees to plant tomorrow morning if the weather holds. Got to get my beauty sleep."

Moments later as they stood on the porch, Daniel gave George a mischievous look. "You mind those curves on the way down."

"Don't you worry about me. My old truck knows the way home."

Daniel laughed.

George walked over to Cody, who was sitting in the same spot on the porch, and stroked the dog's head. Then he ambled down the steps. "Take care, Daniel. When it finally starts, I believe it's going to be a hard winter."

Daniel returned to The Great Room. He picked up the mail that George had delivered and sat by the fire. The letter from Madison was from Debbie's attorney. It contained papers for him to sign, finalizing their divorce. When Debbie learned of her husband's whereabouts, she wasted little time in seeking one. This hastiness surprised Daniel somewhat, but he concluded that he deserved such treatment for leaving in the manner in which he did. He had stunned both Debbie and her attorney by granting the divorce, and offering as well to sign over the house and all their Madison assets. His one stipulation was that she would make no claim on Mountain Farm. Debbie had agreed to his terms.

Daniel poured himself another glass of brandy before he opened the letter from his daughter. He knew that Jeannie would be troubled by some of the things he had told her in his last letter. At the same time he believed she would understand his decisions. He had presumed correctly. Jeannie wanted to visit him, and spring was as soon as she could make the trip. Daniel tilted his head back and looked out the window. He wasn't sure that he would still be at Mountain Farm then.

-28-

The winter weather finally came. It started with heavy, wet snow in late November followed by weeks of intermittent freezing rain and then more snow. Donald Nicklow drank his way through the wet fall, cursing the mud. The building of homes on mountain sides was a lucrative business in fair weather, but it was shut down in a winter such as this. In mid December, the temperature dropped below freezing, where it would remain for six weeks.

Maurice had urged his son to bid on jobs in town, regardless of the profit, to slow the financial bleeding and to keep his crew together. In truth, Maurice knew that with the money Donald made during the construction season, he could afford to sit out every winter, but he was trying to keep him from doing so on a barstool.

Two days before Christmas, Maurice pulled behind the Lick Hollow Tavern and parked next to his son's truck. The parking lot was a graveled area located behind the old stone building, which had been the tavern since Lick Hollow was founded. There were two ancient maple trees in the center with limbs stretched in all directions. The lot was bordered to the north by trees and shrubs that lined the bank of Lick Hollow Creek.

Maurice entered the tavern by the back door. Across the

room he saw a hazy silhouette of his son, defined by the afternoon sun, streaming in through the front windows. Corky Teets, the proprietor, nodded hello. When Donald saw his father, he tilted his head back and blew smoke in the direction of the ceiling, as if he were letting off steam. He knew that Maurice had not come to have a drink with him.

As if to emphasize that point, Maurice skipped any cordialities. "They're going to add on at Foodland, another ten thousand square feet plus a loading dock. I just talked to Hugh, the owner . . ."

"Save it, Dad," Donald interrupted. He held up his lit cigarette between them as if to block Maurice's voice. With his other hand, he took a drink of beer.

It angered him to be interrupted at any time, by anyone. What bothered Maurice more was to see his son drunk again in the middle of the day.

"No. I don't have time for that bullshit s-stuff. Those jobs er always a pain in yer ass and there's no goddamn money in 'em."

On the way to the tavern, Maurice had coached himself to remain calm, regardless of how Donald took his advice. But he was tired this afternoon, tired of working so hard every day building his empire and tired of worrying about this wayward son whom he hoped would one day rule it. Even in the dim light, Maurice could see that Donald looked bad, old and worn beyond his years. The cigarette smoke rolled up across Donald's face and framed dull, half-closed eyes. Maurice knew that he was losing the fight to save his son. Frustration spilled out in jagged words.

"There is more money in those goddamn jobs than there is in sitting on your drunken ass here all day."

Corky wiped the counter in his routine manner, but his

hand now moved in circles that led him away from the conversation.

Donald heaved a long sigh and turned toward Maurice. The aggravation his father was pressing upon him caused the alcohol in his blood to course more rapidly to the brain. It was transforming him into the mean, violent Donald that many people feared. Fortunately, some faint paternal respect lingered, and Maurice would at least not experience the physical basis for their fear. Donald was silent for a moment. He just stared at his father with vacant eyes. When he spoke, he did so in a coarse whisper, emphasizing each word carefully so as not to slur them.

"Go to hell old man."

Maurice said nothing, but he might as well have been physically struck. He stood up and walked away, touching the walls of the back hallway to steady himself as he went to the door.

Donald snatched his glass and drank it down. He spotted Corky at the far end of the bar. "Fill'er up, boss," he said, defiantly.

Corky came for his glass.

"And a shot of Jack Daniels, while you're at it," Donald added.

The back door of the tavern closed behind his father.

Ten minutes later, Maurice Nicklow was leaning back in his office chair, staring at drawn blinds.

"Go to hell, old man," he said softly.

What hurt the attorney most was the contempt in his son's voice as he said it.

Of three children, Donald had always been his favorite for

Wooden Spoons

some unclear reason. Samuel, the oldest, was an attorney and a partner in a law firm in Pittsburgh. Jenny, the youngest and the most intelligent of his children, lived in San Francisco. She had a good marriage, two children, and a successful career. Donald had been trouble since he was a young boy, breaking windows, vandalizing, and fighting, always fighting. He began drinking in high school, which compounded the problem.

After a succession of dead-end jobs, Maurice got his son started in the construction business. For a number of years it seemed Donald had finally gotten aligned on a track that suited his nature. It was during this period that he met and married Sandra Bell, a woman from Morgantown, West Virginia. The couple had two children in four years. Sandra was pretty and intelligent and she had a sense of humor that Maurice liked. When Sandra came to his office one day and removed sunglasses to reveal a dark bruise under her left eye, Maurice wept with her. When he confronted his son, Donald promised to quit drinking, and he did for a short while. Four months later Sandra moved back to Morgantown with the children.

Ten years ago, the terrible accident occurred involving Robert Cranston. The librarian had been an avid walker and would hike up to the top of Hemlock Knob and back on any given day. He was walking home from the library one evening when he was struck from behind by a vehicle that was moving fast down Tuesday Alley. He was nearly killed, and his hiking days ended abruptly. Strong circumstantial evidence pointed to Donald, but when he swore that he did not do it, Maurice had no choice but to defend him. He defended well. Donald was acquitted and R. Cranston came away with a limp and a cane.

Maurice had suspected that his son was the driver, hurrying down the back alley on his way home from the bar.

Dennis Ruane

Everyone else in Lick Hollow was certain of it. The attorney knew that a conviction meant prison, especially in the light of Donald's past offenses. He yielded to paternal instinct rather than a sense of justice.

Some time after the trial, Maurice approached R. Cranston and asked if he could be of some help to him, particularly in a monetary way. When the librarian realized what the attorney was asking, he squared his shoulders and said no in a frigid tone of voice. Maurice meant well but shuffled away, embarrassed and ashamed.

The last major incident occurred four years ago. It was an altercation in a bar in the town of Connelsville, twelve miles north of Uniontown. Donald and some of his crew had been at an equipment auction and they stopped for a beer on the way home. Another man of similar disposition sized Donald up for the fighter that he was the moment Donald swaggered into the bar. It took but a few glances, some pointed words with a few beers thrown into the mix, and they were upon each other viciously.

Although a veteran of many bar fights, Donald soon realized that he had met a good match. His adversary was younger and determined to defend his territory. But Donald would not go down, especially in front of his crew. He eventually maneuvered himself behind the opponent and scrambled to find a crippling hold. When the younger man countered with forceful elbow strikes to the ribs, Donald impulsively grabbed the corners of his adversary's mouth and pulled. The shriek of pain silenced the crowd and ended the fight. It was the most mean and dirty fighting that any of the spectators had ever seen. Medics came, police came, and finally, Maurice arrived to unravel the mess.

The winters that followed were relatively mild. Donald

Wooden Spoons

worked through them with relative sobriety and Maurice began to believe again. This afternoon, in that dismal setting, when his son turned to him and uttered that simple sentence, Maurice decided that there was nothing more he could do for Donald.

Maurice looked at the clock and saw it was four-thirty. On his phone, he noticed the message light flashing. He pushed the play button and heard Tom Arnold's voice. The message was similar to others Maurice had received over the past six months, but it ended differently:

"Now listen," Tom Arnold said in an irritated tone of voice. "I'm losing my patience. Call me."

Maurice stared at the phone as his face reddened. He picked up the receiver and speed-dialed Tom Arnold's office. A secretary answered and informed the attorney that Mr. Arnold was gone for the day.

"Well, yes, then could you give him this message? This is Maurice Nicklow and I am profoundly sorry to have inconvenienced Mr. Arnold with my ineptitude. That will never be a problem again for as of this moment, I will no longer represent his interests in Lick Hollow, Pennsylvania."

The secretary hesitated for a few seconds, but remained professional. "I will give Mr. Arnold the message," she replied.

Maurice looked at the clock again and then stood to put on his coat. He decided to do something that he had not done in many years. He was going home early to ask his wife, Martha, if she would go to dinner with him.

-29-

On a Saturday morning near the end of January, Joe Harmon opened the door of the Lick Hollow Mercantile. It seemed deserted, but the lights and the aroma of coffee welcomed him in. A professional writer from Pittsburgh, he had passed through Lick Hollow on numerous occasions, always on the road to somewhere else. In spite of a general fascination he held for small towns and the proximity of this particular one at the foot of the Allegheny Mountains, he had never stopped. It was a neighbor who had prompted him to do so. A neighbor who had bought a wooden spoon here and then told him pieces of what Joe suspected was a good story. The winter weather had eased somewhat with temperatures rising above freezing. The writer took the opportunity to get out of the city for a day.

In his late fifties, Joe Harmon was interesting in appearance. He wore his gray hair long. It protruded from under his wide-brimmed leather hat and fell across the shoulders of his deerskin jacket. Buck was his nickname, and he liked people to use it. He had a kind face, a red, Irish complexion, and a personality that most people soon appreciated. He and his wife of twenty-five years had divorced four years before and Buck was determined to remain single now, devoting his life to writing.

Wooden Spoons

He glanced into the corners of the room until he saw the rack of spoons. Reading the sign that explained where the spoons were made and by whom, he smiled. These were different from the one his neighbor had shown him. The pieces hanging before him were more artistic, particularly the spoons which had human figures worked into the handles. One in particular sparked his imagination. It was a spoon upon which a slender, androgynous human figure adorned the handle. The figure's arms were folded, its head tilted back, and wide Martian-like eyes searched the sky. The figure had no obvious clothing and yet it did not appear to be naked. It was an intriguing little work of art on the end of a wooden spoon. He decided to buy this one.

"Good morning," came a voice from behind that caused him to turn.

"Why, hello. Good morning," he answered as he searched for a face. He eventually saw Nora Campbell's head just above the counter.

"Can I help you?" she asked.

"I think you can. My name is Joe Harmon. People call me Buck. I'm a writer for *The Commonwealth.* Are you familiar with the magazine?"

Nora shook her head and did not introduce herself.

"I'm interested in writing an article about Daniel Whaley and what he is doing here," he said, turning and pointing at the spoon rack with the spoon he held in his hand.

"I can't speak for him, but I don't think he's much for publicity," she said, in her scolding manner.

Buck hesitated, and then smiled. "I can assure you, Ma'am, that my intentions are good. A neighbor of mine bought a spoon last summer and told me the story of Mr. Whaley's efforts on behalf of the little girl with leukemia. Actually, this

189

is my day off. I want to write about it because I believe it is a great story. I want the public to know."

Nora sniffed. Actually, she believed the man, but she did not know what to tell him. John and George had departed half an hour earlier for an estate auction in Ligonier and would not be back for several hours. She decided that it was probably best to discourage the idea.

"He doesn't have a phone. I could tell you how to get to his house, but Daniel likes his privacy."

"I understand fully and I will certainly respect it." Buck answered, most congenially. "If you don't mind, I could begin by asking you a few questions to gain some background knowledge. Then I'll leave a note for Mr. Whaley requesting that we meet sometime at his convenience."

Nora stared. She didn't like that idea either.

Buck started to speak again, hoping to inspire a bit more enthusiasm for his project but stopped when he heard footsteps on the porch. The door swung open and Daniel Whaley entered the room. His hair and beard were longer and his complexion was darker than when Nora saw him last. Although she would rather have spared Daniel the intrusion of a reporter, Nora was relieved that he appeared. She knew that he was capable of handling the situation.

"Hello, Nora," Daniel said, smiling and nodding in her direction.

She nodded quickly and then glanced toward Buck.

Daniel turned toward the man and nodded.

"Daniel Whaley, I'm Joe Harmon," he said, extending his hand. "I'm a writer for *The Commonwealth*, if you're familiar with the magazine. Could we talk a moment?"

Daniel shook his hand, wary after the introduction. Yet there was something about Buck that he liked.

Wooden Spoons

"Where did you park?" Nora asked.

Daniel turned toward her. "I didn't park. I walked."

"Is the jeep broken down?"

"No. It's a nice day, and my load is light. I decided to walk." He knew Nora would not approve of this form of conveyance. "Besides, now I don't have to worry about Sheriff Pinto catching me with my illegal plates," he added quickly. Nora thought about that and nodded as she returned to her work.

Buck listened to this dialogue with amusement.

Daniel turned toward him. "Mr. Harmon, I uh, I want to say right up front . . ."

"Buck, call me Buck. And let me interrupt here, if I may. I'm here only because I think that what you are doing, particularly what you are doing for the little girl, is a good story. It's a story that should be told. Hey, I came to help the cause in whatever way I can, and writing is what I do."

"What sort of writing did you have in mind?" Daniel asked with resignation.

"Just the basics, Daniel. Connie Pavloc and her plight and how you are trying to help. Of course, the more background I have on you, the more interesting the story becomes. But I'm totally and, I might say, uncharacteristically, flexible in this case. I want to help. Can I buy you coffee?"

Daniel hesitated, and then nodded.

Nora quickly grabbed the carafe and poured the remaining coffee down the drain. Within seconds she had a fresh pot started.

The two men sat at a table by the window and interviewed each other for some minutes, eventually relaxing into conversation. Nora followed their discourse, tuning in when it got interesting. She was glad to see Daniel sit and relax. She warmed to Buck for this reason and courteously brought the men coffee.

"*The Commonwealth* is a magazine committed to telling the stories of the people of Pennsylvania, to preserve the state's remarkable history, and last but not least, to suggest wonderful places to visit. That is roughly the mission statement and roughly true," Buck proclaimed. Then he sipped his coffee. "Mmm, this is excellent coffee," he said loudly.

Nora did not look up, but she heard him.

"I think the story of Connie Pavloc and the particular way you are trying to help, with your art, is a perfect fit for our magazine."

"But, I uh, don't want publicity. I did this on impulse, this spoon idea. I felt bad, I felt compelled to help. I want to do so quietly. I don't want attention drawn to me. My primary purpose in being here is to restore the family home."

"Then so be it. The story will only go so far as you wish. I don't even have to mention your name. But I can tell you this, *The Commonwealth* now has more than one hundred thousand subscribers, and is read by an estimated half a million people. This is generally a more proactive, socially conscience audience. If they like the story, and it is my job to see that they do, the financial concerns of the Pavloc family could end quickly."

Daniel sipped his coffee, considering this information. "Well, let's do it, then. Why not?"

Buck raised his mug cheerfully. "I won't disappoint you, Daniel. This is truly a good story."

Having settled that matter, the two men drank their coffee in silence until Buck could no longer contain his curiosity. He guessed correctly that Daniel was about his own age. Having recently gone through some dramatic changes in his life, he wondered what had prompted this man, a university professor at the apex of his career, to undertake a project such as restoring the abandoned, family homestead.

"Daniel, strictly off the record, how did you happen to . . . "

"It's a long story," Daniel interrupted, guessing his thoughts. "I was having some problems and they took a turn for the worse. I suddenly wanted to see Mountain Farm one more time." Daniel gazed out the window as he said this and then turned and looked directly at Buck. "And away I drove," he added whimsically.

Buck laughed, delighted that Daniel was willing to talk. "I can understand that," he said nodding. "Quid pro quo."

He then went on to tell Daniel that five years before, he was suddenly jolted to the reality that his marriage was in serious trouble, when he came home from a working weekend to find that his wife had packed and gone. Nora's head was turned to one side with this revelation. Daniel shuffled in his chair, uncomfortable with what he was hearing.

"But I got over it. I got out and I got over it. I threw myself into my work, I traveled, I got over it."

But he wasn't over it. Daniel knew that.

"So Daniel, can you tell me about your project on the mountain?"

Nora brought the men more coffee.

Daniel leaned back in his chair. "Well, Nora, where do I begin?"

"Don't start too far back, or you'll have him here all day," she answered on her way back to the counter.

The men smiled at this response, not quite sure how to take it.

Buck reached inside his coat and withdrew a small flask. "Want to sweeten that up a bit?" he asked. "A little Irish creme whiskey is all."

Daniel shrugged and nodded, which prompted Buck to add a generous dose to each mug. Then Daniel outlined the history of Mountain Farm down to its current state of repair.

The writer was enthralled. "Are you planning on living there, not returning to Wisconsin?" he asked excitedly.

Daniel shook his head. "No to both questions. I'm not returning to Madison but I won't be living on the mountain long. Hopefully long enough to put Mountain Farm back in some sort of order but not another year." He said this with such a strange, distant expression on his face that Buck decided not to probe further.

Daniel was beginning to feel the effects of the whiskey and he wanted to talk more. "You know Buck, one thing that has occurred to me as I spend so many hours alone on the farm is just how relaxing and simple life can be, especially in the woods. Mountain Farm represents a lifestyle that is as basic as it gets in these times, and yet I never wish for more convenience or miss modern comforts. I've never enjoyed working like I do now and yet I spent most of my adult life far away, pursuing a career that somebody else designed for me."

Buck did not respond, but it was obvious that he was interested.

"And the old tools that I use are slow, but the job gets done and I'm involved with every step of the process. The act of working is part of the reward. I guess what I'm trying to say is that with all our technology and modern gadgets, maybe we're rushing ourselves past what is really enjoyable about making a living. It's occurred to me that this might be one reason why so many people reach our age dissatisfied with their lives. They have a feeling they've missed something and they're right."

Wooden Spoons

Buck agreed with what Daniel said and wanted to hear more of his opinions. "Do you think that is why there are so many homes being built in the mountains now? Are people looking for a simpler life?"

Daniel rolled his eyes and sipped from his mug before responding. He knew he was being baited, but still wanted to answer. "I think that many people delude themselves with the notion that a house on a mountain will automatically balance the grind of their life in the city. All they are doing is dragging the city into the woods and pretending that they left it behind. If someone wants a simple life in the mountains, they should build a small cabin that fits the landscape and then work outside with their hands a little. People should experience a mountain on its terms and not always try to shape it to theirs."

"It's an interesting point of view. I couldn't agree more. Why not put it in print and pass the idea along to the public?"

Daniel shook his head and waved his hand. "I'm no activist, and even if I wanted to be, I don't have time for it now. Besides, I have no room to preach to people about how to live their lives. It's just an opinion."

"But I *am* an activist and I *do* have time. Over-development of the mountains has long been a sore spot with me. If you'll give me the green light to tell of your experience on Hemlock Knob, I know I can write a story that will prick at people's conscience. It's just a long shot at making any real difference, but if it isn't taken, there's no chance."

Daniel seemed uncertain and he glanced toward the counter. "More coffee, Buck?"

"No, I'm caffeined out for the day."

"Me too, but I want an excuse for more whiskey."

"It's better straight anyway," Buck said, laughing. He divided the remaining contents of the flask between their mugs.

Daniel took a drink, savoring the taste, letting his mind drift for a moment, then he turned toward Buck. He rolled the last bit of whiskey in his glass and sighed. "I don't want to stir up trouble. I really just want to do one last thing, something good, and then fade away."

"Well let's get the ball rolling. You continue to do what you do best, making these works of art behind me, helping Connie Pavloc, restoring Mountain Farm, and I'll do what I do best. And I'll be honest with you, fading away, if it's at the right time, when everyone is watching and listening, might help in the bigger scheme of things."

"What?"

"No, really. Nothing stirs the public's imagination like someone who disappears. You, your work and your ideas will stay in people's minds for a long time."

Daniel was listening carefully and staring into his mug. He swirled the whiskey several times and took the last drink.

-30-

Donald did take his father's advice and inquired at Foodland about the proposed construction. The owner, Hugh Michael, was a longtime friend of Maurice and was happy to see Donald. In spite of the season, the advantage of hard roads made the job relatively easy for Nicklow Developers Inc., and it was underway within a week. While not as profitable as new construction in the mountains, the supermarket enlargement did get Donald out of the Lick Hollow Tavern.

He would look up whenever a vehicle drove by slowly, always expecting his father to pull into the construction area to see how the job was going. That was the usual pattern, no apology and never admission of a mistake. Donald simply went back to work. Maurice would eventually come around to the job site, thus reassuring Donald that whatever had happened was forgiven. Until that point came, the family accountant acted as their medium.

The job progressed. Ten days went by, but the Cadillac did not appear. Donald thought about the last conversation with his father, particularly the last sentence. As his mind cleared, it became increasingly obvious that he had gone too far this time. "Well, damn it, I'll say I'm sorry," he growled one day over the blue prints. "It was a stupid thing to say, that's all. He

Dennis Ruane

knows I sometimes say stupid things when I've been drinking."

An hour later, Donald heard the crunching of icy gravel from a vehicle that was approaching slowly from behind. He glanced over his shoulder to see a long, dark car. He paused briefly over the blueprints, wondering if an apology would still be necessary, then turned to see that it was not the Cadillac. A middle-aged man emerged from a beautiful charcoal-colored Jaguar. He was casually dressed in stylish clothing, which fit his agile physique well. It was obvious that this was not someone looking for work.

"Donald Nicklow?" the man asked, approaching with an outstretched hand.

Donald just nodded as he took the man's hand.

"Tom Arnold, out of Pittsburgh. I've done some business with your father."

It took a moment, but Donald eventually recalled the conversation he had with his father in Martin's Restaurant. This was the man who wanted to build on Hemlock Knob. Donald shook Tom's hand with a nod of recognition but remained silent. He was uncertain as to why Tom Arnold was approaching him especially since he had not spoken to his father in three weeks.

"It seems that Maurice and I have had a communication breakdown of sorts. I was passing through and thought I would air it out with him, face to face. That's the way I like to do things."

Donald looked him over. Tom Arnold was a big man, about Donald's size and though apparently wealthy, his speech and mannerisms were of working class Pittsburgh background. He had big hands which showed some use. *Definitely not old money*, thought Donald. This presumption bettered his opinion of the man. In fact, it was Donald's own, great ambition, to one

Wooden Spoons

day be looked upon as *new money*.

"But his secretary told me that he and your mother had taken the grandchildren on a cruise." Tom Arnold smiled and nodded as if to make a point that he thought this was nice.

Donald knew nothing of this trip in spite of the fact that it might involve his own children, and this irritated him. "How can I help you, Mr. Arnold?" he asked, with obvious coolness in his voice.

"Call me, Tom. I was hoping we might discuss business." Tom glanced from side to side as if looking for a better location to talk, and then he looked at his watch. "Say, it's almost lunch time. Want to grab a sandwich and a beer?"

This offer caught Donald off guard and appealed to his weakness. He accepted without much thought.

Moments later, the two men were on bar stools at the Lick Hollow Tavern. Donald noticed that Tom was at ease with the surroundings as well as the common practice of having sandwiches delivered from Martin's. Tom Arnold noticed how quickly Donald finished his first two beers. After Donald answered some general questions about Lick Hollow and was given a chance to complain about the winter's effect on business, Tom came to the point of their meeting.

"I want to build on Hemlock Knob in a big way. It's been my dream for many years and I can't let it go. When I contacted your father a year ago and learned the history of the place, about the absentee owner from Wisconsin, I thought it would be no problem. I wanted Maurice to get me the best price possible, but I was prepared to drop whatever money it took. Then after thirty years, this Whaley fellow appears out of the blue to live there."

Donald nodded as he took another bite of his sandwich. "Yeah, I know about all that," he said, and then swallowed.

Dennis Ruane

With that revelation, Tom decided to press forward with his proposal. "Well, I know your father has done his best but lately, well, I feel he's lost his enthusiasm. And, hey, I'm a pain in the ass, I know that." He patted Donald roughly on the shoulder and laughed. "I'm pushy and loud. That's just the way I am." He leaned backwards and threw his hands up. "I am what I am, like Popeye sez." Then he bounced his fist off the bar. "But, that's the reason I got what I got."

Donald laughed. He liked Tom, and now he knew the point of this meeting. "So you want me to get the mountain for you," he said, pushing his glass forward to get Corky's attention.

Tom was surprised at this astute statement. When Donald grinned, Tom reached for his own glass and nodded as he drank it down. "I'll be honest with you, my man, I have come into money these days that I never would have dreamed of. I got big plans for Hemlock Knob. I don't mean to kick this Whaley fellow out into the cold. He'll be paid more than well. He'll be able to go wherever he wants, live better than he ever has. I just think he needs more of a push than your father is willing to give."

"Well, I never have met him but it sounds like The Professor is a character," Donald said over the rim of his glass.

With that statement, Tom remembered a ploy he had planned to use. "That's what I hear too. I could hardly believe the way this professor fellow treated your father."

"Huh?" Donald asked, turning.

"Your father didn't tell you about that?"

Donald shook his head.

"Well, Maurice tried to talk to him face to face, which was my suggestion. This Whaley fellow apparently got hot and more or less told your father where to go and how to get there."

"No. Dad told you that?"

"Well, I uh, not in those exact words. I had to read between the lines a little."

"And the old man took it?"

Tom Arnold raised his eyebrows and rotated his head to one side as if to say, *seems that way.*

Donald stared into his beer. "I kinda thought the old man's been losing his punch lately." Donald's mind was working quickly. He saw an opportunity to jumpstart the construction season and at the same time gain a measure of independence from his father. He took a long drink as he thought about it.

"Million bucks. That's what I'll pay."

Donald nearly inhaled what was left of his beer. "Jesus Christ, that's what, ten thousand an acre?"

"Hah, that's right. I want that property bad. Course you don't have to play him that high to open, but that's what you can take to the table."

Donald was impressed. "Well Tom, I'll see what I can do," he said with a confident smile.

"Good, good. Hey, this will be big for both of us, believe me. I got lots of plans and I want you to build them."

Tom looked at his watch. "Damn, I'm due in Clarksburg at three. Never make it. Gotta run."

He shook Donald's hand firmly. Then he pulled a money clip from his pocket, fished out a fifty-dollar bill and tossed it on the bar. "Keep in touch. Call me anytime at this number." He gave Donald a business card along with a light slap on the back and left the bar.

Donald was pleased with this meeting. He lit a cigarette and grinned over it. Calculating that the bill on the bar had some distance to go before it approached Corky's tip, Donald decided to relax and celebrate this turn of fortune.

-31-

When Donald Nicklow awoke, he was hot and uncomfortable. Although it was February, the afternoon sun had been directed on him through a truck windshield for half an hour. Donald was tired and thick-headed, having consumed too many beers with lunch. Biscuit was driving. Mike Miller was a fifteen-year veteran of the Nicklow Developers crew, and few of his co-workers knew that he had any other name than Biscuit. He was not an intellectual, but he was a good man, dependable, and loyal to the boss who slowly awoke beside him. Today Biscuit had been Donald's companion on a trip to Frederick, Maryland, for a machinery auction.

They had bought no tools in Frederick and Donald was disgruntled. Grumpy and hung over, not a good mix to let stew in the afternoon sun. As his head cleared, he realized they were on Route 40, passing by the town of Markleysburg, Pennsylvania.

"Hey, sleeping beauty," Biscuit hollered.

His boss turned and looked at him with bloodshot eyes, definitely no beauty. "Go to hell, Bis," he croaked.

Donald peered out across the landscape, irritated about the auction, mad about the winter. He needed a break in the weather and he wanted to get back on a big job. There had still been no contact with his father. Then the recent discussion with Tom Arnold seeped into his thoughts.

What a damn sweet deal that would be. That's the kind of work I should be doing, not this odd job crap, enlarging a supermarket.

Donald had a headache and a queasy stomach, but he knew how to remedy both. Opening the glove compartment, he withdrew a flask of bourbon. After taking a quick, hard swallow, he offered it to his companion. Biscuit waved it off, as Donald knew he would.

"Too early for me, boss,"

"Wimp," Donald said. He took another swallow, looking out the window, thinking about Hemlock Knob. That job was something that had to happen, and now. One thing his father had impressed upon him was the importance of making the right business moves at the right time.

After another ten miles, Donald sat up straight and pointed to the left. "Turn onto Furnace Road there, Biscuit," he commanded.

"Huh, what the, what's out there?"

Donald turned and looked at him with a grave expression. "Biscuit, yours is not to question why, yours is but to do or die."

Biscuit looked at his boss and grinned.

Four miles down Furnace Road, Donald directed him to turn right at the next dirt road.

"Hemlock Road? Can't always get though from this direction, specially this time of year."

"We'll get through."

"It's your truck, boss."

Donald took another drink from the flask. When Mountain Farm came into view, they saw a pick-up truck parked beside Daniel Whaley's jeep.

"Shit," Donald muttered.

"That's George Haynes' truck," Biscuit said.

"I know who it is. Pull in," Donald said, motioning toward Reilly Lane.

Biscuit was surprised that they were stopping here, but he did not question why this time. Cody was sitting on the front porch, staring at the truck.

"That's an old Cur dog," Biscuit exclaimed. "Ain't seen one in a long time. My great-uncle Pete had the last one I knew of."

Donald nodded without really listening or caring about the dog. Cody was watching him intently. Donald was uncomfortable; this was not the end of the business he was used to. His father had always done the negotiating. He took one more long drink before they pulled up to the house.

Daniel appeared on the porch before the truck stopped while George remained in the doorway. Cody continued to watch but did not move. Not recognizing either of the men, Daniel assumed they had stopped to ask permission to hunt on his property. George recognized them, and the friendly smile from Donald Nicklow made him uneasy.

Donald had been coaching himself to speak with Daniel Whaley ever since his meeting with Tom Arnold. He had little of the oratory prowess of his father and none of the eloquence, his particular social skills being better suited to the job site. But he had calculated that with the monetary margin that Tom Arnold had given him, he should be able to discuss business with this oddball living alone on top of Hemlock Knob.

"Can I help you, gentlemen?" Daniel asked in a formal but friendly tone of voice.

"I hope so," Donald answered, still smiling. "I'm Donald Nicklow of Nicklow Builders, er uh, Developers. Nicklow

Wooden Spoons

Developers, I mean. Um, this here is Michael J. Miller, known far and wide as Biscuit."

Donald turned toward George Haynes. "George," Donald said, grinning and nodding.

George nodded but did not speak.

Donald quickly turned back to Daniel. "Come to talk business, and I mean big business. Got a man who's willing to pay half a million bucks for your property here, maybe more." Donald spoke with a noticeable slur. "We're talking ten, er I mean, um, five thousand an acre. Don't get much better than that around here."

Daniel recalled all that George had told him about this man, and so he knew that he had to choose his words carefully. "I don't want to sell. This is my home place, built by my great-great-grandfather. The man you represent has . . ."

"Hey, this man might go as high as eight hundred grand."

"The money doesn't really matter to me."

Donald was incredulous. He moved a step closer. "What do you mean, money doesn't matter to you? It matters to everybody."

"Not to me. I have everything I need right here."

Donald took another step and was now within a few feet of Daniel. This was not going as planned and Donald was becoming warm and irritated. The bourbon was coursing through his bloodstream, threatening whatever professionalism he had hoped to muster. "What are you, insane? With that kind of money you could buy a whole goddamn mountain and build a home palace. You don't even have running water here, do ya?"

Daniel did not answer. He steadied himself, preparing mentally for what he felt might be coming.

"A project like this would mean jobs," Donald blurted out, remembering another point he had planned to make. It was an

205

argument he had worked out one night with nodding heads on nearby bar stools. Here in the open air, with a sober audience, it sounded idiotic. "Boys need work. Been a rough winter. What I'm saying is, this is a big project and a big project means, uh, big jobs. Or what I mean is, more jobs." Donald opened his mouth as if he might elaborate further. Then he bobbed his head up and down in seeming agreement with himself.

It was obvious now that Donald had been drinking. Daniel's anxiety level rose and then his temper began to smolder.

George watched with alarm, his mind racing for a method to diffuse the situation. "Donald," he said, "Daniel does not want to sell right *now*. Maybe another time, he and you and your father can discuss it." Unaware of the rift between father and son, and certain that Maurice would never have condoned this, George thought his suggestion would remind Donald that this was not his role. George's words only incited him.

"Back off, George. I'll handle my business, my old man can handle his, and you mind yours."

Daniel's eyes narrowed and his jaw set. "I have absolutely no intention of selling this property, especially to you," he said through clenched teeth.

Donald turned back to Biscuit with a look of disbelief. "Did you hear that? I have absolutely no intention of selling this property," he repeated, imitating Daniel's voice. When he faced Daniel again, it was with an ugly sneer, an expression that seemed more natural on his face. He took another step toward Daniel.

"Well, goddamn it, maybe people down there, people that work, are getting sick of supporting the likes of you with their taxes, professor or not. Who the hell do you think you are?"

"Donald," George shouted.

Wooden Spoons

"Shut up, old man."

Daniel glared at Donald now. His eyes were ice-blue crystals, sparkling with anger.

George feared that Daniel could be killed. At first he looked for something to hit Donald with should the situation call for it. Then he glanced anxiously toward Biscuit. Mike Miller had known and liked George Haynes since he was a child. He read the expression correctly and knew that he would have to corral Donald and pull him off if his boss lost control. It was a job he did not desire, but because of his great size, he was capable of it.

Donald took the last step toward Daniel, staring venomously. He pushed him in the chest with the fingers of his right hand. Donald felt some faint alarm in the fact that The Professor's expression did not change, nor did he move backwards. In fact, Daniel's demeanor was suddenly calm, and his voice was low and defiant.

"I'll tell you plainly, Nicklow, Mountain Farm is my family home, my ancestors are buried on the hill behind me, and I'll be damned if I'll turn it over to the likes of you for any reason." Daniel paused and tilted his head. "And don't touch me again," he added solemnly.

Donald looked back at Biscuit. "Did you hear that?" he asked with an ugly grin.

Biscuit looked at his boss vacantly. He knew a fight was imminent, and he was not so sure whose side he was on anymore. Donald did not really need Biscuit's support at this point. He turned back toward Daniel and stuck a gnarly finger in his face. His voice was low and vicious, like a growl.

"Now I want you to understand something, you simple ass, you. I ain't like my old man. I've been as nice about this as I'm going to be . . ."

Dennis Ruane

He did not really know what he was going to say, but that was not important anymore. Nor was negotiating this deal for Tom Arnold a concern now. Donald was acting on brute instinct. He needed to put the man in front of him firmly, and if necessary, violently in his place.

But as he jabbed his finger forward to emphasize each word, it lightly touched Daniel's chest and the effect was as if an electrical switch had been flipped. Daniel took a half step backwards, squared his shoulders and raised his fists in a rigid, old-fashioned boxing pose. George did not know what to make of it; he never would have guessed that Daniel could box. Daniel looked different to him again, it was like the day he engaged Maurice at the Mercantile. His expression was angry and unyielding and his eyes showed cool resolve.

Donald was as surprised as George and for that reason, he hesitated. He stood motionless for several seconds while The Professor pulled back his right fist and punched him squarely on the jaw, propelling him backwards. He caromed off the porch railing, tumbled down the stairs and floundered to the ground on his back. Pain streaked through his side where his ribs had hit the railing. A few seconds of confusion were followed by an eruption of rage.

He struggled to his feet with an assortment of grunts that grew louder until they merged into a roar. Donald charged up the stairs like an enraged bull. Then he saw the dog coming, teeth bared, head low. The transformation in Cody was remarkable. The quiet, somewhat aloof animal was now a snarling beast, moving toward Donald with obvious intent to harm him.

Donald had never been fond of dogs, but he was never intimidated by one either, until now. He was unnerved by the way this dog was approaching him and he froze. Cody stopped two feet from Donald, pacing rhythmically, barring passage to Daniel. Donald hesitated. His side hurt and was beginning to stiffen. He stood a moment longer until Biscuit came up behind him.

"Hey boss, why don't we hit the road?"

"I'm all right, dammit," Donald said over his shoulder. Then he looked up at Daniel. The pressure of the punch was fresh on his jaw and he wanted vengeance. But he saw the same grim resolution on the face of the man and unyielding ferocity in the dog at his feet. Donald knew that he could not win this fight.

"I know you're all right, but we ought to hit the road now, I think."

"OK Biscuit, if that's what you think," Donald murmured. He turned toward his employee and nodded. Then he looked up at Daniel. "We're not done," he said with bitter contempt. Daniel did not respond.

Donald shuffled slowly toward his truck. Biscuit hovered behind, ready to help, but being careful not to imply that his boss needed it. Donald eased himself into the passenger seat. His head hung as the truck drove away.

George laughed, more a sound of nervous relief than of amusement. Daniel did not even smile. He knelt and rubbed Cody's head while the dog stared after the truck. When the vehicle was out of sight, Daniel looked up at George.

"I can't tolerate people like him anymore," he said calmly.

George shook his head and laughed again.

-32-

Behind the penmanship of Joe Harmon, Daniel Whaley's efforts on behalf of Connie Pavloc did reach a receptive audience. As Buck predicted, the Pavloc's monetary concerns began to dissipate soon after. Although it was not his desire, Daniel became a minor celebrity. Despite the fact that it was the middle of winter, the remaining spoons at the Mercantile sold out quickly.

Had the public discussion of Daniel remained on Connie Pavloc and the spoon business, there could have been no question of his motives. It was after subsequent publications in *The Commonwealth* that controversy stirred. In an article entitled *Life on the Mountain,* Buck told the history of Mountain Farm along with Daniel's description of his restoration project. This was harmless information and was well received by the public. It was when Buck wove in Daniel's opinion on the shortcomings inherent to the modern approach to living in the mountains that some readers began to get uncomfortable.

The author remained true to his word and quoted Daniel carefully. He did, however, add his own opinion that perhaps the very thing that was desirable about living in the mountains was being destroyed by the building of such elaborate homes there. Some readers agreed fully with this point. Many were ambivalent, uncertain about the development of the mountains, but convinced that the area reaped much needed economic benefit in the process. Those people who were directly involved in the development, particularly those who were making their living by it, became a bit hostile.

Controversy is news. The articles in *The Commonwealth* spawned coverage in other periodicals and all the press added to Daniel Whaley's notoriety. His fame eventually extended into the dim interior of the Lick Hollow Tavern.

One Saturday evening, Kent Madison was reading aloud an article from the *Uniontown Herald Standard*. It made the observation that more tourists were passing through the village of Lick Hollow as a result of the stories about Daniel Whaley in *The Commonwealth*. The *Herald Standard* article went on to state that shop owners felt that this was improving business in the town.

It had been a rough winter for Donald Nicklow, who was sitting in the stool beside Kent. He was hunched over a beer and a smoldering ashtray. After three weeks, his bruised ribs were healing, but his pride still bore a festering wound. Now his nemesis, Daniel Whaley, was attacking him on another front, his livelihood, and becoming famous while doing it. During his convalescence, Donald had been particularly disagreeable and belligerent. Biscuit, the most loyal of employees, was eventually driven away. He began taking on small building projects independent of Nicklow Developers, Inc.

"Whaley received his PhD at age twenty-four," Kent read. "Let's see, at twenty-four, I was still carrying block for old Mike Raffle. Man, he was a slave driver. What about you, Don?"

Dennis Ruane

"Huh, I don't know. What about me?" He had read the article over breakfast at Martin's Restaurant and was trying not to pay attention to his bar mate.

"What were you doing at twenty-four?"

"Hey, I don't know, workin' or in jail. Drinkin'. I dunno." He was playing with his lit cigarette, slowly rolling it in the ashtray. The smoke sifted through his fingers and blended into the hazy shroud of the room.

Kent laughed at this response, not realizing that Donald was being truthful. Kent Madison was an old acquaintance whom Donald tended to associate with when he was drinking most heavily. He was a big man with a thick mop of black hair and a boyish face, which belied the fact that he was actually a year older than Donald. Kent drifted from job to job or into business and out of business, always drinking too much. He was a harmless and likeable man. Because the Lick Hollow Tavern was the only bar in town, he would occasionally find his path running alongside Donald Nicklow. He knew nothing of Donald's disastrous stint as a real estate agent on Hemlock Knob, or he would not have chosen this particular article to read aloud.

Kent started to read again.

"Hey, enough. I don't want to hear about that asshole anymore," Donald growled. He was gazing at his own image in the mirror behind the bar.

"Wait, just this last sentence, you'll love this," Kent insisted, laughing. "In the end Whaley lives alone on the mountain to follow his dream of restoring the old family home and also to have the peace and quiet he needs to pursue his art."

Donald didn't respond.

"Isn't that wonderful?" Kent asked in a teasing way.

Wooden Spoons

Donald continued to look at his image in the mirror, gripping his mug with increasing force. He hated The Professor and wished that he would walk through the door right now.

Just then the door did open and two young men entered. Nathan and Edward Redmond had never been in the Lick Hollow Tavern, and everyone in the room knew that at a glance. Their parents had built a house on Chestnut Ridge the previous spring, a holiday and summer alternative to their home in Pittsburgh. More people like them were in the area every year, but rarely did they appear in a bastion of the local culture such as the Lick Hollow Tavern.

The Redmond brothers were on Christmas break from college, and while their parents vacationed in Buenos Aires, the brothers had opted to stay in the mountains of southwestern Pennsylvania. By the second evening on the ridge, they needed more stimulation and ventured into town.

They approached the bar and politely asked for two draft beers. While they were being poured, Edward nudged Nathan and nodded toward the pool table. The older brother bobbed his head in agreement, and Edward went over to set up a game. When Kent saw this, he tapped Donald on the arm and rolled his eyes toward the pool table. Donald glanced over his shoulder through the mirror, and a smirk spread across his face as he picked up his cigarette.

They let the brothers play through most of their game, and then Kent wandered over to put two quarters on the rail of the table. When Nathan made eye contact, Kent nodded and smiled.

"Guys want a game?" he asked, nodding toward Donald.

The boys looked at each other, shrugged and then nodded. When their game was over, Donald approached the table,

213

more alert and animated than he had been in weeks.

"Hey, how about ten bucks on the game to make it interesting?" he asked casually. The brothers agreed.

"I'm in," Kent said loudly.

He immediately pulled a ten-dollar bill from his wallet and laid it on the rail of the table, placing a piece of cue chalk on top of it. Donald then quickly slid a ten of his own under the chalk. Nathan and Ed realized that they had either misunderstood or been misled. Nathan did not change his expression and casually laid a twenty-dollar bill down.

In their day, the team of Kent Madison and Donald Nicklow rarely lost at this table. Although this was well past their day, they could still be a formidable challenge when the mood and blood alcohol content were right. They presumed that they would have no trouble with these greenhorns, but they were wrong. The Redmond brothers' father was an accomplished pool player who had competed professionally. While the sons had never aspired to follow in their father's footsteps, they had grown up playing pool. Donald and Kent realized from the break that they were in a run for their money. The brothers were not only good, but had a classy playing style and demonstrated teamwork never before seen in the Lick Hollow Tavern.

The game attracted a crowd as the tavern began to fill for the evening. It was a foreign audience to these two young men from Pittsburgh, and they were somewhat unnerved by the noise around the table. They grew less certain of their shots, and an early advantage eroded. Naturally, Donald and Kent thrived in this atmosphere.

After Nathan executed an incredible bank shot, the game had come down to the eight-ball for victory. The young man had a difficult shot, but one he was capable of making. As he

Wooden Spoons

moved along the table, considering how to play it, he faced Donald, who was parked against the rail slowly chalking his cue. Donald gave no indication that he intended to move.

"Don't shark me, boy," Donald said in a low, sinister voice as Nathan walked around him. Then Donald circled the table until he was behind the pocket Nathan would be shooting for.

The young man got into position and slowly aimed his shot while Donald stared maliciously. He did not like this cute boy in fancy clothes and with a little gold chain around his neck. The sweet-smelling cologne disgusted him. Donald gripped his pool stick firmly and imagined swiping it across his opponent's face.

That would be a fun way to end the game, he thought, laughing aloud.

Nathan Redmond was the more pugnacious of the brothers, especially after a couple beers. He was determined to defeat these two old rednecks, whatever the consequences. He shot suddenly and with uncharacteristic force, wanting to slam the ball into the pocket to emphasize the victory. He even imagined careening the ball off the big, bloated face that loomed over the pocket.

As determined as the shot was, some law of pool physics acted against it. Nathan shot too hard, too quickly, resulting in an uneven spin on the eight-ball. When it glanced the left corner of the pocket, it didn't continue forward and drop as Nathan had planned. Instead, it spun to the right and struck the opposite corner squarely. Then the ball shot back to the left, finally rattling back and forth across the mouth of the pocket until it drifted harmlessly away.

The cue ball did worse. Nathan's design was for it to bounce off the distant cushion after hitting the eight and then come back toward him victoriously. Instead, it rebounded

215

awkwardly, edging toward the left side pocket where it hovered for a second and then dropped in. The game was suddenly over. Kent was quick to collect the money, and Ed was quick to collect his brother.

"Let's go, dammit. Are you trying to get us killed?"

Nathan hesitated fumbling in his pocket for more quarters.

"Let's go," Edward pleaded.

Nathan finally looked at him and nodded.

The crowd forgot the Redmond brothers quickly and settled in for the next challenge to the old champions. The young men left, mostly unnoticed. As they approached their car, which was parked at the side of the building, they heard footsteps on gravel.

"Hey," came a voice from behind them. The brothers turned to see a man approaching with a bottle in one hand and a lit cigarette in the other.

"Hey, I don't know you, but I just wanted to tell you that, hey, you guys are good, man. You really won that game. Just bad luck on that old table is all it was. I was pullin' for ya, me and some others in there. We wanted you to beat those old birds in the worst way."

"I'm Jim Durst," the stranger said, quickly putting the cigarette in his mouth so that his right hand was free. He shook hands with each brother emphatically. Jim was taller than the Redmonds with a muscular build and a powerful grip. "Hey, you guys are good, man. I mean it. You play like it's supposed to be played. Don't let those guys get to you. That's all I wanted to tell ya."

The Redmond brothers were so surprised at this encounter that they never said a word.

Jim Durst turned back toward the bar, but reversed and

faced them again. "Hey, come back around. You guys are good. Those guys," he said, thumbing over his shoulder, "freakin' dinosaurs, man." He tilted his head back and laughed. Nathan and Ed laughed with him.

"Hey, take it easy," Jim said and turned back toward the bar.

"Take it easy, Jim," the brothers answered simultaneously.

But for tonight, dinosaurs ruled. When Jim reentered the bar, Donald and Kent were on their way to defeating the next challengers. Donald was in his old groove again, back in the glory days. He quickly forgot how close he and Kent had come to defeat. When they had won the second game, which was never much of a challenge, a shot of whiskey and a beer appeared at Donald's side. He looked around the room, trying to locate the source of this generosity. He spotted Spike Summer, another old construction veteran, grinning at him from the other side of the bar. Donald lifted the shot glass toward Spike and drank it down. He couldn't lose now.

Kent had moved to the juke box and punched in some songs to celebrate victory and to inspire his team onward. Donald broke to begin the next game. He was singing along to *Can't You See* by the Marshall Tucker Band as he ran several balls off the table. He was a winner again. He would show Tom Arnold that he was. He would show his father too. Donald called for another beer and a shot of whiskey.

After they had won their fourth game, Donald announced that he and his partner were retiring for the evening as supreme champions. Kent looked up from a bar stool in dumb surprise. Donald brushed past him on the way to the men's room.

"Meet me out back."

Dennis Ruane

"What for?"

"Business," Donald answered, grinning back at him.

Kent had not seen Donald so motivated the entire winter. When he joined him in the parking lot, Donald was standing beside his truck with the door open, lighting a cigarette.

"Come on. Let's go for a ride."

"Where to?"

"To disturb a little peace and quiet."

-33-

Daniel Whaley lay on his back gazing out the bedroom window in the direction of the little cemetery. He did not know what time it was but knew it was late. He had experienced an excruciating headache earlier in the day, and although it had passed, he was nervous and restless in its wake. For some careless reason, Daniel had allowed himself to believe that he would leave this problem behind in Madison. For many months as he settled into his new life on the mountain, that seemed to be the case, but the headaches returned as he knew they must. Daniel was determined not to yield to them this time but rather to push forward with his plans in spite of them.

He was chilled, and got up to check the fire. In the light of the full moon he could see Cody sitting near the wood stove. It was as if the animal had been up and waiting for him. He went over to the dog and stooped down. Moonlight was reflected in Cody's dark, mysterious eyes. Daniel rubbed the knobby head affectionately, wondering about this creature who had wandered into his life at such a strange juncture.

Suddenly Cody's head turned and then tilted. He was alert and listening. Daniel eventually heard the sound of a motor. Few vehicles came through at any time, so it was odd to hear one so late at night. Perhaps some kids fooling around, or maybe a resident of Furnace Road who had been drinking and opted to take the police-free route home. As he watched, the headlights turned down Reilly lane, and it was obvious that the vehicle was moving fast and recklessly.

"Get me the sh-shotgun there, my man. On the floor behind ya. Shells too."

"What? Hey Don, what the hell?"

"Give me the shotgun, damn it. I ain' gonna shoot the sonova bitch. Juss dissturb his peace and quite."

Kent did not entirely believe this, but he pulled the semi-automatic shotgun over the seat. Donald bore down on the house with a wild look on his face. He turned sharply to the right when the truck was forty yards away and stopped. He grabbed the shotgun, stepped from the truck, and without hesitation, fired at the log house. The blast resounded off the forest as the shot pummeled the roof.

That had been his intention, to fire above the house, to scare the occupant and then leave it at that. Donald wanted to give Daniel Whaley a sample of what life on the mountain *could* be like. He wanted The Professor to know that there was no guarantee on peace and quiet around here.

As they charged up the mountain, Donald had added to an already considerable alcohol consumption by drinking liberally from the glove compartment flask. The rush of adrenaline, stimulated by the gun's roar, stirred the brew and unleashed the monster. Donald lowered the barrel, aimed at the dark outline of a window, and this time the sound of shattering glass accompanied the roar of the gun.

Daniel had watched the approaching truck from the window of the big room and sprawled to the floor with the first shot. The second shot exploded the window above him, and the third, his bedroom window. He looked up and saw Cody, pacing in a tight circle by the stove. The dog was staring in the direction of the firing.

"Donny, stop it," Kent yelled.

"Shut up," Donald answered without looking at him.

He couldn't stop. Taking a few steps toward the log house, he fired two shots at the door in rapid succession. The first shattered the latch. The impact of the second caused the old door to sag open with a groan.

Kent Madison was not a hero, and he had been somewhat afraid of Donald Nicklow most of his life. But Kent was no weakling either, and when forced into a fight he could be a formidable opponent. Convinced that Donald was going to kill the man in the cabin, he knew that he had to do something.

When Kent moved close, Donald spun around and pointed the gun at his chest. "Back off, coward. I say when the party's over," Donald shouted.

Kent stopped, but the word 'coward' triggered anger in him.

Then there was movement at the house accompanied by a growl. Cody leapt from the porch and raced toward the intruders. Donald turned automatically and fired. The dog did not slow down. With the second shot, the animal yelped but kept coming. With the third shot, Cody collapsed and slid to a halt ten yards from the men.

"Cody," came a frantic shout from the house.

Donald and Kent looked up as a figure stepped from the porch and began pacing toward them. Donald raised the gun and fired at the roof, but Daniel Whaley kept coming.

"You asshole," Donald muttered and lowered the barrel. He shot quickly and was off to the right. Daniel's left arm flinched, but he did not stop. Donald's face twisted into an ugly sneer as he aimed carefully for Daniel's chest.

Dennis Ruane

Suddenly the barrel thrust upward and the gun was wrenched from his hands.

"Get in the truck. I'm driving," Kent yelled. He pushed Donald backward with the gun, nearly knocking him to the ground. Donald was stunned, and suddenly very drunk.

"Get in the truck," Kent roared, pushing him again. Donald looked nervously toward the figure that was stalking toward them and did as his companion ordered. Kent jammed the gun behind the seat.

"Hey, watch, you'll s-scratch the varnis-sh."

Kent did not acknowledge the remark. He wrenched the truck in gear and lurched away.

Daniel called for Cody once more as he approached his dark form lying on the grass. He knelt down and put his hand on the dog's chest. It was wet and still. Dark patches were oozing into the sleeve of Daniel's shirt. He looked up as the truck turned onto Hemlock Road and saw that it had a cracked right taillight. He looked down and saw moonlight reflected in Cody's lifeless eyes.

On the way down the mountain, Kent drove the truck hard, saying nothing.

"Juss wanded him to know it's not alls peace an quite, issall," Donald muttered once, in his defense.

Kent did not answer.

When they reached the parking lot of the Lick Hollow Tavern, Kent lurched up close to the maple trees and turned the key. He bowed his head and shook it from side to side.

"Shot the man's dog. Shot the man's dog, damn it. And you would have shot him too, you no-good son of a bitch." Donald was barely conscious now. Kent shook his head again, as if he were trying to dislodge the memory of what had just taken place on the mountain.

"Coward, is that what you called me?" Kent hollered, suddenly grabbing Donald's shirt at the neck with a determined fist.

Donald scarcely noticed. He was soon to pass out.

Kent let go in disgust and exited the truck, slamming the door behind him.

-34-

Unless there were direct repercussions such as jail or personal injury, Donald Nicklow was never one to regret his actions. As a result of the shotgun incident on Hemlock Knob, he had suffered no injury or was he in jail. In fact, one month later, he was happy and optimistic about life. Spring had come and serious construction would soon begin. The fact that neither Biscuit nor Kent Madison associated with him any longer was their problem as far as he was concerned.

He was at the Lick Hollow Tavern on this night, drinking with Spike Summer. Fifteen years before, a drunken argument over a game of horseshoes turned into a vicious fistfight between him and Spike. It was an even match, finally halted by Harry Pinto. Both men were treated at the Uniontown hospital and then housed at the Fayette County jail. In the years after the fight, they mostly stayed out of each other's way. Spike had steered toward road construction and could boast of some large state jobs he had contracted. Most would agree that the two men were alike in many ways, except that Spike did not possess Donald's inherent meanness.

Not only were these two construction veterans drinking together, they were discussing business. As reckless as it seemed, they were considering some sort of merger to form a

Wooden Spoons

company in the likeness of Nicklow Developers, Inc. The idea originated in the same spot where they were talking tonight, so they were still a long way from starting their first job.

As the men talked, they noticed that the Lick Hollow Tavern was unusually busy, even for a Friday night. It was obviously a younger crowd; Donald and Spike were the old men at the bar. Corky even had a young partner now, which was a strange sight after all the years. Naturally, Donald didn't like him.

Donald looked across the room at the crowd around the pool table, watching Nathan and Edward Redmond put on a show against one challenging team after another.

"Sucks, doesn't it?" Spike commented as he peered over his cigarette in the direction of Donald's gaze.

Donald nodded.

"Things gotta change, I know, but this used to be a kick-ass bar. I juss hate to see it turn into some yuppie, preppie-type deal, ya know what I mean?"

Donald bobbed his head. He knew what Spike meant. "Well Spike, my man, all the more reason for you and me to make our millions and get the hell out of Dodge."

Spike laughed, a rough, wheezy, coughing laugh which caused him to exhale smoke in short bursts, like an old engine with the idle set too low. "You think I'm bullshittin', don't ya?" he asked, leaning backwards on his stool in an attempt to better focus his eyes.

"Naw, I'm in. I think it can work. With the experience and the equipment we got, it's a pretty wicked combination."

"Here, here," Spike exclaimed, raising his glass.

Donald raised his and they drank them down, apparently sealing the partnership.

"Say old man, what do you know about that dude over

there cheering on the kid brothers?" Donald asked, motioning toward a man standing close to the pool table.

"Jim Durst? Not a whole lot. Been around. Was in the Marines for a while. Heard he did some boxin' in the service and was pretty good. Why?"

"I got a feeling he's layin' for me."

"What?"

"It's the way he looks at me. I know what he's thinking. He wants to take me down in a bad way."

"What's he got against you?"

"Might be cause I knocked around his brother a few years ago. Didn't hurt him bad. He got mouthy one night and I let him have it."

"Well, partner, I suggest you keep your belly up to the bar and forget about it. You're too old to mix it up with that buck."

"You think so?"

"I know so." Spike had learned to avoid bar fights years ago, and he did not want Donald starting something tonight while he was with him. He was also being honest in his assessment of the match-up.

"Well, you're no fun anymore, Spike."

"Whew, maybe not. But I'm still alive and have most of my teeth."

"OK partner, I'll behave," Donald said as he stood. "Now if you'll excuse me, my good man, I must go forth to the gentlemen's room," he said with a sloppy attempt at an English accent.

"By all means, sir knight," Spike responded. Then he pointed to the empty glasses and raised his eyebrows.

Donald merely stared and tilted his head to demonstrate surprise that his companion would even ask such a question.

As Donald moved away through the crowd, Chuck, the

new bartender, quickly approached the empty glasses. "Two more, sir?" he asked cheerfully.

Spike was caught off guard by the rush of enthusiasm and nearly looked over his shoulder at the word 'sir'. He just nodded.

"And?" Chuck pointed to the shot glasses.

Spike winked.

"Coming right up," the bartender said as he rushed away.

"What the hell?" Spike said, to the man next to him. "I might just get used to this, after all these years with that old curmudgeon Corky."

As Donald ambled down the hallway to the restrooms, a woman burst from the ladies room and nearly ran into him.

"Ma'am," he said, stopping in his tracks ceremoniously.

She was young and pretty with curly black hair that hung down across her back. The woman looked up at him with slight acknowledgment of his presence but moved close to the opposite wall and hurried by.

Donald laughed and shrugged it off. "It's your loss, baby," he said over his shoulder.

When he tried the knob on the men's room, the door was locked. Donald drummed his knuckles on the door to alert the occupant that a line was forming. It was only recently that the practice of locking the door began. The men's room at the Lick Hollow Tavern was a dingy, ancient facility, and all of its contents were revealed whenever the door swung open. This was never a problem in the preceding decades, but with a growing clientele, privacy had become more of an issue. In fact, Corky and his new partner had plans to expand out the back of the building and add new restrooms. Donald thought about this as he waited and was sure he would miss the current arrangement.

Dennis Ruane

He shortly lost his patience, rattled the knob vigorously and then stepped out the back door. He walked in a meandering line through the parked vehicles to Lick Hollow Creek at the far end of the lot. It was running high and fast from the combination of spring rain and melting snow in the mountains. Donald pulled up to a well-used opening in the trees that lined the stream. As he relieved himself, he tossed his head back and breathed in the cool night air.

Who would have thought it, Spike Summer and me, partners? Wait'll the old man hears this. He'll have a damn coronary.

Then his mind drifted back into the bar and he thought about the man who he sensed was challenging him. He couldn't take Spike's advice and forget about it.

Why the hell else would he be sucking up to those two pups that are riding on my table if it wasn't to piss me off? Maybe I'll just challenge one of those boys to a game and insist they play man to man. If G.I. Joe Boxer gets cute, I'll break his nose so fast, he won't have time to do any fancy punching.

So Donald's mind worked as it often had in the past, setting the stage for a fight. Adrenalin was pumping. He felt a twisted, nervous excitement, the thrill of violence that he was addicted to.

When he finished relieving himself and turned, he had a sudden sensation that a person was standing close beside him. As Donald squinted into the dark, he was struck in the stomach. Doubling over, he staggered backwards to the edge of the water, finally steadying himself by placing one hand on the ground. Coughing and vomiting, gasping for air, he looked up toward whoever had hit him. He saw no one. Donald forced himself to stand. Then he was struck again, this time directly in the face. The blow was accompanied by a sickening thud, like the sound of a jack-o-lantern being hit with a baseball bat. Donald Nicklow was propelled backward into the raging torrent and disappeared.

-35-

In late February, there was a break in the weather. Daniel sat astride a shingle horse, shaving rough shakes he had split from the red oak log. The shingle horse is a combination vise and bench, upon which a shake is firmly mounted by foot pressure. One end of the shake is then thinned with a draw knife to produce a smooth surface and a slight taper. This results in what is known as a shingle.

The oak shingle horse that Daniel used had been hauled to Mountain Farm by George Haynes on an early visit. George had purchased it at an estate auction for twenty-five dollars. Daniel had hoped to shingle all the buildings, but he knew now that it would be impossible. He would do well if he finished the log house. Once the basic technique had been mastered, shingle-making was a simple task, repetitive and relaxing. Daniel had become quite skilled at it.

It was the first spring-like day on the mountain, but a headache was threatening to ruin it for Daniel. Since Cody's death they seemed to come more often and to emanate from a specific location. He focused on his task, hoping that the pain would fade, but he was determined to make shingles in spite of it.

Then there came a scuffling sound on the road. Without the keen senses of his lost companion, a man had walked onto

Wooden Spoons

Reilly Lane before Daniel was aware of his approach. The visitor wore a white ball cap, sunglasses, and casual outdoor clothing. His hiking boots seemed to be new and there was a camera slung around his neck.

"Now what?" Daniel muttered as he placed another shake under the clamp. He was determined to keep working until there was no choice but to deal with the visitor.

In his articles, Buck had done his best to remind the public that Daniel needed privacy. As surely as the majority could understand this and contain their curiosity to Lick Hollow, there was a determined minority who had to meet the man of so much discussion. The greatest bother came from those who felt that Daniel had discovered some universal truth about life. They lingered the longest and were determined to have him impart it to them.

However, some came because they believed in Daniel's cause and wanted to help. Buck was a member of this group. He would come to talk and to gain more information for his writing, but he always came to work. Buck seemed to enjoy whatever task was placed before him and worked at it as if the restoration of Mountain Farm was his dream as well.

There was no person more welcome on the homestead than George Haynes. Along with his vast knowledge of construction and his desire to help, he brought a charming philosophy of work and life that aided Daniel's cause in immeasurable ways. More than anyone Daniel had met over the years, George reminded him of his great-grandfather. Daniel would forsake all activities to sit by the wood stove to discuss the curiosities of life with George.

But this was neither George nor Buck coming. When Daniel finally turned, he saw that the man was grinning and tilting his head in a familiar way.

"Daniel, is that you?"

Daniel was startled by the voice but said nothing. A few steps closer, sunglasses off, the face so extraordinarily out of context, finally registered.

"Victor?" Daniel cautiously asked.

The man laughed and walked up to him.

"Victor, I don't believe it."

"Hey, if I can believe that you are you, than surely you can believe that I am I. If the kind folks in Lick Hollow hadn't described you to me, I'm sure I would have walked right past you. In fact, I might have run past you."

Daniel laughed. The two friends clasped hands warmly. They stared at each other for a moment without speaking, each man trying to adjust to the sight of the other in this unusual setting.

"Well, Victor, I know you must have come here to see me, but how in the world did you happen to walk down my lane today?"

"That is a bit of a story, friend."

"Coffee?"

"Mmm, yes, that would be great."

"Have to be black."

"That's OK. I can rough it, too."

Daniel smiled and motioned toward the cabin. Victor followed him eagerly. He maintained his casual demeanor, but he was obviously in awe. It was all so foreign compared to the life he had lived. The interior of the cabin enveloped him in mystery. He turned a slow circle in the center of the Great Room and was uncharacteristically silent. Daniel prepared the coffee and watched him with interest. He had placed the percolator on the wood stove, having filled it with boiling water from the kettle. Coffee was brewing within a minute.

Wooden Spoons

"Victor, why aren't you lecturing in Biochemistry 301 this afternoon?"

"I'm in the process of retiring. I'm sixty-seven now, I've paid my scientific dues. Blanche and I are en route to Florida to explore the possibilities of relocating there. Not interested in the beach, just a quiet little town where it's warm in the winter. You know I love Madison, but the winter up there is cold on these old bones."

Victor turned to face Daniel. "You had a lot to do with the decision. Your sudden departure made all of us old-timers pause and think. Besides, I've always wanted to give writing a try. Now I'm going to do it."

"Really? You mean the great-American-novel type writing?"

"That's exactly what I mean."

Daniel smiled and nodded his approval.

When Daniel had answered Victor's questions about the log house, they made their way to the woodshed. Once again, Victor was turning circles, examining the firewood and then admiring the tools on the back wall. He stopped when he saw the large cherry sculpture. The piece had recently been completed, and Daniel watched nervously as his friend moved close to it. It was obvious to him that it was a woman, and though it lacked detail, Victor thought she was sensuous and beautiful. It was a simple female form separated into facets that loosely followed anatomy. Ridges and indentations suggested musculature and facial features.

"My Goodness, Daniel, this is wonderful," Victor said when he turned.

"Thank you," Daniel softly replied.

"What have you titled it?"

"Long Woman."

233

Dennis Ruane

Victor nodded. He liked the sculpture, and felt that the title fit well. He also knew it represented Debbie.

"So Victor, what do you hear of Debbie? Do you ever see her?" Daniel asked.

Victor looked at the sculpture as he spoke. "Only once since you left, and that was months ago. We didn't talk long. It was on the Union Terrace. We practically walked right into each other. She was friendly but seemed uneasy around me. I hear bits and pieces. I, uh . . . He hesitated for a moment. "She remarried, you know?"

"No," Daniel said, shaking his head. His shoulders sagged and he looked toward the ground. "When?" he asked in a weak voice.

"December, I think."

"That was right after the divorce was final," Daniel stated with obvious surprise and hurt in his voice. "That must be why her attorney pushed me. After all the years we were together, how could she have met someone and remarried so soon?"

Just as Victor had suspected, Daniel knew nothing of the two-year affair between Debbie and Tom Stringer. Fortunately, he had left Madison a few days before the storm broke. Myra Stringer had called Victor when she could not reach Daniel and then detailed her grievances to him. It would seem that she had made a similar call to half of the city, considering how many people eventually knew of the affair.

There was an uncomfortable silence. When Victor tried to say something, Daniel interrupted, purposely changing the subject. "Tell me more about this book you are going to write, Victor. I would think that writing fiction would be difficult after so many years of thinking science." He had straightened up, and his voice was calm again. Daniel motioned toward the door.

Wooden Spoons

They walked slowly in the direction of the house as Victor explained.

"Yes, but for two decades now, I've been a part-time scientist and part-time administrator. I've had ample opportunity to observe people and no shortage of problems to deal with. That's the stuff of novels, people and problems."

Daniel laughed and nodded in agreement.

"What if I were to write a novel about something as far-fetched as an eminent professor of biochemistry who walked away from his career and turned his back on civilization, so that he could devote his life to carving wooden spoons on top of a mountain?"

Daniel frowned. "That would, indeed, be fiction," he answered with tension in his voice. "Victor, there is something you need to know now, something that I should have already told you. Despite what you said about your own experience with headaches, I had some tests run by Will Barton. One day when I ran into Willy, I mentioned that I was doing fine but could not seem to shake the headaches. You know how he is. He insisted that I come in for tests that day."

Daniel paused and took a deep breath before he started to speak again. "He called me at my office and insisted that I come personally to discuss the results. That should have told me the story right then. What Willy told me was that . . ."

"You needn't go on, Daniel. I know what he said. Willy came to me not long after you left and told me about the results. He didn't want to. He said that he promised you that he would not tell anyone, but he was worried by the time he came to me. Willy had heard about your disappearance. He had expected you back soon to discuss treatment options."

"Daniel, he told me that without treatment, you would only live another six months, a year at the most."

Dennis Ruane

"That's right. He told me that, too. And with treatment I might live a little longer." He shrugged his shoulders. "I nearly ended it right then. I didn't even want these last months. I literally had a gun to my head. Then, I got the notion that I wanted to see this wonderful place one more time."

"I understand what you've said so far, but I think you have to be practical about this. Are you aware of the scenario you face?"

"Yes, I am." Daniel stopped near the sawhorse and placed his right foot on a short sycamore log. The felling axe was leaning against the log and he placed his right hand on the end of the handle.

Victor positioned himself about six feet away. "You can't just stay up here and die alone," he said with a quiet, pleading voice.

Daniel sighed. During the months of solitude he had worked through the rationale behind his decision.

"In the end, Victor, we all face death alone, whether it's here, on a mountain top or in a room crowded with people. It took me thirty years to get back here where I belong. Regardless of the circumstances, I won't leave Hemlock Knob again."

"Daniel, you have so little time left," Victor said with a sigh, almost as if he were thinking out loud.

"None of us have much time left. I'm at least using each day to do something that I believe in. It's a wonderful feeling. That's all we can ask for in life, just a little time to do something good for the world. Whenever our time runs out, whether it's tomorrow or fifty years from then, we can only hope to go with a measure of dignity and perhaps, pleasant thoughts of what we've accomplished."

Victor felt that he should try to change Daniel's mind, but

Wooden Spoons

this time, he had run out of words. No verbal maneuvering could sidestep the cold logic in front of him.

"It'll be OK, Victor. I have a plan right up until the end," Daniel said in a reassuring tone.

When Victor did speak, his voice was choking. "C-Could I take a picture of you, Daniel, a picture right here? I want to remember you as you are right now and not from some photograph in a faculty catalogue."

Daniel nodded. "Would you send a copy of the photograph to Jeannie? I would like her to remember me this way too."

"Certainly, Daniel. Certainly."

As he photographed his friend, Victor felt that after all the years he had known him, he was only now seeing what Daniel Whaley really looked like. The low afternoon sun highlighted the gray in long brown hair. The wide brim of his hat cast a shadow over swarthy features, framed by a rugged beard. Victor looked into clear blue eyes in which he saw neither despair nor resignation. The plain, worn clothing completed the picture of a man who was a natural part of his surroundings. It was hard to imagine that he ever walked the halls of the biochemistry building in an ill-fitting blue suit. Victor thought that Daniel looked magnificent. He looked like he belonged here, like he had always been here.

It was late afternoon and Victor still had a hike ahead of him. He did not want to leave his friend, and yet it seemed appropriate at this point. His eyes were tearing as he approached Daniel and clasped his hand.

"Goodbye, Daniel. I should be heading back down."

It troubled Daniel to see Victor so uncertain and sad. "You've got about an hour of daylight left and a bit longer in walking time before you make the hard road," Daniel said ominously.

Victor looked up the lane and back at Daniel as if an alarm had gone off.

"You have time, Victor. I'm just being mean. You'll have no problem."

At that, Victor finally smiled. He held Daniel's hand a moment longer, knowing that when he let go, it was forever. "Goodbye, my friend," he said, and then turned toward the road.

Daniel watched him walk away. "Good luck with your novel," he called.

Victor stopped.

"I mean that, sincerely."

"Thank you, Daniel," Victor said, and then turned back toward Hemlock Road.

-36-

In late March, Daniel awoke to the sound of rain pelting the newly-shingled roof of the log house. Then he sat up rigidly in bed when he realized that he had no feeling on the left side of his face. It was finally happening, just as Dr. Barton said it would and roughly on the timetable that he had projected. Daniel was suddenly scared. *I've waited too long*, he thought. *Maybe I shouldn't have stayed here this long.*

The room was cold. The weather had been so mild that a fire throughout the night had been unnecessary. But this morning, cold rain was falling and a gray day dawned. Spring seemed to be losing its claim to the season. Daniel shuddered as he lit the fire. He was quite adept at it now and soon had a crackling blaze. Sitting near the stove, he rubbed the side of his face as if it was frostbite he was afflicted with and the fire would alleviate it. The heat did serve to calm his fear, at least.

After Will Barton's somber diagnosis that afternoon in Madison, Daniel did not hear much of the doctor's advice. As he struggled now to remember it, he thought of the journal. That was Will's suggestion, for him to keep a journal that could be used as a tool in the end, when his memory began to fail. At the time Daniel found the idea depressing, but he had written in this journal almost daily, ever since leaving

Dennis Ruane

Madison. It had become an outlet for the swirl of emotions that were stirred up by the upheaval in his life.

The room was warming as he crossed to the table where the journal lay. Opening the book, he was alarmed to find the most recent entries disconnected and nonsensical. With some effort, he could recall what he had meant to write, but what he saw were just bizarre collections of words.

This is it, then. This is the end. Somehow, in this new setting, in this new life, he was able to entertain hope that the prognosis was incorrect. He rubbed the side of his face and it felt to him as if there was a slab of rubber being pushed from side to side against his jaw. There was no doubt about his fate now. His head drooped forward and hung for a moment. "Life isn't fair," he murmured. "I don't deserve this." Momentarily, he drifted with self-pity but then straightened up.

No. I've thought this through. I knew this was coming. There is no time for crying. I've got to do this one last thing. He paged back through the journal until he found the plan he had worked out, a course of action for when he felt the end was near. He read it with interest, almost as if it had been written by someone else. The words encouraged him to be strong at the end and to deal rationally with the unfolding situation. Will Barton was right, the journal did prove to be a useful tool.

First Daniel cleared the table of everything but his journal. Then from it, he removed a note for Nora, John and George, which he had written one month before. Going to the bedroom, he retrieved his father's gun from a top dresser drawer along with a leather pouch. He placed the pouch on the table alongside the journal and tucked the gun inside his coat pocket. The woodcarving tools were to be placed on the table as well, and Daniel welcomed the opportunity to visit the woodshed

Wooden Spoons

one last time.

He opened the door and inhaled the intoxicating aroma of musty planks and freshly cut firewood. There were over five cords of wood just inside the door that would never be burned by him. Daniel walked toward the tools and steadied himself against the workbench. For a moment, he lovingly examined the display on the wall. He knew the tools well, the feel of the handles and the pitch of each blade. Now they must pass into other hands.

Finally Daniel turned toward *Long Woman*. He had worked many hours on this sculpture, and his goals for restoring Mountain Farm were compromised as a result. He felt no guilt on this account. Daniel now believed that he had to create this piece, that it was part of his destiny. Months before, R. Cranston had readily accepted his offer to donate the sculpture to the Folk Museum, in spite of the fact that the librarian had never seen it. Knowing that it would reside there among his family's artifacts was a great comfort to Daniel.

His eyes studied the form and lines of *Long Woman*, this work of art, which represented the memories of an era. It was a study of the woman who had altered the course of his life, and while he worked on the piece, he thought about Debbie. Daniel tried to focus on the good memories, but recollection of what was bad in their relationship was unavoidable. His thoughts influenced the decisions he made with mallet and gouge, and this was subtly reflected in the finished sculpture. Daniel knew that he should go, but he continued to stare. He didn't want to leave her yet.

"It was all worth it. You were worth it," he whispered. "I loved you at first sight and I still love you. It was worth it, all the years and all the pain, if only for that wonderful time when you loved me, too."

Several more minutes passed and Daniel finally turned. He walked to the workbench and arranged the carving tools in the canvas roll, and then tucked it inside his coat for protection against the rain. At the door he turned and looked through the woodshed one last time. *I did it,* he thought. *I came back here and lived and worked, just like I always wanted to, just like Paw did.*

As he crossed the yard, the scenery seemed different to him. It was as if he were observing it from a distance and no longer part of it. He noticed a deer standing at the edge of the meadow, among the apple trees. The animal was staring at him intently but without alarm, almost as if it had been expecting him.

Then he heard the sound again, that resonant vibration. When he learned of his illness, he assumed it was one of the side effects, pressure affecting his brain. But now he knew better. He felt it from without and all around, from somewhere beneath him. Closing his eyes, Daniel turned a slow circle, listening, feeling. Perhaps it was some deep tectonic grinding. Now he knew it was the mountain itself, calling him.

That night, the rain fell in heavy droplets. When an arctic front moved down from Canada, these crystallized into large wet snowflakes. Soon Mountain Farm was covered with a heavy white blanket. It clung tenaciously to the trees and within an hour, branches were breaking and falling to the ground. As the storm intensified, there began a great cracking and booming throughout the forest as massive limbs broke off, and whole trees split under irresistible weight.

Wooden Spoons

Although the weather was less severe at the lower altitude, Lick Hollow was given a fair sample of what was taking place on the mountain. Power lines came down and darkness engulfed the village. Those who ventured out looked toward the mountain with unease. They heard eerie popping and cracking noises reverberating down into the hollows. Some said it reminded them of sporadic gunfire. It was as if a ghostly military skirmish had broken out on Hemlock Knob.

-37-

The freak storm was winter's parting blow. By the following day, the sky had cleared and mild temperatures erased the snow from Lick Hollow. The effects of the storm did not dissipate so easily. It was afternoon before electrical power was restored to the entire village, and it would be several days before many of the secondary roads were passable. The whine of chainsaws sounded throughout the area, like a giant, robotic, bee-swarm.

During a coffee break at the Lick Hollow Mercantile, members of the cleanup crew shook their heads and made comparisons to the great spring snows of the past.

"Never seen anything like it for the volume of timber that's down," claimed Roy Teets, leaning back in his chair, the brim of a well-worn hat pulled low over his eyes. While no man was working harder to restore the town to normalcy, the truth was that Roy lived for these challenges that nature threw at civilization.

"Been a while," George Haynes said. He was twenty years Roy's senior.

"Trees got used to it and spread too far. That's why it's so bad this time," Tom Lowry explained.

The men nodded.

"Say, how far have you moved up Hemlock Road?" George

Wooden Spoons

asked.

"Not far," Ben Hillen answered from behind him. "Hope to reach the first houses this afternoon. Be another day at least, before we reach the last."

George knew that Ben was not referring to the log house at Mountain Farm when he said *the last*.

Roy, who was the municipal engineer, overseeing the cleanup, realized George's concern. "Can't spare the men to clear the road to the top, George. You know how that goes. But when we get close, I'll send one of the boys up on an ATV to make sure The Professor's OK." George smiled and nodded.

One week later, a Ford pick-up truck slowly ground its way through mud and wet snow toward the summit of Hemlock Knob. It was Mike Miller's new truck and 'Biscuit' was proudly displayed on the front plate. Beside him sat his new partner, Chuck Madison, Kent's youngest brother. After parting ways with Nicklow Developers, Inc., Biscuit found his niche in the local construction business. He was the first in the area to specialize in the renovation of buildings in town. Many thought that he was foolish to stray from the proven formula of building new homes up high, but Biscuit enjoyed the challenge of this sort of work. Time would prove the wisdom of his inclination.

The two men had talked business nonstop since the truck left Lick Hollow. They had been recruited for this expedition by members of their grandparents' generation, George Haynes and John Campbell who sat quietly in the back, bearing somber expressions.

John spoke, silencing the occupants of the front seat. "When do you figure is the last time anyone saw him?"

Dennis Ruane

"It was late February, if I remember right," George answered, turning toward John. "That was the fella from Wisconsin, his friend who walked up to see him during the break in the weather."

"That's right, that's right. It's been about five weeks, then," John said, shaking his head and turning back to the window.

They were on this drive because Ben Hillen had not seen smoke coming from the chimney of the log house when he circled it on the county ATV. He also reported that no signs of human disturbance were evident in the snow. Most notably, there were no tracks to the woodshed or to the outhouse. The jeep was there and obviously had not been moved since before the storm.

"He wouldn't leave the mountain without telling us," John stated.

George shifted his gaze from the passing landscape, but his expression did not change. "Uh uh," he answered.

Just past The Bend, they had to stop because a massive red oak tree lay directly across the road.

"Here we go," Biscuit said. He went to the back of the truck to get his chain saw. After several mighty pulls on the starter rope, the cold engine coughed into a high-pitched roar. He skillfully trimmed his way through the tangle of branches while Chuck thrust them into the air and down the side of the mountain. The butt log of this forest giant was forty inches in diameter. The tree had sprouted more than one hundred and fifty years before it's catastrophic end. It was a sapling when a horse-drawn wagon rolled by, bearing Adam and Sadie Reilly to the summit of Hemlock Knob.

The eager teeth of the chain saw quickly cut through moist wood, reducing the trunk to small logs, which the men rolled to the side of the road. John and George helped by moving branches. They worked impatiently, often glancing up the road with anxious expressions.

After dealing with another roadblock of similar magnitude and a dozen smaller ones, they reached Mountain Farm. There was still an abundance of wet, heavy snow, such that tire tracks from Ben Hillen's survey were still evident. Halfway down Reilly Lane, the truck tires started to lose traction.

"She's boggin' down," Biscuit announced with agitation in his voice. "I'm in four-wheel, too." He put the truck into reverse and slowly backed into shallow snow.

"Let's not mess with it, Mike. We'll walk in from here," John said, naturally taking charge.

Biscuit and Chuck trudged their way through the snow, toward the house, while John and George followed in the rough path they created.

On the porch, John fumbled impatiently for the key, obviously anxious to get inside but privately scared at what they would find. The setting and the mood brought back the memory of his great-uncle's death. *Why does the Reilly side of the family insist on living up here alone, anyway?* John thought as he inserted the key.

He unlocked the door and the men cautiously entered. It was much colder within, as if they had walked into a freezer. Their breath came out white, hanging in the sunlight that slanted through the windows. Eyes adjusted to the dimness and then glanced around the Great Room in all directions. Daniel Whaley was not there. George went quickly to the bedroom and the skin on his neck prickled when he thought there was a form lying on the bed. But as he approached, he could see that it was a fold in the blanket and some clothes, a trick of shadow and imagination. There was momentary relief, but George emerged from the room with no answers.

"Everything's here except Daniel," he said to John.

Biscuit and Chuck came down the stairs with a similar report.

John looked up at George from across the room, where he was bent over a collection of items stacked neatly on the table. He had a strange look on his face and was shaking his head. "Maybe you should check the other buildings."

George hesitated. It was obvious to him that John planned to stay where he was. When John continued to stare at him with a deliberate, puzzled expression, he did as suggested.

"Let's check the woodshed, men," George said with a sense of urgency.

Biscuit and Chuck jumped at his command.

When they trudged to the woodshed and opened the door, the intrigue only deepened. As with the log house, everything was in place, even the firewood. John joined them shortly and they divided up to widen their search to the other buildings, including the outhouse. Still, they found no recent evidence of Daniel's presence.

When it was decided that they should stop and continue on another day, with more help, John stated that the materials on the table should go with them. George turned his head in a questioning manner, but when John nodded emphatically, he agreed.

As they drove down Hemlock Road, the men in front talked about what a wider search might entail and recalled other cases of people who went missing on the mountain. The older men nodded when it was appropriate, but did not join the talk. Eventually the discussion drifted back to the construction business, and John and George watched the passing scene outside their windows in silence.

Wooden Spoons

From the porch of the Lick Hollow Mercantile, John and George thanked their two companions who stood on each side of the truck.

"They're good boys," George said as the vehicle rolled across the gravel toward Main Street.

John nodded. "Let's go inside and pull up a seat near the stove. I need some nerve tonic, and then I have something to show you."

Once inside, John went to the back room and returned with a bottle of bourbon and two glasses. A day in the cold mountain air, a seat near a hot wood stove, and then a bit of whiskey, caused them to glow with warmth. The two friends sat in silence for a short while, letting the events of the day settle in their minds.

"What is it John? What is it you have to show me?" George eventually asked.

John looked up and cleared his throat. "It seems that Daniel has gone away."

"How so?"

"I found this with the items on the table. Daniel obviously assumed that we would be the first to enter the house."

John gave him a handwritten note. George held it in two hands.

> *My Good Friends,*
> *Thank you for all your help with my project. I have no choice but to stop now. Mountain Farm has been sold to the State of Pennsylvania and will become part of the Forbes State Forest. The deed specifies that the buildings must be preserved and that Mountain Farm remain intact. Could I trouble you to send the carving tools to my daughter Jeannie and the journal to my*

249

friend, Victor DiAngelo? Their addresses are in the journal.

Good luck with all you do in life and goodbye.

Daniel

George was dumfounded. "Well, maybe he was planning to go, but then something happened. Daniel wouldn't just walk away and leave everything he owns."

"He did it before."

"Maybe he did. But I don't think so this time. I think something has happened to him, maybe in that storm."

"Maybe." Then John picked up the leather pouch and handed it to George. "Go ahead, open it. I've already seen what's inside."

George nervously undid the zipper. Inside were two stacks of one hundred dollar bills, bound with rubber bands. He turned them over and over "There are thousands of dollars here," he exclaimed.

"I'm sure Daniel meant for us to deal with this money however we see fit," John said

"But he didn't say anything about it in the note."

"If he had, then it would be on record," John said with a sly smile

"I'll be damned," George said, shaking his head, "Just like old Tom."

-38-

Sheriff Pinto was informed of Daniel's disappearance the next day, and with reluctance that was obvious, he committed to organizing a search party. The following day, after the story spread throughout Lick Hollow, it was subsequently learned that Mountain Farm *had*, in fact, been sold to the Commonwealth of Pennsylvania in December. Along with the provisions outlined for the buildings, the deed carried the stipulation that Daniel could live there until the following spring.

It was two days later, on a beautiful Saturday morning, that Harry Pinto and twenty-four volunteers gathered at Mountain Farm. The sheriff noted with some suspicion that half of them were newcomers. There were women too; that was a first for Harry.

"Hello, Harry," George said as he entered the log house through the back door.

The sheriff was staring at the shillelagh above the main door, and turned quickly from it when George spoke.

"George," he growled in a friendly manner. "Considering the fact that all of Whaley's possessions seem to be intact and having studied the note that you and J.C. found, it could be that he was planning to go and got hurt or else killed. I don't know. Can't rule out suicide either."

Dennis Ruane

George did not like any of these choices and simply nodded.

"We have the personnel, so we'll give it a look," Harry said.

Outside, Sheriff Pinto directed the volunteers to form a circle around the house and then to slowly expand outward. He specifically instructed them to walk through any snow of significant depth, to look under and throughout the buildings, and to push through all foliage, particularly the laurel and rhododendron, which grew thick in certain areas.

"Don't have a person in mind so much as clothing, that's what will stand out in the brush," he droned, to put the searchers in the right frame of mind.

Harry did not directly participate in the search, but lingered at the house as the team fanned out. Soon he retired to his truck and the ever-present newspaper. Jim Durst was one of the volunteers, and Harry had put him in charge of the field operation.

At noon when they stopped for lunch, the search team had covered over half of Mountain Farm, and no sign of Daniel Whaley had been discovered. Harry simply bobbed his head as Jim informed him of this. By early afternoon, the entire farm had been covered with the same result. With several hours of daylight remaining, they expanded their search into the state forest and along both sides of Hemlock Road, but still they found nothing.

Tired and annoyed, the sheriff assembled the volunteers just before dark. He cleared his throat loudly before he spoke. "First of all, thank you for your help. Now folks, considering the evidence, I think it's safe to say that the man we're looking for has been gone for awhile, since before the storm at least. It's not hard to figure that if he *is* out here somewhere, we can't help him now. Anyone is welcome to continue searching, it will be much appreciated, but I'm officially calling it off."

Harry cleared his throat again, nodded and turned toward his truck.

The searchers turned toward each other in surprise, and at least one of them was upset. George Haynes followed the sheriff to the truck. Harry knew whose footsteps he heard before turning.

Over the years, Harry Pinto and George Haynes had always respected each other at some level. This made it all the more difficult for the sheriff when he turned and saw the look of disbelief on the older man's face. Harry raised both hands as if to block words so that he could speak first.

"Now George, if it were you or Nora or, uh, Ed Martin over there we'd search till you were found. We know you and we would know for certain that if you were missing, that something was wrong. But, I'm sorry, this Whaley fellow, he appears one day out of nowhere and then one day he disappears into nowhere. I'm supposed to tie all these people up for days on the chance that he is out here, or the even lesser chance that we can help him now if he is?"

"But don't you think it's odd that a man would leave all his possessions behind like this?"

"It's not like he left a pot of gold. Is it more strange than parking your vehicle and walking, instead of just transferring your damn license to another state?"

George was silent. Harry did have a point.

"George, I've seen cases like this before. Well, I take that back, nothing exactly like this. People missing in the woods, I mean. If he is up here, which I'm not so sure of, then he's not alive. The cabin's been empty for weeks, you can see that. The body will be found, if not sooner, than by hunters later in the year."

Dennis Ruane

Sheriff Pinto opened the door of his truck and worked his way in. He had put on weight over the winter, and his hip was bothering him again. "Best I can do, George. I know it sounds cold, but that's the way I'm gettin' in my old age."

Minutes later, Harry was rumbling down the mountain, alone with his conscience. He *was* getting older, and his hip bothered him most days now. Although he had not announced it, he was not planning to run for reelection in the fall. Harry had grandchildren that he wanted to spend time with, and his wife wanted to travel. The sheriff was backing Jim Durst for his replacement. He knew the young man was tough and smart as well. Besides, he was good with newcomers. Harry thought that Jim was the man who could best deal with the changes that were coming.

Daniel Whaley had been a great mystery to the sheriff since the day he first heard there was a man living in the old Reilly place. Regardless of what he had said at Mountain Farm, he believed that The Professor had gone away. He wanted to close the matter quickly, and let the man go. In so doing, he felt the Pinto family would have returned the long-ago favor from the Reilly family.

Kent Madison had come to him a few weeks before, upset and wanting to talk. Harry had known Kent since he was a boy and had been a playmate of Harry's own son. Kent told the sheriff about the incident on Hemlock Knob with Donald and the shotgun. He said that he didn't care about the trouble he might be in, that his conscience would no longer let him remain quiet. Harry asked Kent to not tell anyone else about what happened. The sheriff pushed him on the shoulder, told him to let it go for now, and said that the matter would be

Wooden Spoons

looked into. He did advise Kent, as he had on other occasions, to stay away from Donald Nicklow.

Sheriff Pinto decided to approach Daniel about the incident the next time he saw him. That's when he learned that The Professor had started walking to town, through the forest, on unmarked paths. Harry hadn't yet spotted him when Donald Nicklow disappeared. His suspicion was aroused, but his instinct was that it was just a coincidence. When he examined Donald's bloated body after it was pulled from Lick Hollow Creek, he took note of the dramatic indentation of the face. He reasoned that this could have resulted from the force of the water driving the body into a blunt object. Harry wanted to agree with the general consensus, that Donald Nicklow had simply stumbled out the back of the tavern to urinate, and was so drunk that he fell into Lick Hollow Creek.

What changed his opinion was the story his niece told him several days after the body was found. Penny worked at the Mount Laurel Rest Home, located several blocks from the Lick Hollow Tavern. The night Donald Nicklow disappeared, she had been making her rounds and looked into the room of Ray Seiler. At ninety-seven years of age, Ray Seiler was the oldest living inhabitant of Lick Hollow. A docile man, Ray rarely spoke and passed most of his time, day or night, sitting in his wheel chair, staring out the window toward Tuesday Alley.

According to Penny, when she entered the room, his chair was pressed against the wall and he was awkwardly leaning forward, nearly touching the window pane.

"Mr. Seiler, what's wrong?" she asked rushing to reposition him.

The old man was breathing hard when he looked up at her. "I saw the ghost of Adam Reilly."

"The ghost of Adam Reilly?" Penny questioned, surprised

that he had spoken at all.

Ray nodded emphatically. "Yes, Adam Reilly. I saw him. He was marching up the alley and, by God, he's carrying his war club again."

Harry didn't believe in ghosts.

A surprising number of people did continue to search on the days that followed. Except for George Haynes, they were all newcomers. These were people who had read about Daniel Whaley in *The Commonwealth* or had heard his story from someone else. They were a merry group for the most part, and it did George good to circulate among them. He gladly shared his knowledge of the man they sought. Some were there because they were curious, and others, simply for the adventure. Many came because they believed in what Daniel Whaley had been doing and they wanted to pay this tribute to him.

Joe Harmon was amongst them by the end of the week, by which time the number of volunteers had nearly doubled. Buck remained anonymous, quietly searching and often thinking about his conversation with Daniel at the Lick Hollow Mercantile.

Despite their efforts, Daniel was not found that spring, or that summer, or even that fall during the hunting season.

In the months that followed, word of Daniel's mysterious disappearance spread beyond Lick Hollow. Not long after *Long Woman* was put on display in the Lick Hollow Folk Museum, local newspapers began to pick up the story. Then there was extensive coverage in the Pittsburgh Press. Journalists began

Wooden Spoons

to appear in Lick Hollow and in Madison, Wisconsin, collecting details about Daniel's life. The story eventually became newsworthy for national media. In time, the trickle of people that had been coming to Lick Hollow because of Daniel Whaley became a flood.

-39-

During the ten years following Daniel Whaley's brief stay at Mountain Farm, the village of Lick Hollow changed dramatically. No trace of Daniel was found over this period. There were many people who shared Harry Pinto's belief that he had simply gone away for some private reason. Others believed that he died by accident or maybe had been murdered, and his body was simply not found. Some, however, say that Daniel Whaley never lived on the mountain. The story is told that it was Adam Reilly himself who came out of the grave to save his home.

The State Forest assumed ownership of Mountain Farm in the spring of Daniel's disappearance and moved quickly to control the onslaught of people that began to ascend to it. Through a volunteer program, the restoration of the homestead continued. Throughout this process, historical architects were consulted, old photographs were studied, and testimony was taken from people who had seen Mountain Farm before its decline. Beyond restoration, the goal was to develop the homestead into a living exhibit of pioneer life in the Allegheny Mountains.

The Lick Hollow Folk Museum received many generous donations as a result of the now famous Reilly-family artifacts, and the grand new centerpiece, *Long Woman*. The sculpture had been viewed by thousands of people and photographs of it had circulated around the world. It seemed to evoke a wide range of emotions in viewers, from those who were filled with a sense of exhilaration to those who felt such great sadness that they were moved to tears. Regardless of where they found themselves emotionally, most people believed they were in the presence of a masterpiece. Six years before, a new building was proposed to house the museum. In time, these plans expanded into an art and cultural center, which now included a new library.

People from all over the United States followed Daniel Whaley's effort to help Connie Pavloc, contributing enough money to cover all her medical expenses. In fact, so much money accumulated that a foundation was established to help all children in the Allegheny Mountain region with cancer-related illnesses.

Daniel Whaley's story and his unexplained disappearance intrigued the world. People from all directions began to plan Lick Hollow into their travels. The village adapted and was soon making its own reputation as an eclectic blend of fine shops, restaurants, galleries, and artisan studios.

The *Lick Hollow Association* was formed to guide the transformation of the village. While property owners were encouraged to renovate buildings for the sake of historical preservation, the overall plan for the town was not mere restoration. The goal was to weave tradition with a contemporary look, to preserve the past while looking toward the future. Thus, an abstract metal sculpture was showcased in a small public park, between two buildings built in the early nineteenth century. The architectural firm that designed the new Allegheny Art and Cultural Center, which now housed the Folk Museum, was selected on the basis of its contemporary

Dennis Ruane

and innovative portfolio.

When it was proposed that the village sponsor a spring festival commemorating Lick Hollow's favorite son, Daniel Whaley, R. Cranston, a founding member of the Lick Hollow Association, was opposed to the idea. His fear was that such an event would merely capitalize on Daniel's fame and inevitably overshadow the simple ideals that his life on the mountain represented. However, when he was approached privately by another prominent member of the Association, Martha Nicklow, he was convinced that it could be a meaningful occasion if planned properly. Martha Nicklow and R. Cranston were chosen to co-chair the festival.

A decade before, when Donald Nicklow's body was found in Lick Hollow Creek, his parents were shattered as their worst fear for their rogue son came to pass. The punch that Donald once suspected his father was losing, was lost, never to return. Maurice phased himself out of his law practice and sold the construction business. He retired to the large stone house on the south edge of Lick Hollow, which he and Martha had built thirty years before. It had spacious grounds of nearly ten acres with a pond and numerous gardens. It was here he passed his time, tending the gardens. Maurice was rarely seen in public, and then only when he went to dinner with his wife. On these occasions it was noted that the attorney was congenial and smiled easily, but rarely spoke.

Martha moved away from the tragedy in a different direction. She chose to concentrate on living. Lick Hollow was her hometown, and she wanted to be part of the change that was unfolding. Never fully aware of the extent of her husband's business holdings, she was surprised and somewhat embarrassed to learn of how many buildings were owned by Nicklow Developers, Inc. Martha and her accountant devised a

Wooden Spoons

plan to slowly release the Main Street buildings in a way that would facilitate the plan of the Lick Hollow Association.

Martha Nicklow and Robert Cranston meshed into a perfect team and developed the spring festival without compromise into a classy event that was both enjoyable and educational. At their suggestion, it was simply titled *The Wooden Spoon Festival.*

This year marked the third annual Wooden Spoon Festival, and also the tenth year since Daniel Whaley's disappearance. One of the highlights of this year's event was the dedication of a new metal sculpture, *The Spoonmaker.* It had been commissioned by the Lick Hollow Association from blacksmiths Dane and Becky Allen and was recently installed on the public green. The Allens had bought George Haynes' house at the end of Pine Creek Road three years before. They were part of a general migration of artisans into the area

As she strolled up Main Street, weaving back and forth against the flow of the crowd, Jeannie Whaley was amazed at the vibrancy of this little town in the Allegheny Mountains. She had arrived the day before, determined to experience for herself the phenomenon which she had been following in the media surrounding Lick Hollow and her father. She eventually wanted to meet all the personalities he had described in his letters, but for now she wished to remain anonymous.

Jeannie was thirty years old and had experienced a measure of success with her painting, including several one-woman shows at noted galleries in Amsterdam. In recent years, the bohemian life had lost its charm and she grew weary of her location. Soon after a long-term relationship sputtered out, Jeannie decided to return to the United States. She had a

Dennis Ruane

general plan of buying a little house and then transforming it into her dream studio. Years ago, she had wisely invested the money her father had sent her from the sale of Mountain Farm.

She was tall like her father and pretty like her mother. Jeannie had short brown hair, classical, sharp features, and dark eyes. In her pleated tan pants and white safari shirt, she stood out in this crowd although that was not her intention.

Jeannie stopped at a booth, bought a bag of roasted peanuts and picked up a festival brochure from the counter. She leafed through it as she turned the corner onto Bennington Road. On the inside back cover was a picture which caused her to stop. At first, she thought it was her father, but she saw that it was a reproduction of an old photograph. Then she read the inscription: *Adam Reilly, circa 1895.* It was her great-great-great-grandfather.

Jeannie was amazed at the similarity between this old photograph and the one that Professor DiAngelo had sent her ten years ago. Adam Reilly was standing in the same location, in front of a log house, and as in the photograph of her father, he had one foot on a piece of wood and his right hand on the end of an ax handle. The only striking difference between the images was the light-haired dog on the porch in the old photograph. It was sitting at attention behind Adam and was obviously watching the photographer intently.

Folding the program under her arm, Jeannie continued along the street until she was drawn toward a stone building, which a wooden sign designated as *The Village Pottery*. Inside, a crowd surrounded a man at a pottery wheel who was casually throwing mugs and talking. She guessed that the potter was about her age. He had long hair, pulled back into a thick ponytail, and he sported a full beard. She thought he was

Wooden Spoons

handsome in a rugged way. Jeannie watched as perfectly shaped vessels seemed to appear from small lumps of clay on a revolving wheel, as if it were a magic trick. Able to work by feel, he casually looked up from his work to answer questions.

"Are you from this area?" a man asked.

The potter looked at the man and shook his head, smiling. "No, actually, I'm from the Midwest. Kansas. I moved around some and came here five years ago when I learned that . . ." The potter's eyes had moved to Jeannie and he stopped talking. He tilted his head with such an obvious look of surprise that the crowd turned to follow the direction of his gaze. She was startled by this sudden attention and nervously looked from side to side, finally turning to see if this concerned someone behind her.

"Uh, I, uh moved when I learned what was happening here in Lick Hollow," the potter said, regaining the attention of the audience.

Jeannie nodded to the people who were still looking at her and backed toward the door. She had no idea as to what had taken place. She crossed the porch, went quickly down the steps and entered the crowd.

"Jeannie," someone called from behind.

She turned to see the potter coming toward her, smiling. He had something in his hand.

"Jeannie Whaley?" he asked.

She nodded as he came up to her. He was carrying a wooden spoon.

"I'm Bruce Planter. I was a graduate student in the Biochemistry Department in Madison, about ten years ago."

She smiled but struggled for recognition.

"I was one of your father's graduate students."

Then Jeannie remembered. She was a senior in high

263

Dennis Ruane

school when Bruce had entered her father's lab. She recalled that he had always spoken politely to her when she passed through the lab to see her father. She had thought he seemed out of place in the biochemistry department. He didn't seem out of place here.

"Yes, I do remember you," she said. "Pardon my surprise. I would have sooner guessed you to be a fourth generation potter from the Allegheny Mountains rather than someone I used to see in the Biochemistry building in Madison."

Bruce laughed. "I take that as a compliment," he said. "Your father gave me this when I left the department." Bruce held up the wooden spoon with the spiraled handle.

Jeannie smiled. "My father sent me a spoon just like that many years ago."

Bruce smiled. "Uh, Jeannie, I really should get back to the wheel," he said, glancing toward the cabin.

"Oh, OK. I understand, I have to run, too. I want to attend the dedication of the statue in the park."

"Want to meet later for something to eat?" Bruce asked quickly.

"Sure, sounds good."

"Meet me here around six?"

Jeannie smiled and nodded.

"I wish I could attend the ceremony, too," Bruce said. "Don't miss George Haynes' talk. He is a great guy and he and your father were good friends."

"I'll be sure to see him, and I'll see you later."

They shook hands nervously and hurried away in opposite directions.

When Jeannie arrived at the park, a crowd had already

Wooden Spoons

gathered around the podium. An elderly, attractive woman who introduced herself as Martha Nicklow was welcoming the audience. *The Spoonmaker* stood to the left of the podium. As Jeannie had noted earlier in the day, the sculpture was surprisingly contemporary for this small town in the Allegheny Mountains. She could see the rough shape of a human, perhaps leaning into the wind, a long coat, and the suggestion of a hat. It was a fleeting image, not a definite shape. The more Jeannie looked at it, the more she liked it and the more appropriate it seemed to the subject.

"Welcome, folks. My name is George Haynes," the first speaker began. "I was an acquaintance of Daniel Whaley when he lived on Hemlock Knob."

The crowd quieted and turned toward him. George looked good for his eighty years. His unofficial business partner, John Campbell, had died three years earlier. J.C. was found in his office chair inside the little barn. He had his green visor on and was going over the *Antique Quarterly* in the end. Two upcoming estate auctions had been circled. The following year, George worked out a business arrangement with Nora. After building himself a small apartment in the barn, he relocated there to carry on the antique business. He also served as resident handyman on the Mercantile property. Nora was still going strong at eighty-two years of age. She excused herself from today's ceremony, however, because she had to mind the store.

George began his talk in an interesting way. "Daniel Whaley lived his first fifteen years in that stone house over there," he said, pointing across Main Street to the Martin House. That's where the story begins."

The crowd turned.

"One fine afternoon while Daniel and I were sitting by his

265

wood stove, sipping brandy, he told me of what he thought was his earliest memory. He was not yet two years old, and he was on the back porch of that house with his great-grandfather, Tom Reilly. Tom picked him up and pointed up at the mountain. 'That is Hemlock Knob, Danny, my boy,' Tom said to him. Daniel told me that he always remembered that moment because of the happy smile on his great-grandfather's face." George looked toward the mountain after he said this.

The crowd shifted its gaze toward Hemlock Knob. For all the changes that had occurred in the area, the mountain appeared the same as it did over sixty years ago when Tom Reilly brought it to his great-grandson's attention. It appeared much the same when Adam and Sadie Reilly made their way up Hemlock Road, over one hundred and fifty years ago to build their home on its summit. It was an image stamped in every native child's memory, and now that most of Hemlock Knob was part of the State Forest System, the vision would remain for future generations to see.

With the restoration of Mountain Farm, the public could follow Adam and Sadie Reilly's tracks up Hemlock Road to a place where they might imagine a simple and independent life on top of a mountain. And now it would still be possible for a child to sit high on the rock outcrop overlooking Lick Hollow, to gaze at a distant horizon and dream of the future. Someday, if the need should arise, that child might be the one to beat up a bully that was ruining Lick Hollow or perhaps become so famous that they could share their wealth with everybody in town.

"The gray patches near the top are the rocks that make up what is called Point Lookout. About a half mile beyond that is Mountain Farm," George continued.

Jeannie stared at the mountain as he spoke. She

Wooden Spoons

remembered the name *Point Lookout*. The memory took her back to a conversation she had with her father when she was very young. That day, Jeannie's Aunt Cathy was visiting with her three children, two girls and a boy who were near Jeannie's age. Her cousins were tough and loud; Jeannie was quiet and timid. She never enjoyed playing with them for long and they seemed to sense this, often making her the point of their jokes.

She was sitting on her father's lap in his study. She was crying, and he was comforting her, explaining that her cousins *did* like her but were from a big city and different than her.

Jeannie's mother suddenly opened the study door. Debbie and her sister had sensed that there had been trouble. "Here she is, in Daniel's cave," she called back over her shoulder to Cathy. The women laughed. Debbie leaned into the room. "Is everything OK?"

"We're fine," her father answered, calmly

Her mother and Aunt Cathy went back to the patio.

Jeannie's father settled back into the big chair and smiled.

"I actually had my own cave once, Jeannie."

"Your own cave?" she asked, wiping her eyes and quickly forgetting her trouble.

"Yes, I've never told anyone. When I was young, I had my own secret cave. It was at the base of a rock cliff on Hemlock Knob, at a place called Point Lookout. I found it by accident while looking for a jackknife that fell over the cliff. I have never told anybody where it is." Her father had her total attention now. "I often thought that someday when I finally have had enough of people, when I want to get away from everybody, I will hide in it. I will go to my secret cave and just stay there."

"Somebody will find you, Daddy," Jeannie said. "You

Dennis Ruane

couldn't hide there forever."

"Oh yes I could, too. My cave is hard to find. The laurel grows so thick and gnarled that it is impossible to walk through. You have to get down low and crawl along the base of the cliff to get inside the thicket. Even then, the entrance is underneath a rock overhang and not easy to see."

"But it's not a secret cave anymore because I know about it now," she had said to her father, very seriously.

Jeannie felt a nervous tingle on the back of her neck and shuddered as it pulsed across her shoulders. She did not hear what George Haynes was saying now, her thoughts were focused on Point Lookout. Jeannie recalled that her father had smiled mischievously at her remark, and she remembered well what he had said next.

"You're right, Jeannie, you know my secret. Now, if I ever decide to hide from everybody once and for all, you will be the only one in the whole world who knows where I am."

Epilogue

The broadaxe looked like a weapon from the Middle Ages, but it is actually a woodsman's tool, used to hew rough logs into building timbers. Adam Reilly swung a broadaxe with precision that was unmatched in any age. He had only to square another half dozen logs and the frame for a forge would be ready. The logs had been cut from the tall trees that grew on Hemlock Knob. Adam worked with dogged resolution. Since he and his wife moved to the mountain, he had built a two-story log house and several outbuildings of hemlock and stone. Adam and Sadie Reilly had named their homestead Mountain Farm.

Pausing to refresh himself in the cool mountain air, Adam peered across lush green meadows, looking for deer that often fed there. He was a tall man with a lean, sinewy frame. He had well-defined cheekbones and chiseled features which were half-hidden behind a full beard. His hair hung from under the wide brim of his hat and touched his shoulders. He peered over a vegetable garden of half an acre, the harvest from which, along with the occasional hunt, fed his family. Adam loved his home on Hemlock Knob and in all outward respects seemed to be a man at peace with the life he lived.

Yet his thoughts were often clouded with images of other fields where, by his own admission, he once did the Devil's work. Adam had viewed gentle meadows such as this, covered with dead and dying men, in some places so thick that it was difficult to walk around them. Over fifteen years had passed since those desperate battles, yet he remembered vividly the agony of the wounded, the vacant stares of the dead and, worst of all, the pitiful cries of the men who died by his own hand.

Adam and Sadie had emigrated from Ireland twenty years before, settling in Philadelphia with her relatives. Adam found that America was not the immediate land of opportunity that he had dreamed of, and he also learned that citizenship did not readily gain him acceptance. His hope had been to attend art school in Philadelphia and to become a painter. Instead, his time was consumed by rough and menial jobs with no sympathy for a young Irishman's dreams.

As the threat of civil war loomed over his adopted country, Adam enlisted in the 116th Pennsylvania Infantry Regiment, which was composed primarily of Irishmen from Philadelphia. Like many of his fellow soldiers, Adam joined the Army with the desire to demonstrate that he was worthy of opportunity. The Regiment joined the New York Irish Brigade at Harpers Ferry, Virginia, in 1862 and was assigned to General Edwin V. Sumner's Division, Army of the Potomac.

Throughout the war, the Irish Brigade was always at the foremost position in the major battles and suffered high casualties as a result. It was two years into the war, at The Battle of Chancellorsville, that a musket ball tore through Adam's calf, nicking the femur as it passed. Another ball plowed a quarter inch furrow across his forehead before he collapsed to the ground among his fallen countrymen.

When Adam returned from the war, he suggested that they might live to the west, away from cities and politicians

Wooden Spoons

and Sadie began packing that day. The young couple traveled by horse and wagon to the mountains of western Pennsylvania. and after searching the ends of the available roads, bought land on the summit of Hemlock Knob. Here they wanted to build a home and raise their family, without further molestation from the governments of the world.

Adam Reilly wielded his broadaxe once again. He had learned that focusing on simple, repetitive tasks such as hewing a log into a square beam, diverted his thoughts from the haunting memories. After settling on Hemlock Knob, Adam swore an oath that he would never again raise his hand against another man unless Mountain Farm itself was attacked. As a symbol of this he hung his bata, his fighting stick, above the door of the log house.

Adam could smell the aroma of food coming from the house where Sadie was preparing their evening meal. Sadie Reilly had developed a similar philosophy concerning the benefits of simple tasks. She had lost a brother to The Bloody Lane at Antietam and a cousin to The Wheatfield at Gettysburg. She nearly went out of her mind with worry while the men were gone, and with each tragedy that she endured, her grip on reality loosened. Once Sadie moved to Hemlock Knob, she left it less than a dozen times throughout the remainder of her life.

Over the years, she grew to be superstitious and accumulated a repertoire of rituals and oaths to ward off bad luck or else to bring good fortune. It was after she and Adam's first child died of cholera that Sadie became preoccupied with the afterlife. She came to believe that the dead could influence their living ancestors.

When Adam came to dinner, it was the occasion of his fortieth birthday. It was after his meal, while he sipped a glass

271

of cider, that Sadie approached him with an unexpected surprise.

"I wanted to give this to you before our guests arrive and you men get lost in your toasting and laughing," she teased. She set before him a package wrapped in brown paper and bound with twine. Adam opened it to find a canvas roll, crisp and new, tied with leather straps. Tears came to his eyes when he undid the bindings and realized the present Sadie had made for him. The canvas roll contained the woodcarving tools which had been given to him by his grandfather. The collection was a family heirloom, originating from an ancient relative who had been a woodcarver by trade. The tools had been passed down ever since, sometimes skipping a generation, to whomever showed artistic promise.

Sadie had designed the roll around the tools, and each of the twelve chisels and gouges were protected in its own pouch along one side of the roll. An oak mallet, sharpening stones, and carving knives balanced the array on the opposite side. In a small space that remained was embroidered a sentence in Sadie's neat penmanship.

"This is for my husband, a great artist," Sadie said, placing her hands on his shoulders.

"Thank you, my dear wife. This is a most wonderful gift," Adam replied, taking one of her hands. "But you flatter me. I know now that I am not the artist that my grandfather hoped I would be. A skilled craftsman, yes, a good woodcarver, perhaps, but not an artist. To be an artist requires a rare spark of imagination, the genius to look at the world in a way that nobody has before. It is not in me. I can follow a plan or copy from nature, but the genius is not there."

When Sadie protested, he shook his head and smiled. "It's

all right, my dear, I am content with that. I do my best, and my effort is its own reward. Someday though, I hope these fine tools will serve a great artist. I believe that good tools that are well made and cared for will eventually come into the right hands. The genius will emerge someday, and a masterpiece will come." He looked over his shoulder at the infant in the walnut cradle behind him. "Perhaps little Tommy here," he said with a grin.

Adam looked back at the tools, so handsomely displayed in the new canvass roll. "So what does this mean?" he asked, pointing to the words embroidered on the corner of the canvas."

"You can read it, Adam, try."

"Hmm, you wrote it in the old language."

"It's not the *old* language. It's *our* language and you mustn't let it die in you."

"No, no, you're right, I mustn't. But you see, it's just that I don't have my spectacles on and I'm too weary, after the long day's toil, to walk the distance to the bedroom."

She looked at him with one side of her mouth turned up slightly, and then smiled. "All right. It is your birthday, after all." Sadie pointed to each word and read slowly as if it were a school lesson. "Art is a good idea."

"Art is a good idea," he repeated. "What made you think of that?"

"It is from listening to you talk. It is from things you have said at times, although with more words. I only had a small space, so I shortened it. It is a saying to bring you good luck while you work. Maybe it will bring forth the genius."

Adam laughed and took Sadie's other hand. "Art is a good idea."

"Do you think it is silly?"

Dennis Ruane

"Not at all," he answered, looking up at her. "I think you have said it just right."

The End

Printed in the United States
131213LV00004B/5/A